A Life in Full
and other stories

The Caine Prize
for African Writing 2010

D1173359

A Life in Full
and other stories

The Caine Prize
for African Writing 2010

cassava republic
feeding the African imagination

JACANA

New Internationalist

The Caine Prize for African Writing 2010

First published in the UK in 2010 by
New Internationalist™ Publications Ltd
Oxford OX4 1BW
www.newint.org
New Internationalist is a registered trademark.

First published in 2010	First published in 2010
in Southern Africa by	in West Africa by
Jacana Media (Pty) Ltd	Cassava Republic Press
10 Orange Street	Edo House
Sunnyside	Plot 75, Ralph Sodeinde Street
Auckland Park 2092	Central Business District
South Africa	Garki, Abuja
www.jacana.co.za	Nigeria
	www.cassavarepublic.biz

Individual contributions © The Authors.

Cover painting: 'And Sings My Soul' by the Kenyan artist Njuguna.

Design by New Internationalist.

Printed by T J International Limited, Cornwall, UK
who hold environmental accreditation ISO 14001.

Mixed Sources
Product group from well-managed
forests and other controlled sources
www.fsc.org Cert no. SGS-COC-2482
© 1996 Forest Stewardship Council

British Library Cataloguing-in-Publication Data.
A catalogue record for this book is available from the British Library.

Library of Congress Cataloguing-in-Publication Data.
A catalogue record for this book is available from the Library of Congress.

National Library of Nigeria Cataloguing-in-Publication Data.
A catalogue record for this book is available from the National Library
of Nigeria.

New Internationalist ISBN: 978-1-906523-37-4
Jacana Media ISBN: 978-1-77009-899-2
Cassava Republic ISBN: 978-978-907-877-6

Contents

Introduction

IN 2010 THE CAINE PRIZE has writers from Zambia and Sierra Leone on its shortlist for the first time, bringing to 17 the number of African countries represented on the shortlists over the Prize's 11 years. This year's shortlisted authors and their stories were as follows:

- Ken Barris (South Africa) *The Life of Worm*, from *New Writing from Africa 2009* published by Johnson & King James Books, Cape Town.
- Lily Mabura (Kenya) *How Shall We Kill the Bishop?* from *Wasafiri* number 53, Spring 2008, London.
- Namwali Serpell (Zambia) *Muzungu*, from *The Best American Short Stories 2009* published by Houghton Mifflin Harcourt, Boston MA.
- Alex Smith (South Africa) *Soulmates*, also from *New Writing from Africa*.
- Olufemi Terry (Sierra Leone) *Stickfighting Days* from *Chimurenga* volume 12/13, Cape Town, 2008.

Ken Barris was also shortlisted for the Caine Prize in 2003. *Muzungu* is Namwali's first published short story.

The winner will be decided by a panel of judges chaired by Fiammetta Rocco, literary editor of *The Economist*, and including Ellah Allfrey, deputy editor of *Granta*, Professor Jon Cook of the University of East Anglia, and Samantha Pinto, professor at Georgetown University, Washington, USA, where the winner will be offered a month's residency.

These stories are accompanied by those written at the 2010 CDC Caine Prize African Writers' Workshop, which was held in the incomparable surroundings of the Gellmann Conservancy at Ol Ari Nyiro in Laikipia Province, Kenya, where impala, elephant and even lion showed a close interest in the proceedings and a puff adder settled right by the entrance to the workroom. The 12 workshop participants, from six different African countries, were guided on this occasion by Veronique Tadjo (Ivory Coast) and Jamal Mahjoub (Sudan), whose critical analysis and commentary some found scarcely less daunting than the presence of the wildlife.

Once again, the principal sponsor of the Prize was the Oppenheimer Memorial Trust. The CDC Group sponsored the Workshop. Extremely valuable support has been received from Miles Morland, from the Booker Prize Foundation and from Actis, as well as a grant from the British Council and other generous private donations. Valuable help in kind has been given by the Royal Over-Seas League, the Bodleian Library, Kenya Airways, the Rector of Exeter College, Oxford, and the Institute of English Studies, London University. We are immensely grateful for all this help, and we would also like to acknowledge a grant from the Thistle Trust towards last year's workshop expenses, which reached us after our 2009 anthology went to print.

Nick Elam
Administrator of the Caine Prize for African Writing

Caine Prize 2010
Shortlisted Stories

The Life of Worm

Ken Barris

WORM, AS I CALL HIM, is quivering. He needs to go for a walk. I have nothing to fear with Worm on the leash. He shivers with untapped energy, his muscularity itself bristles at the thought of violence: even his walking is violent. His eyes have a lugubrious quality, they are liquid with soul. It is a deception. He crouches at the doorway, hair bristling, his ribs standing out, outrage in his eyes, a sort of terror that he might be denied his walk. I sometimes picture him stripped of fur and skin, a flayed beast walking.

I need to make preparations. I check that the electric fence is working – there is a panel in the garage that makes a ticking noise – and preset the alarm. I take the remotes out of their cabinet. Then I fetch the leash, which I keep in the scullery. There is no line of sight between the scullery and the front door. It is inadvisable for Worm to see his leash.

I have the leash behind my back. I have to approach him carefully. Until it is fastened he is potentially psychotic. His eyes roll as I approach, showing the murky corneas. Then I snap the leash on in a smooth and practised movement, aware of a certain nausea, a sour taste in my mouth. A curious ripping sound rolls out of him, neither bark nor snarl, strangely high-pitched, alto rather than tenor. He rises on his back legs, foreclaws ripping at the door. I have to jerk him back in order to open it. He lunges out, and I grab the handle from outside, using his momentum to slam the door behind us.

He tugs me rapidly towards the electric gate, while I lean back, a staggering land anchor, slowing him down long enough to reach into my pocket to find the gate and burglar alarm remotes. I am skilled now, I can take out both and juggle them in one hand, well enough to open the gate and set the alarm. It activates, the siren giving a single blip. The gate has a seven-second delay before it closes. I hear its trundling noise behind me as we set off at a ridiculous pace. Worm tugs madly, trying to go at his natural speed. He ranges left and right, right and left, testing the leash. Sometimes he chokes on his collar, strangling and gargling, but never relents. I would like to let him go, but it wouldn't work: this is an animal one dare not unchain. It is difficult to live with a dog of this nature, but it is necessary. I have no choice.

I look back, unobtrusively as possible, difficult at this speed, difficult to keep balance and scrutinize the street. There is no-one behind me. So far, so good. There is obviously no-one ahead. I feel apprehensive as we approach the intersections – who can tell what (or who, more to the point) might be lurking down the road unseen? You cannot tell, until you are right in the mouth of the intersection, and can gaze left or right, and reconnoitre. The first intersection on this morning's route is Avenue Picardie, which rises to a gentle crest above my current position. There is someone – in the distance, there is a human figure, and a small dog trotting – she wears a dress, there is no threat there. Worm lurches towards them, dragging me up the hill, trying to sprint while his claws scrabble at the tarmac. Can he see the little dog? I wonder about his eyesight sometimes. I know that he is blinded by rage, by battle madness. When he gets that look, blood films his eye, its blood vessels thicken and swell to bursting. Surely that must damage his sight?

The woman is a stick figure wearing a dress. Her dog sniffs the ground and struts about, oblivious to the approach of terror. The distance closes swiftly, though they seem to stand still, as if the street rolls towards me on massive and silent gears. We are on the right-hand side of the road, the side on which you face oncoming traffic. It is better to walk on this side, but the woman and her dog are on this side too. I glance backwards, hastily, confirm that nothing approaches from behind, and swerve out behind Worm, dragging him to the other side of the road.

I begin to make out details. She wears a raincoat, an unpleasant yellow. It is this I mistook for a dress. Beneath it she wears beige slacks and sensible shoes. She appears to be middle aged. Despite the overcast weather, she wears white-rimmed sunglasses, of a type I would think were old-fashioned, with thick white rims. She comes nearer, and I see a spray of silver shot in her cheeks, and sprays of silver in her hair. The woman positively glints, she is metallic with manners and face powder.

To my annoyance – to my consternation – she crosses the street, and comes to a halt right in front of Worm. Before I can warn her, she bends down over him. Is she mad? She takes both his cheeks in her hands, and says, looking up at me, 'Isn't he a love? What's his name?'

I am so astounded I cannot speak at first. Worm's tail wags madly, his hindquarters shake. He pays no attention to the small dog at all, all his sensibility focused on her attention. The little dog sniffs at a pile of droppings just inside the curb, with the utmost delicacy, reading its information, keeping its distance. My dog makes excited guttural noises, sounds I have never heard before.

'Worm,' I say at last.

'What a strange name for a dog like this!' she exclaims gaily.

I clear my throat, unsure how to respond. I take in as much slack on the leash as I can, without pulling him backwards. Does she realize her danger? Does she know he might take her face off?

She straightens up, wiping her hands down on her hips, against the unforgiving yellow of her raincoat. No doubt he has slathered over her fingers.

'Such a frantic young man,' she remarks, amused.

The dog is tugging at the leash again, vibrating.

'Well, yes,' I reply, feeling quite foolish. 'I think we'd better move on.'

We spring away briskly. I feel intense relief. I cannot be responsible for foolish people who risk their lives and faces. I close my eyes for an instant, unable to suppress an image of her scalped, exposed. Turning back, I see her departing frame, a splash of yellow. Then I stumble, tugged forward, and scramble after Worm. A gentle, squeezing pressure makes itself felt in my chest, with a single clear tendril of pain moving upwards on the left, and curling into my heart. It is not unpleasant.

✳ ✳ ✳

There is a threat to my security that I cannot do much about. It is an oak tree growing on my neighbour's property, right next to our shared boundary wall. I know for a fact that this tree is rotten to the core. The trunk is hollow. My neighbour, a wizened and stubborn old fool, has confirmed it. I've asked him repeatedly to cut it down, but he refuses. 'Can't go around cutting down trees,' he mutters. 'Not old trees like this. Too much history in them.' He points to the fresh leaves growing from its upper boughs, as if that's proof of its health. When the winter wind blows from the north-west, I cannot sleep. I fear the tree. How much does a medium-sized oak weigh? I try to calculate the direction of its fall. This is difficult, because the tree bows in my direction, the lower half of its trunk leaning slightly over the wall; then it bends back, inclining the other way. The bulk of its branches are on his side, tipping the centre of gravity back towards him; but the northwester would push it onto my side. The soil here is of poor quality, with terribly low compressive strength. If you push a steel rod in the ground to test it, as engineers do – as I have done in front of this neighbour – it goes right in, easily sinking 600 millimetres or more. How stable can the roots be in this soil? It is so precarious.

To make matters worse, he has allowed a bougainvillea to grow up the trunk and into the branches, so a matted, massive network of vegetation – virtually a hedge in the air – hangs from these branches. More accurately, it grows up into the branches; in any event, it must act as a sail; it inevitably must catch and amplify the force of the wind.

I sometimes try to estimate the height of the tree, and mentally convert that to horizontal distance. How far will it reach? It will obviously destroy my lounge and chimney, probably scatter the coals in my fireplace and start a fire. It could well bring down the roof and outer wall of the dining room adjacent as well. I do not think it will reach my garage and so destroy my car. But it is difficult to translate height to length without instruments of survey. I have a number of valuable paintings in my lounge. These are uninsured. How might one replace these? I often consider removing them, but surely the lounge is where one hangs valuable paintings? They are my only heritage – paintings by Boonzaaier, Stern, Jensch, Maggie Laubser, Ignatius Marx – paintings that capture the country of my youth. I refuse to displace them. No doubt this is unwise. No doubt I will regret it one day.

One thing is certain: this oak tree will shatter the boundary wall. It will cut the electric fence. Once that is down, my first line of defence is gone. This presents no immediate danger, not in a storm. Criminals are as sensitive to bad weather as we are. However, it will take days to repair. In a bad storm, many trees go down in this city. It will take time to get it cut up and removed, the rubble cleaned up, the wall rebuilt. Only then can the fence be restored, only then. Fortunately, I have Worm.

* * *

I follow a certain protocol at night. I begin with the garage, checking each night on the electric fence charge energizer panel. It has five LEDs to indicate the level of charge. They are arranged vertically, light runs upwards, one after the other, arriving at the topmost with a snapping sound if all is well. Tonight, as usual, there is full charge. It is an excellent unit. If we have a power cut, there is a battery. It cannot provide power indefinitely, of course – not if the power cut runs for several hours – which concerns me. I will install a generator if these power cuts go on. Then I go through each window in the house, and each external door, making sure that it is secured. I do not neglect the windows of my study upstairs. People who believe that thieves only break in on the ground floor delude themselves. I leave open a single fanlight in the bedroom, as fresh air is so important when you sleep. I have burglar bars, but they are easily removed. These are flat strips of metal. All one has to do is adjust a large shifting spanner to the apposite thickness, brace the flat bar in its jaw, and twist. The burglar 'bar' will snap soon enough. Of course, that will make a noise, and arouse my dog, but they are aware of this. Now they have battery-powered metal-cutting torches that can remove the bars almost silently. All it takes is expertise. Whatever measures you take, they will bring the counter-measure to bear.

I set the external beams and activate all the window sensors. While I am awake, I bypass the infra-red motion sensors inside the house, though not those on the two patios. My perimeter is secure as I can make it. I would like to leave Worm outside the house, patrolling my garden, snaking his way into the dark shrubbery, into every corner. I have reason to believe his hearing is not particularly sharp, though like all dogs he must have a keen sense of smell. But I cannot do this. He barks and howls all night. It was my practice not long ago, but the neighbours complained, particularly the man with the oak tree. One rude, anonymous letter threatened to get the municipality on to Worm. I was not disturbed by this threat itself – the municipality is incapable of doing anything at all other than sending one wildly inaccurate accounts –

but I like to keep the peace.

Now he patrols inside the house, which is acceptable, if not ideal. I would rather he dispatched intruders outside, before they come in reach. And even if he didn't – for example, if they sprayed him with some kind of disabling toxin, pepper spray or insecticide, or even shot him, none of which is uncommon, it would make a great cacophony, I can assure you. He would not die easily. Another problem is that my security beams are set to ignore any animal weighing less than 40 kilograms. I don't know what Worm weighs, but sometimes he trips off the beams, and sometimes he doesn't. It upset the neighbours again, many times, and there were complaints. They are stupid and short-sighted: there is no boundary between my security and theirs, despite the walls that divide our properties.

On completion of my first-level security protocol, I am free to read, or watch television. Sometimes I listen to music, or prowl the internet. I keep track of incidents in my area through the local Neighbourhood Watch website. It is an excellent service. They email Crime Incident Notifications every day – I call it a CIN – usually two or three, with a synopsis of the event and news, if any, of arrest. They circulate the number plates of suspicious vehicles, and even photographs of people who are suspected of being a danger to the area. These are police mugshots, which proves their danger.

* * *

I listen to the wind. To say that it howls, as people do, is inaccurate. Howling is a curve of sound that lifts and dies smoothly. This wind surges, mounts raggedly, drops off. It builds up its power unsteadily, using many instruments to steal or manufacture a voice, having none of its own: sheeting slapping under cement roof tiles, the thump of that poorly fitted door against its frame, creaking gazebo timbers, whining telephone cables, the choir of branches that sing as the gale scuds through them. Then rain drums on the skylight, a nerve-wracking percussion, growing high-pitched and more frantic still as hail bounces off. I believe I feel the night go pale at the climax. But none of this matters: my attention is endlessly drawn to that corner of the property above which the oak tree stands, fragile and yet monstrous.

Worm cannot sleep either. His nerves are frayed too. He paces about the house, around the sleeping quarters at least. They are blocked off from the remainder of the building by a steel security gate in the passage, so his area of patrol is confined to three rooms. His claws click on the passage tiles, robotic but anxious, and on the sprung floor of the empty bedroom beside mine. Then he comes back in and flops down beside my bed. He sleeps briefly, snoring and grunting through his flabby lips. A particularly sharp peal of thunder sets him on his feet again, howling in outrage. Howling again is inexact. It is a slobbering, manic voice that lifts at last into a bloodcurdling, high-pitched groan.

'For God's sake, shut up!' I hiss at the dog. A dying cornetto of sound, and then he subsides, slumping against the side of the mattress. Somehow – I do not know how – I sleep again. I dream of Worm torn open like a bloody exploded diagram, his organs and limbs detached and spread out. I struggle to read the total meaning of these hieroglyphs, to picture the animal from which they spring. The wind mounts up too, building up its batteries of spiritual violence. I dream this too, caught between waking and sleep. It grows louder and stronger, a blast sustained. Then there is a crumpling sound, not very loud, as if thousands of voices whisper in resignation, but never in unison. And one meaty percussion, which I feel even in my chest, that unites these voices and gives them a single meaning. No doubt the tree has come down. But as my waking mind assembles itself, I realize that the alarm is silent. The electric fence is obviously intact. I am flooded by relief. Just to make sure that the system has not malfunctioned, I check the control pad at my bedroom door. There is no report of malfunction. I must have dreamt the tree collapsing, though this remains inevitable. It is only a matter of time.

* * *

The storm has blown over. The clouds are sullen and bruised, their edges stained iodine. As Worm and I turn the corner and pace swiftly down Avenue Provence, I realize that my dream was not entirely misplaced. A large section of a neighbouring oak tree has indeed fallen. It is not the whole tree, but it is far more substantial than a branch. I recognize the tree, of course – I walk past it every day. It is one of these oaks with a somewhat bifurcated trunk; or perhaps over the years, its lowest branch grew almost as broad across as the trunk itself, so that it is hard to distinguish branch from stem. In any event, a massive section of oak tree lies halfway across the road. The sight worries me deeply: not the fresh, almost pink inner wood exposed where it sheared off, or the sweaty odour of its sap. It is rather the depth and spread of inner rot exposed in the supine part, a clotted chocolate mould, dense with bacterial and insectoid life. And spreading along what would have been the inner arm of this bifurcated branch or trunk are giant funguses of some kind, a leathery brown mushroom that protrudes, like half a generous soup plate embedded in the rot, feeding off it. This is not strength, legendary or otherwise: it is corruption.

The damaged tree triggers something: I choke with anger. I want to drag that old fool next door by his collar round the corner to see this spectacle of ruin. I want to show him the inner life of oak trees, their weakness, their corruption, the bloated mass of their history. I want to prove to him that his tree, at last, will break open my property. But my dog has done as much sniffing and urinating on the corpse of the tree as he is going to, and now he tugs wildly at the leash, impatient to get on. I tug back, hard, trying to discipline him, but it makes no difference. We lurch round the tree and carry on, Worm exulting in his furious movement, and I merely furious.

By the time we reach Avenue Le Seuer and pace beside the green belt, things are easier. He has used some of his excess energy. I would love to let him go, let him hurtle down the green belt, but this is a dog one dare not unleash. As if to illustrate the point, a cocker spaniel in his prime comes trotting towards us. His body language is worrying. He is confident to the point of arrogance, blind to his danger. I cross the road, trying to avoid the dog, but he swerves in towards us and comes to a halt before Worm, challenging him, growling. I begin taking in the slack, aware that Worm does not indulge in threat behaviour. Then weariness overtakes me. I cannot explain this. It is so extreme that I feel queasy, and all the colours of the street, the greenery, become too rich, seem to float off their objects and fill the air. I let go the leash. There is a brief pause; Worm hurtles forward and sinks his teeth into the neck of the lesser animal. Perhaps he growls, I am not sure; his mouth is muffled by fur, by flesh and no doubt blood. He gives an occasional shake, tightening his grip each time. The spaniel is oddly silent, eyes stricken with disbelief. I think he is being throttled. Slowly, he collapses; Worm lowers him in stages, allowing him to keel over.

My arms are weak, the edges of my hands tingle. There is the cream and liver of Worm, and the copper fur of the spaniel. I've always thought – I realize it afresh – their ears are ridiculous. But life and motive return gradually. The spaniel appears to be dead. I cannot get Worm to release it. He growls if I try to pull him away. He does not try to eat his kill, merely to tighten his grip. To give his victim redundant death, I suppose. Or perhaps this moment is just the completion of his nature. Luckily, so far, no-one has seen us. If I can only detach Worm, make him open his jaws somehow, we will walk on, leaving the spaniel behind us. There will be no consequences. I am filled with a grim satisfaction, which I do not really understand. It is a relief, however, a kind of pleasure. I stand holding Worm's leash, hoping he will soon let go.

Ken Barris lives in Cape Town, and teaches at the Cape Peninsula University of Technology. He has twice been shortlisted for the Caine Prize for African Writing, and his most recent novel, *What Kind of Child*, was shortlisted for the 2006 Commonwealth Prize Best Book Africa. He has won a number of South African literary awards for fiction and poetry, including the M-Net Book Prize, the Ingrid Jonker Prize, and the Thomas Pringle Award. 'The Life of Worm' appeared in *New Writing from Africa 2009*, published by Johnson & King James Books, Cape Town.

How Shall We Kill the Bishop?

Lily Mabura

IT WAS FR YASIN LORDMAN who had asked the question – nothing more than a joke. A most inappropriate joke since he loved the bishop. It was Easter besides. But the three other priests in the vicarage heard him. Dafala, the cook who had set a breakfast in keeping with Holy Saturday, heard him. Perhaps it was the weak kettle of black sugarless tea that was to blame, or the sleep raging in his mind, or the pain in his knees for bearing his weight all night, or his fellow priests who would not join him for their usual morning cigarette.

"I'm fasting cigarettes today," the youngest priest, Fr Ahmed, had declared. He had been ordained at the beginning of the year and had been trying to quit smoking since.

"The bishop would want us to," Fr Seif had said. He smoked more for the company than anything else.

"He is ill and he is watching us, Yasin. What do you think he says to the Archbishop in Nairobi, to the Nuncio, to Rome?" Fr Dugo had asked.

"He is the problem, then, I suppose," Fr Yasin had said. "Tell me, how shall we rid ourselves of him? How shall we kill the bishop?"

The three were now staring at him under the flickering light of a candle, which was set in the middle of the dining table. The generator had been shut down on Maundy Thursday and the vicarage stood dark and pensive like the arid land surrounding it. "You should whip yourself," Fr Dugo said.

Fr Yasin rose from the table and walked into the kitchen. Dafala retrieved the bishop's breakfast tray from the wood oven. Dafala was almost as old as the bishop. In his lengthy white kanzu, regularly mistaken for a priest's frock, he was no less of a priest than any of them. His life was single-mindedly devoted to the vicarage. He had no property that he could call his own. He was celibate. He was a man who had lived out his priesthood unwittingly, Fr Yasin thought. With his conscientious hands, Dafala now covered the bishop's sconce and scrambled eggs with a purple crocheted napkin. Next to them he placed a flask of tea and chinaware. Then a small glass vase, often used in the chapel, with a single purple rose stem. Dafala had roses for all occasions and kept a kitchen garden even in the worst of droughts. He skimped on everybody's drinking water if he had to. He handed the tray to Fr Yasin without a word.

Fr Yasin knocked on the bishop's door twice before entering. The knock was perfunctory. The bishop was knelt on a prie-dieu at one end of his room. There the wall jutted out like an apse and served as his own private chapel. He was awake and fully dressed as usual. His bed was made even though he had taken to returning to it by midmorning. Fr Yasin had begun judging his daily disposition by the length of his random siestas. The bishop's broad back was to him and he stared at it under the smoky yellow light of the candelabrum burning on his desk. It was a back still unbent by age or illness, and his neck rose from it like a ship's mast. Above his white shirt collar was the familiar edge of his hairline from which it was so easy to see a clear throbbing vein under the sun. He was always the last man to break into a sweat on the hockey pitch. He looked very much his old self from the back, but his face had begun to change – it resembled his father's more and more each day, Fr Yasin thought.

There was a photo of the bishop's father on his desk. Having one made a difference, Fr Yasin had always felt. It was the only thing he envied in other men. Perhaps that was the reason he loved this photo. Raji Lal Sandhu stood there beside his Kenyan wife in his white turban and generous Sikh moustache. He had the face of a man who had worked hard his entire life; a man who, in exchange for a piece of land that he could call his own, had left the Sikh units of the Indian Colonial Army for the ballast pits feeding the construction of the Kenya-Uganda railway. Every time Fr Yasin looked at this photo, he noticed something new. Holding the bishop's breakfast tray that morning, for instance, he noticed that here was a man who had determined to forget India.

It was the condition of man, he was inclined to think. Fr Ahmed, for example, was hard bent on forgetting cigarettes; Fr Seif, in his determination to forget the woman he loved, intruded on everyone's quiet time because he could not stand his own; Fr Dugo determined to forget that the bishop had tested him most before admission; and Dafala determined to forget that the bishop was sick at all and carried on as usual. If the bishop ever determined to forget anything, though, it was sealed in his heart, well hidden beneath the surface of his face.

That face was now cast upwards, to the crucifix nailed onto the innermost recess of the apse. This was the only crucifix still standing in the vicarage. The rest had all been taken down and replaced with bare wooden crosses the evening before. The bishop's crucifix, however, was still standing: Christ's head like a drooping flower, his cranium a framework of metal petals crowned with barbed wire; his cheekbones high and pointed above the hollow flesh; his nose a sharp edge of metal; his beard an emerald mixture of rust and solder; his splayed hands broken at the joints, with ragged strips for fingers; his chest the very semblance of a fallen warrior's breastplate – severely punished and bloodied; below that a gaping hole, as jagged as a cave's mouth, exposing a metal vertebrae blackened with soot; his penis a small and humble-looking rod of metal, placed at an odd angle, as though the sculptor had considered leaving it out all together and then, upon further pondering the matter, had realized that it could hardly be ignored, that it would be more visible in its absence than actuality; and his legs, of course, those corroded buttresses that still held up the church long after Golgotha.

"Fr Yasin."

"Your Grace?"

"Have breakfast with me," the bishop said, rising from his knees. There was a faint smile on his thin face. "And what has Dafala made this morning?"

Fr Yasin placed the breakfast tray on a table facing the patio and lifted the purple napkin. "Hmmm. There is no cook like Dafala, don't you agree, Yasin?" he asked. "In his mind's handbook are an explicit set of rules on how to cook for a sick priest, a disobedient priest, a vain priest, a good priest …"

Fr Yasin laughed and pulled him a chair.

"How is his garden faring?"

"Well, let's say that the birds will have none of it and neither will the locusts if they come this year. They would need pliers for teeth from the way he's been working the wire mesh."

The bishop chuckled, but his brown eyes seemed tired and somewhat sunken, like a drying riverbed slowly shrinking away from its banks.

"He'd rather be telling you this himself, of course," Fr Yasin said. He opened the flask and poured the bishop a cup of tea. "He's not used to having someone else bring in your breakfast."

The bishop sipped his tea and said nothing. He was weaning Dafala from himself, Fr Yasin suspected. When he had been posted to this Kenyan northern frontier town 30 years ago, he had come with two things: his mule and Dafala. A young pregnant Borana prostitute, groaning with labour pangs, had stumbled into their camp the very first morning. The bishop had carried her to his sleeping bag, Dafala had boiled some hot water, and Yasin Lordman had been born. He had a mulatto skin for which the only logical explanation out here was a white soldier from the British military training base. The base was a remnant of the colonial legacy standing amongst stunted acacia trees and withered shrubs of solanum. The stunts of sparse grass surrounding the base were too brittle for cattle to graze on – too brittle even for the camels. There were no doum palms close by either, and Dafala always explained this by stating that sacred plants could not flourish near the base.

When Fr Yasin stepped onto the patio and lit his cigarette, he could see the old military base with its floodlights beaming out towards the rising sun, which burned dark purple and red, its brow on the dunned horizon as yellow as ostrich yolk. With time, additional military bases had cropped up, government bases that periodically filled with local troops. They were like Roman garrisons, ever sending out legions through this gateway town into the troubled desert beyond. Rumour had it that there was a huge battalion on the way. It was the talk of the town, a distraction from the sick dogs that would not stop howling, from the dry animal carcasses in the bush and watering holes caked with mud. He should have informed the bishop, but there was no need to tell him right away. He had enough to worry about with the emptying school, falling church attendance and the overcrowded hospital. Fr Yasin wanted him to enjoy his breakfast. If the battalion was arriving today, he would hear it.

The bishop joined him on the patio, a cup of tea in one hand. "The Lord should give us peace for he has given us all else, Yasin. It was what Augustine prayed for at the end."

What Augustine had actually prayed for, Fr Yasin thought, and what the bishop was perhaps praying for, was what Augustine had penned after those words – the peace that is repose, the peace of the Sabbath and the peace that knows no evening. One hardly forgot Augustine, Fr Yasin felt; not if you read him with passion and plenty of time on your hands like he had while on a pre-ordination retreat at the Red Sea port of Massawa. The heat in Massawa was as exhausting as it was here, as exhausting as it must have been for Augustine farther along that North African shoreline. Sometimes days would go by with hardly a breeze finding its way over the water. At such times red algae would appear suddenly and bloom endlessly, miles and miles of it, as if from the very Suez to the Strait of Bab al Mandeb, like streaks of thick camel blood that would not dissolve away. Then it would die, unexpectedly, and the sea would turn from red to rusty. Eventually Fr Yasin would wake up one morning and find the algae gone altogether, the sea blue-green again.

That was how droughts ended here: when you least expected. Out of the blue. You simply awoke one morning to the sound of rainfall. The grass, like it always did, would have budded overnight and the women, who always showed up at sunrise for maize rations, indeed, who were already at the gates, would show up as usual, but with their long hair wet, their clothes dripping wet, their faces already nourished.

"The need to confess overwhelms me today, Father," the bishop said.

His words startled Fr Yasin, and he looked away in embarrassment, unprepared for such access to the bishop's heart even though he had been contemplating it only a moment ago. "I'm hardly the man for it, Your Grace," he said. "I could place a call to the Nuncio, if you like. He's your old friend. He knows you best."

The bishop remained silent for a while, gazing at the sunrise. "I cannot speak to Felice right now, but I have a letter for him. There, on my desk. Mail it for me."

By its weight, Fr Yasin could tell on his way to his room, it was several pages long. He was going to mail it later in the day when the post office opened. There was no hurry. Sometimes it took almost a month for a letter to reach Nairobi. Dafala had poured half a pail of water into the washbasin. He used it to shave and bathe. Then he lay on his bed and slept.

The rumble of diesel engines and the laboured rotation of crankshafts woke him up. The air was already tinged with the smell of dust, hot rubber and exhausted clutches. It was the battalion slowly pouring in. Soldiers' voices and soldiers' hard combat boots, hitting the dry sandy ground in unbroken descent, could be heard alongside the rolling machinery.

When Fr Yasin emerged from the vicarage, there were soldiers everywhere, milling about in desert camouflage fatigues and standard issue rifles. The town, generally sleepy and desolate, was now an anthill of tough unfamiliar faces from other provinces. Fr Yasin made his way towards the post office slowly, the bishop's letter in his shirt pocket, the smell of soldiers' sweat in his nose, as old and as rank as a nomad's. He was standing at the doors of the post office when he saw the altar girl, Salima, across the street. Their regular set of altar boys had left town with their families when the drought had begun in search of more reliable waterholes for their livestock; they were deep in the sun-scorched land where wars were fought over whatever little water and pasture remained. Salima had landed their job inadvertently when she had scaled the vicarage's walls and Fr Ahmed, taking an early evening walk, had spied her in Dafala's garden. It had taken two mad dashes around the vicarage for him to corner her. Her penance, it was decided, was to serve as an altar girl and join the priests every Sunday afternoon in the chapel where they practised the hymn 'Salve Festa Dies' in preparation for Holy Saturday. It was Fr Dugo who had come up with the idea – to surprise the bishop. Without the altar boys their in-house choir had somewhat diminished in strength, not to mention that they were sorely lacking in the alto department. Salima was the panacea. Such was the strength of her soprano! It was amazing that it could be found in so scrawny a creature. Added to that was the fact that she had memorised the entire Gregorian melody, in

Latin no less, during the first practice while they, to learn it, had been listening to a taped version the entire Lent. For her prodigious memory, they had dubbed her Giordano Bruno.

Salima, however, had not shown up for the last choir practice. Fr Ahmed was convinced that her family had moved. Fr Seif differed and revealed that he had sent her home with excess rations every time she had shown up for practice. Fr Dugo, distrusting the exact excessiveness of Fr Seif's rations, had told him off. Fr Yasin thought that they were all unnecessarily worried, but did not have adequate conviction for his opinion. Consequently, when he saw her milling in the chaos of that afternoon, his heart lurched and he screamed her name. She did not seem to hear him and, as he pushed against the soldiers to cross the street, she disappeared into the dilapidated clip joint his mother had worked in till her death.

The two men at the door, designated to shake up tight-fisted clients, absconding clients and the like, let him through because they were too surprised to stop him. A huge strobe light rotated from the iron sheet ceiling and dancing soldiers bumped against him under its intermittent glaring lights, swirling about to the music like they would to a war dance: in a frenzy of waving hands, kicking feet and faces as dark and gleaming as Dafala's eggplants.

"The guards at the door swear that you've lost your mind, Father." It was a woman who spoke to him, a woman like his mother, the kind of woman he always determined to forget.

"I'm looking for someone... a little girl. Her name is Salima."

She put her arms around his neck – little stick arms that came from a little stick body. He could break it, he felt, by merely resting his hands on its sides. It spoke of paucity: conceived and bred as such into the natural state of her being.

"A desert man always thinks of the going out before he enters," she said.

She talked like Dafala and her long hair smelt like his mother's: of ancient Cushitic perfume encrypted into his pre-oedipal senses. "I have to find her," he said.

"You would need money."

The only thing in his pocket was the bishop's letter. "I have none," he said.

"A trick then," she suggested, "something to fool a drunken soldier's eyes for a little while."

"And you?" he asked, reaching for the bishop's letter. "Doesn't a desert woman also think of the going out before she enters?"

"Me? I am like a doum palm, father. My head is always in the fire, but my feet run in the water."

He opened the bishop's letter, removed its contents and handed her the empty envelope. She let go of his neck and smiled – a little broken half-smile that would always remain with him.

"Go back," she said. "I shall send her to you."

In the vicarage living room, after lunch and after the bishop's afternoon siesta, they sang him the poet Sedulius' fifth-century Easter poem: "Hail, festival day, venerable throughout all ages, in which God vanquished hell and took possession of the Heavens/ Behold, the beauty of the reborn world bears witness to the fact that all the gifts of the Lord have returned with Him/ He who was crucified is God, and behold, He reigns over all things; let all creation lift its prayers unto the Creator/ O Christ, Saviour of all things, good Creator and Redeemer, only begotten of God the Father."

The bishop was in full regalia – his pink cap on the middle of his head, the bishop's ring on his hand. He smiled at the tiny set of dust prints across the red floor, which Fr Ahmed had polished to a gleam. The prints ended at Salima's bare feet. Tears welled in his eyes whenever she chorused *salve festa dies...* Dafala cried. Fr Ahmed, Fr Seif and Fr Dugo cried. They all cried because they had never seen the bishop so moved.

But Fr Yasin did not really cry until sunset when he was lighting the sacred fire from which the paschal candle would be lit. When he knelt onto the dry sand, arranged the dry pieces of wood together and lit them up, tears brimmed in his eyes. He wept then for the bishop, whom he loved. He wept for Dafala's pain. He wept for the woman with a little broken half-smile who reminded him of his mother. He wept until a hard rubber boot bit into the back of his neck and yoked his head still. With bleary eyes he saw a familiar envelope fall before his face and into the fire. At that moment he remembered what the woman with a little broken half-smile had said to him – that she was like a doum palm with her head in the fire but her feet running in water.

A rifle barrel dug into his spine and the pressure at the back of his neck increased, forcing his face closer to the fire. The hair on his face singed all at once and the flames danced and leapt higher as they consumed the crumpled envelope. The hot ash beneath exploded. Something more than mortal man seemed to be holding him down. He faced, then, a fear that is only known to a nomad as he comes to the realization that he is too deep out in the desert to make it across or to turn back.

Then the boot on his neck lifted unexpectedly and with it the rifle barrel. As Fr Yasin reeled away from the fire, smoke and heat in his lungs, he saw the bishop on the other side. He was standing very still, the desert sunset reflected so deep in his eyes that it seemed to be flaring from within him. In his hands was the towering white paschal candle. Engraved on it, in golden letters, was the alpha at the top and the omega at the bottom. In between the letters were five red grains of glowing incense, one for each holy wound. When the volley of bullets exploded over Fr Yasin's head, the paschal candle suddenly glowed with hundreds more; they sparkled red like rubies. The paschal candle remained standing even as the bishop let go and Fr Yasin blindly reached for his punctured body. It stood, stoic, the candle, at that eerie moment when the dark figure was scaling the vicarage walls and the church bells were pealing to the rhythm of abrupt thunder rumbling from afar.

Lily Mabura is an African and African Diaspora scholar and writer at the University of Missouri-Columbia. Her literary awards include the Jomo Kenyatta Prize for Literature and Kenya's National Book Week Literary Award. She has published several short stories, a novel, *The Pretoria Conspiracy* (Focus Books, 2000), and three children's books. She is currently working on a fictional exploration of Kenya's 2007-08 post-election violence, *Man from Magadi*. 'How Shall We Kill the Bishop?' was first published in *Wasafiri* 53, Spring 2008.

Muzungu

Namwali Serpell

ISABELLA WAS NINE YEARS old before she knew what white meant. White in the sense of being a thing, as opposed to not being a thing. It wasn't that Isa didn't know her parents were white, although with her mother, this was largely a matter of conjecture. A layer of thick dark hair kept Sibilla's face a mystery. And even though as she aged, this blanket of hair turned grey then silver then white, a definite movement toward translucence, Isa never could properly make out her mother's features. More distinct were Sibilla's legs, tufts of fur running like a mane down each thick shin, and her strange laugh, like large sheets of paper being ripped and crumpled. Isa's father, the Colonel, was white but it often seemed as if pink and grey were battling it out on his face. Especially when he drank.

Her parents had settled into life in Zambia the way most expats do. They drank a lot. Every weekend was another house party, that neverending expatriate house party that has been swatting mosquitoes and swimming in gin and quinine for more than a century. Sibilla floated around in a billowy Senegalese *boubou*, sending servants for refills and dropping in on every conversation, distributing laughter and ease amongst her guests. Purple-skinned peanuts had been soaked in salt water and roasted in a pan until they were grey; they cooled and shifted with a whispery sound in wooden bowls. There were Tropic beer bottles scattered around the veranda, marking the table and the concrete floor with their damp semi-circular hoof prints. Full or empty? Once the top is off a Tropic bottle, you can't tell because the amber glass is so dark. You have to lift it to check its weight. Cigars and tobacco pipes puffed their foul sweetness into the air. Darts and croquet balls went in loopy circles around their targets, loopier as the day wore on.

The Colonel sat in his permanent chair just beyond the shade of the veranda, dampening with gin the thatch protruding from his nostrils, occasionally snorting at some private or overheard joke. His skin was creased like trousers that had been worn too long. Budding from his arms were moles so large and detached they looked ready to tumble off and roll away into the night. And as though his wife's hairiness had become contagious, his ears had been taken over – the calyx whorl of each had sprouted a bouquet of whiskers. The Colonel liked to drink from the same glass the entire day, always his favourite glass, decorated with the red, white and green hexagons of a football. As his drunkenness progressed, the glass got misty from being so close to his open mouth, then slimy as his saliva glands loosened, then muddy as dirt and sweat mixed on his hand. At the end of the evening, when Isa was sent to fetch her father's glass, she often found it beneath his chair under a swarm of giddy ants, the football spattered like it had been used for a rainy day match.

Isa had no siblings and when the other expatriate children were around she was frantic and listless in turns. Today, she began with frantic. Leaving the grownups outside propping their feet on wooden stools and scratching at their sunburns, Isa marched three of the more hapless children inside the house and down the long corridor to her bedroom. There, she introduced them to her things. First to her favourite book, *D'Aulaires' Book of Greek Myths*. Second to the live, broken-winged bird she'd found in the driveway. Third, and finally, to Doll.

"And this is my doll. She comes from America. She has an Amurrican accent. Her name is Doll."

Bird and Doll lived together in an open cardboard box. Isabella stood next to the box with her chin lifted, her hand pointing down to them. Due to the scarcity of imported goods in Lusaka, Isa was allowed only one doll at a time, and this one had gone the way of all dolls: tangled-haired-patchy-bald. Forever smiling Doll, denied a more original name by her fastidious owner, sat with her legs extended, her right knee bent at an obtuse and alluring angle. From Doll's arched left foot a tiny plastic pink stiletto dangled. Her perforated rubber head tilted to one side. She seemed interested and pleasant. Bird, also on its way to bald, cowered as far away from Doll as possible, looking defeated. Isa poked at it with her finger. The bird skittered lopsidedly around the box until, cornered, it uttered a vague chirp. Alex and Stephie, prompted by Isabella, applauded this effort.

But Emma, the littlest, thinking that the doll rather than the bird had made the sound, burst into startled tears. She had to be soothed (by Stephie) and corrected (by Isa). Isa was annoyed. So, she sat them down in a row on her bed and taught them things that she knew. About fractions and about why Athena was better than Aphrodite. About the sun and how it wasn't moving, we were. But soon enough, Emma's knotted forehead and Alex's fidgeting began to drive Isa to distraction. Then came the inevitable tantrum, followed by a dark sullen lull. The other three children hastened from the room in a kind of daze. Isa sat next to the cardboard box and cried a little, alternately stroking Doll's smiling head and Bird's weary one.

When she'd tired of self-pity, Isa walked to the bathroom and carefully closed and locked the door. She took off her shoes and climbed onto the edge of the bathtub, which faced a wall about two feet away. Only by standing on the edge of the tub could she see herself in the mirror on the wall, which hung at adult height. She examined her grey eyes, closing each of them in turn to see how she looked when blinking. She checked her face for hair (an endless, inevitable paranoia) and with a cruel finger pushed the tip of her nose up. She felt it hung too close to her upper lip. Then Isa let herself fall into the mirror, her own face rushing toward her, her eyes expanding with fear and perspective. At the last minute, she reached out her hands and stopped herself. She stayed in this position for a moment, angled across the room, arms rigid, hands pressed against the mirror, nose centimetres from it. Then, bored of her face, she jumped down and explored the floor. She unravelled the last few squares of toilet paper from its roll and wrapped it around her neck. Then she opened the cardboard cylinder from the toilet paper roll into a loose brown curlicue – a bracelet. She discovered some of her mother's torn OB wrappers, which twisted at each end like candy wrappers. She stood them on their twists to make goblets for Doll.

Eventually drunken guests started lining up outside the bathroom, knocking at the door with tentative knuckles and then flat palms and then clenched fists. Isa emerged, head high and neck at full extension, her OB goblets balanced on an outstretched hand like a tray. Bejewelled with toilet paper, she strolled past the line of full-bladdered guests. She gave Doll the goblets, modelled the jewellery for Bird. But Isa's heavily curtained bedroom was too cold to play in alone.

Reluctantly, she removed her makeshift jewellery – too childish for her mother to see – and rejoined the party outside. As she marched outside in her marigold dress, she glanced at the other children running around making pointless circles and meaningless noises in the garden. She avoided them, choosing instead to be pointedly polite to their parents, who were still sitting in a half-circle on the veranda, insulting each other. There was something excessive about her attentiveness as she shoved snack platters under the noses of perfectly satiated guests and refilled their mostly full beer glasses, tilting both bottle and glass to minimize the foam, just like the Colonel had taught her.

Finally her mother told her to sit down over by Ba Simon,

the gardener. He was standing at the far end of the veranda, slapping varieties of dead animal onto the smoking brai. He reached down to pat Isa on the head but she ducked away from his hand, ignoring his eyes and his chuckle. The saccharine smell of the soap he used mingled with the smell of burnt meat.

Ba Simon was singing softly under his breath. He'd probably picked up some nasty song from the shabeen, Isa thought emphatically, repeating in her head a condemnation that she'd heard a thousand times from Ba Gertrude, the maid. There are three kinds of people in the world: people who unconsciously sing along when they hear someone else singing, people who remain respectfully or irritably silent, and people who start to sing something else. Isa began singing the Zambian national anthem. Stand and sing of Zambia, proud and free. Land of work and joy and unity. Ba Simon gave up on his quiet song, smiling down at Isa and shaking his head while he flipped steaks he wouldn't get to eat. Ashes from the brai drifted and spun like the children playing in the garden.

Isa watched the other children with a detached revulsion, her elbows on her knees, cheeks cradled in her hands, ashes melting imperceptibly onto the pale shins below the hem of her marigold dress. Stephie was sitting in a chair, depriving a grown-up of a seat, reading a book. Isa was scandalized. It was her mythology book! She stared at Stephie for a while and then decided to forgive her because her nose had a perfect slope. Unlike Winifred, whose nose was enormous and freckled, almost as disgusting as the snot bubbling from Ahmed's little brown one. The two of them were trying to play croquet under the not-so-watchful eye of Aunt Kathy. Younger than most of the adults at the party, Aunt Kathy always spent the day chain-smoking and downing watery Pims cups and looking through everyone, endlessly making and unmaking some terribly important decision. Isa found her beautiful but looking at her for too long sometimes made her feel like there were too many things that she didn't know yet.

Emma, who had cried about Doll, was all smiles now, sitting cross-legged by herself and watching something, probably a ladybug, crawl along her hand. Emma was so small. Isa tried to remember being that small, but the weight of her own elbows on her knees made it hard to imagine. The ladybug was even smaller. What was it like to be that small? But anyway, how could Emma have been so afraid of Doll when she clearly wasn't afraid of insects, which everyone knew could bite and were much more disgusting? Isa had once retched at the sight of a stray cockroach in the sink but it had been a pretend retch because she'd heard at school that cockroaches were supposed to be disgusting. Horribly, Isa's pretend retch had become real and had burned her throat and she'd felt ashamed at having been so promptly punished by her body for lying. But enough time had passed to transform the feeling of disgust at herself into disgust about small crawling creatures. She watched as Emma turned her cupped hand slowly like the Queen of England waving at everyone on the television. The ladybug spiralled down her wrist, seeking edges, finding curves. Emma giggled. Isa swallowed and looked away.

Far off in the corner of the garden, there was a huddle of boys crouching, playing with worms or cards or something. Isa watched them. Every once in a while, the four boys would stand up and move a little further away and then crouch down again, like they were following a trail. They were inching this way along the garden wall, toward where it broke off by the corner of the house. Around that corner was the guava tree Isa climbed every afternoon after school.

Isa got curious. And then she got suspicious. She stood up, absently brushing ashes from her dress instead of shaking them off and accidentally streaking the yellow with grey. She noticed and bit her lip and squeezed her left hand with her right, caught between her resolve to do good and her need to change her dress. But the adults were roaring with laughter and slumping with drunkenness. Whatever inappropriate behaviour was taking place in the garden, it was up to her to fix. She started running across the garden, looking behind her to make sure no one followed. When she was close, she stopped herself and began stalking the boys, holding her breath.

She tiptoed right up to their backs and peered over their shoulders. At first she couldn't see much of anything, but then she realized that they were huddled around a thick-looking puddle. It was mostly clear but, as Jumani pointed out in a hushed whisper, there were spots of blood in it. Isa's eyes widened. Blood in her own garden? She winced a little and looked back at the party: Emma was interrupting Stephie's quiet read; Winifred's freckles were pooling into an orange stain in the middle of her forehead as she concentrated on the next croquet hoop; Ahmed, snot dripping dangerously close to his open mouth, stared back at Isa but he seemed sunstruck rather than curious.

She glared warningly at him and turned back around. The boys, oblivious to her presence, had disappeared around the corner. She followed and found them squatting at the foot of the guava tree, her guava tree, with its gently soughing leaves, its gently sloughing bark. She circled the mysterious puddle and walked toward them with purpose, abandoning all efforts at being sneaky. But the boys were too fascinated with whatever they saw to notice her. A whining and a rustling from under the tree drowned the sounds of her approach. Isa looked between their shoulders, her throat tight.

Lying on its side, surrounded by the four boys, was Ba Simon's dog. She was a ridgeback, named thus because of a tufted line down the back where the hairs that grew upward on either side of the spine confronted each other. At the bottom of this tiny mane, just above the tail, was a little cul-de-sac of a cowlick. Ba Simon had named the dog Cassava because of her colour, though Isa thought Cassava's yellowish white fur was closer to the colour of the ivory horn that her father had hung on the living room wall. But today her fur was crusted over with rust. Her belly, usually a grey suedish vest buttoned with black teats, was streaked dark red.

Isa's first thought was that these boys had poisoned Cassava and were now watching her die a slow miserable death under the guava tree. But then she saw that the side of Cassava's head was pivoting back and forth along the ground. Isa stepped to the left and saw an oblong mass quivering under the eager strokes of Cassava's long pink tongue. The thing was the colour of ice at the top of milk bottles from the fridge, cloudy and clear. From the way it wobbled, it seemed like it was made of jelly, maybe more like the consistency of gravy that had been in the fridge too long. It was connected by a pink cord to a slimy greenish black lump.

The boys were whispering to each other and just then Jumani made to touch the lump with a stick. Isa jumped forward and said, "No!" in a hushed shout. Cassava whined a little and licked faster, her tail sweeping weakly in the dust. The boys turned to Isa but before she could say anything, the oblong thing jerked a little and Isa inhaled sharply. She pointed at it, her eyes and mouth wide open. The boys turned back to look. Where Cassava was insistently licking, there was a patch along the oily surface through which they could just glimpse a grey triangle. It was an ear. Isa took her place beside the boys, sitting in the dust, her precious marigold dress forgotten.

Perhaps out of fear, perhaps out of reverence, the boys didn't touch Cassava until she had burst the wobbling sac and licked away all of the clear fluid inside it. Occasionally there was a tobacco-tainted breeze from around the corner. Sometimes laughter would flare up, crackling down to Sibilla's chortle. But the grownups didn't come. At first the children whispered their speculations but soon they were all watching in silence, gasping only once when the outer skin finally burst, releasing a pool that crept slowly along the ground.

There it was, lying in a patch of damp dirt, trembling as Cassava's tongue grazed along its sticky body. It was the size of a rat; it was hairy and pink; its face was a skull with skin. Below its half-closed pink eyelids, the eyes were blue-black and seemed almost see-through. But that was just the sunlight dappling through the guava leaves and reflecting off their shiny surface; the children looked closer and saw the eyes were opaque and dead.

The boys became restless. Cassava was still licking but nothing was happening; the mystery was revealed, the thing was dead, what else was there to see? They got up and left, already knocking about for other ways to pass the long afternoon. Awed and resolved to maintain her dignity and her difference from the boys, Isa decided to stay, silently shaking her head when Jumani offered her a hand up. She was so absorbed in watching that hypnotic tongue rocking the corpse back and forth that she didn't notice the girl until she spoke.

"He et oh the bebbies? Eh-eh, he et them," the girl asked and answered.

Isa looked around and saw nothing. Laughter fell from the sky. Isa looked up into the tree and saw Ba Simon's daughter sitting in a wide crook, her little head hanging to one side as she smirked down upon the world. Chanda was about six or seven, close enough to Isa's age, but they weren't allowed to play together because of an unspoken agreement between Ba Simon and Sibilla. The two girls had been caught making mudpies together once when they were younger and had been so thoroughly scolded by their respective parents that even to look at each other felt like reaching a hand toward an open flame. Isa's entrance into primary school had made their mutual avoidance easier, as had her innate preference for adult conversation and her recently acquired but deeply held feelings about the stained men's t-shirt that Chanda wore every day as a dress.

Isa glared at Chanda's laughing face.

"He ate what? Anyway, it's a her," she replied with hesitant indignation. She gathered some strength in her voice. "Obviously," she said. Chanda was expertly descending from the crook of the tree, flashing a pair of baggy but clean pink panties on the way down. Isa abruptly decided that Chanda had been secretly climbing the guava tree during school hours and that she had stolen the panties off the clothesline.

As she carefully lowered herself to the ground, Chanda said: "His stomach has been very row. And then pa yesterday? He was just cryingcrying the ho day. Manje ona, jast look: he et the bebby."

Isa was horrified, then dubious. "How do you know?"

Chanda, now standing with her feet planted a little apart, her hands resting on her haunches in imitation of Ba Gertrude, nodded knowingly.

"Oh-oh? Jast watch." Her voice trembled nevertheless.

Cassava hadn't stopped licking the stillborn. Her tongue maintained its rhythm and her mouth appeared to have moved closer to the dead-eyed skull. Isa shuddered and scrambled to her feet. Suddenly, mustering all her courage, she stretched her leg out and with her bare foot kicked the dead puppy as hard as she could away from Cassava. It tumbled away into the dust, a guava leaf trailing from it like an extra tail. Cassava growled ominously.

"Did she do that yesterday too?" Isa demanded, reaching behind her for Chanda's hand. Chanda was silent. Cassava scudded her distended torso across the ground toward the puppy. Isa quickly glanced back at Chanda's face, which, in reflecting her own fear, terrified her even more. Cassava wheezed and growled at the same time. Her legs twitched.

"Let's go," Isa suggested breathlessly.

Their hands still clasped, the two girls ran away, Cassava baying behind them. Isa felt buoyed by her fear, like it had released something in her, and she let her legs run as fast as they wanted, relishing the pounding of her feet on the dusty path to the servants' quarters. It had been a long time since Isa had visited this concrete building at the back of the garden. When she had been a very little girl, like Emma, there had been an emergency when her father had drunk too much from his bleary glass. There hadn't been anyone among the expats to take care of her when the Colonel had tumbled to the ground, football stein clutched unbroken in his hand. So that night, while her mother veiled up and drove the Colonel to the hospital, Isa had gone with Ba Simon to his home for supper.

They'd eaten *nshima* and *delele*, the slimy okra dish that reminded her of the shimmery snail trails on the garden wall. Ba Simon had been as kind and as chatty as usual, but it had gotten cold and the servants' quarters had been very dark and cold. Isa had been grateful to hear the soft shuffle of her mother's hair on the floor when she came to fetch her that night.

Isa stopped running abruptly. Her left foot had stepped on a small but sharp rock. Her halt jolted Chanda, who still held her hand. With the pain in her foot, Isa suddenly felt an arrow of real fear piercing her exhilaration, deflating her back into her sulky self. The vegetable patch behind the servants' quarters was just visible beyond the avocado tree. She lifted her foot and examined the sole. It wasn't bleeding but there was a purple dot where the rock had dented it. As she put her foot down she remembered Cassava and turned to see how far they'd run. The garden was huge and encompassed a small maize field, which Isa could glimpse just beyond the mulberry trees with their slight branches and their stained roots. She really ought to go and tell mummy about the dog.

When she turned back to tell Chanda exactly that in her most grown-up voice, Isa found herself surrounded by three other small children. There was a little boy who looked just like

Chanda and two slightly younger girls, toddlers, who looked just like each other. Isa stared at them. She'd never seen twins before. They stood with their hands clasped behind their back, their bellies sticking forward like they were pretending to be pregnant. Isa sometimes played this game in the bath herself, pushing her belly out as far as it could go until her breath ran out, but this did not seem to be what the little girls were doing. A picture of Cassava's low stomach from the previous week flashed through Isa's head.

One of the girls was probing around her mouth with her tongue and the other was making stuttery noises that Chanda apparently understood because she replied, pointing at Isa and shaking her head. The little boy was staring at Isa and smiling broadly. He stepped forward and held out his hand, making the same upward-turned tray that Isa had made for Doll's goblets. Isa shook her head and stepped back, unsure. Chanda implored, "Bwela. Come. Come." She pointed at the servants' quarters to show where Isa was meant to come. There was blue smoke and the sound of splashing water coming from around back. Isa relented.

They walked together toward the building, which was low to the ground and had no door, just a gap in the façade. There were also no windows, just square grids drilled into the concrete here and there for ventilation. As they approached, the little boy ran to the back shouting something. A young woman whom Isa had never seen before appeared from around the corner carrying a metal pot, her wrists and hands wet. She wore a green *chitenge* and an old white shirt, but Isa immediately noticed that she wasn't wearing a bra: you could see the shape of her breasts and the dark outline of her nipples. The woman smiled at Isa and waved and as she approached, said, "*Muli bwanji?*" Isa knew this greeting and replied in an automatic whisper, without smiling, "*Bwino.*"

The woman shook Isa's hand and Isa noticed that she didn't bend at the knee or touch her right elbow with her left hand as blacks usually did with her. Halfway through the handshake, Isa suddenly realized that she herself was supposed to be deferential. She hurried to bend her knees but they seemed to be locked and she managed only a jerky wobble. The woman lifted her head, sniffing the air imperiously. Then she looked at Chanda and demanded something. Chanda shrugged and ran up the three stairs into the servants' quarters, dribbling a forced giggle behind her. "Ach," the woman said and sucked her teeth. She walked back to the rear of the house to finish her washing. Halfway there she turned and gestured to Isa that she should follow Chanda into the quarters.

Isa gingerly made her way up the steps and into the velvet darkness beyond the doorway. The concrete floor wasn't dirty – it was polished to a slippery shine – but the dust on her bare feet rasped as she stepped inside. The place had a strong coppery smell of fried *kapenta* mixed with a tinge of woodsmoke. As Isa moved further in, the smell took on an acrid note that she dimly recognized as pee. It was so dark that she couldn't see anything except for the gold grid on the floor where the sunlight had squeezed through the ventilation grill. The fuzzy squares seemed more radiant for having been through that concrete sieve. Isa walked toward them. The patch of latticed light travelled up her body as she moved into it and eventually glowed on her stomach. It was like being in church or on Cairo Road. She held her hand in front of it and the light made her hand glow like the orange road lamps...

A chuckle from the corner interrupted her reverie. Isa looked around, her heart thudding, but she still couldn't see anything. She stood still and concentrated her eyes on the darkness, willing them to adapt.

She could just make out three figures sitting in the corner. There was a young woman, younger than the one outside, an old woman, and Chanda, who sat cross-legged, fiddling with an ancient cloth doll with a vaguely familiar shape. Isa worked out that it was the faceless ghost of the Doll who had preceded Doll; she felt a little shocked that it should be here and then even more shocked that she should have forgotten it to such a fate.

She walked toward the women, who were mumbling to each other. Only then did Isa notice the baby sitting on the young woman's lap. In fact – she moved closer – the child was sucking on the woman's breast. Isa knew about breastfeeding but she'd never seen it before. She couldn't tell whether the baby was a boy or a girl; it had short hair and was naked except for a cloth diaper. She wanted to turn away but she couldn't stop looking at the way the child's lips moved and the way the breast hung, oblong and pleated like a rotten pawpaw. The women continued to deliberate while Chanda, who was responsible for this intrusion, for this straying, sat staring at Isa, absently twisting the doll's dirty arm as though to detach it.

The child started crying: not the wailing of a newborn, but an intelligent sobbing. Isa stared at it and then realized that it was staring back. Its mother lifted it and began bouncing it up and down on her lap. After a moment, the old woman began laughing, a rattling laugh that devolved into coughing and then rose back up again to the heights of gratified amusement. She said something. Then the young woman began to laugh too and finally Chanda joined in with a high-pitched trill.

"What?" Isa asked. "What?" she demanded.

But they kept on laughing and then the woman stood up and held the baby in front of her. Isa stared at its sobbing face, distorted with wet concentric wrinkles like its nose was a dropped stone rippling a dark pool. The child began to scream, wriggling its little body as its legs kicked. Was she supposed to take the child in her arms? The room echoed with laughter and wailing.

Isa shouted "What? What?" again.

The laughing woman kept shoving the child at Isa's face in

jerks until their noses suddenly touched.

"*Muzungu*," the woman said.

As though at the flip of a switch, Isa began to cry. Her breath hitching on every corner of her young-girl chest, she turned and ran out of the room, tripping down the steps in her haste. As she ran past the mulberry trees, the beat of her feet released a flock of birds from their boughs. They fluttered past her and flickered above her bobbing head, their wings a jumble of parentheses writing themselves across the sky.

The night brought the breeze and the mosquitoes. The guests waned in number and spirit. When she'd had enough, Sibilla planted bristling kisses upon their cheeks and sent them to navigate the intricacies of Lusaka's geography and their drunken dramas on their own. Colonel Corsale was still in the garden, dozing on his chair, one hairy hand holding his football glass clasped to his belly, the other dangling from the armrest, swaying like a hanging man. In the early days, Sibilla used to drag her husband to bed herself. But over the years, his boozing had swollen more than just his ankles. These days she told Ba Simon to do it.

"A-ta! I'm not carrying the *cornuto* to bed. The man's earlobes are fat," she'd grumble, leaving her husband to the night, the breeze, and the mosquitoes.

Isa wandered around the yard, yawning, picking up Tropic bottles of various weight under Ba Simon's direction. She hadn't told anyone about the dog yet, or about all the inhabitants of the servants' quarters – did they realize how many people lived there? – or about the laughing. She felt tired and immensely old, old in a different way from the times she played teacher to the other children. Old like her father was old, a shaggy shambling old, an old where you'd lost the order of things and felt so sad that you simply had to embrace the loss, reassuring yourself with the lie that you hadn't really wanted all that order to begin with.

Ba Simon was singing something spiritual, not in English, but Isa could barely muster the energy to gainsay his song with her own. She only got halfway through "Baby you can drive my car" before she collapsed on the grass beside her father's chair. The wicker creaked in rhythm with his snoring. She put her fingers in his dangling hand and he muttered something.

"Papa?" she asked softly. "*Dormendo*?"

She only spoke Italian to him when she was very, very tired. The international school she attended had compressed all her thoughts into English, but some of her feelings remained in the simple Italian her parents had used on her as a toddler.

"I went to the servants' quarters," she said.

The Colonel's whiffling snore continued. Isa slapped a mosquito away from her shin. She stood up and walked over to Ba Simon, who was vigorously scrubbing the grill.

"What does *muzungu* mean?" she asked, sitting on her stool.

He kept humming for a second. "Where did you hear that word?" he asked.

Isa didn't reply. Ba Simon hesitated. Then he made a face and said, "Ghost!" He waved his hands about. "Whoooo! Like that katooni you are always watching." He smiled and moved closer to her with his hands still waving. "Caspah Caspah the shani-shani ghost," he sang in the wrong key.

"Whoooo!" she giggled back at Ba Simon in spite of herself and they chatted about nothing for a few minutes. Ba Simon wasn't very bright, she thought and then forgot. But Ba Simon noticed her thought even though she hadn't said it and soon enough, he told her to go to bed. When she looked back from the doorway to the house, Ba Simon was just getting ready to carry her father to bed. His body was pitched awkwardly over the Colonel, his face contorted, his long stringy arms planted beneath the Colonel's neck and knees. But when he saw Isa turn back, the strain on Ba Simon's face dissolved instantly into a smile.

"Go," he whispered, and she did.

Namwali Serpell was born in Lusaka, Zambia, in 1980 and moved to the US when she was nine. She is currently an assistant professor at the University of California, Berkeley. 'Muzungu', her first published short story, originally appeared in the African Diaspora journal *Callaloo* and was selected for *The Best American Short Stories 2009* (Houghton Mifflin Harcourt, Boston). She has also contributed non-fiction to *Bidoun* and *The Believer.* She is working on her first novel and on a book of essays on uncertainty in narrative fiction.

Soulmates

Alex Smith

MARY OF THE BEES and thorns, Mary of the porcupines and nubbly roots, *namelijk Maria, genaamd Magdalena, van welke zeven duivelen uitgegaan waren*, Maria minus seven devils, Maria after whom I have been named, help me, *please*! Outside spiders were spinning webs, bees were waiting, motionless, for day, and porcupines were chewing through the frost and rutty bulbs of the *renosterveld*. Inside Maria was tearing. The door to the room was closed, but windy wind, tumultuous as Maria's loss, violated the locks and cracks and came in with grit and insects, to witness the splitting of the elliptical entrance to Maria's physical soul, and, regardless of the fragile circumstances, boorish wind rampaged about the room with all the rattle of seven devils. Maria was laid out on a bed of coarse sheets. Bewildered by the soft creature he had acquired, and more eagerly aggressive than clumsy, her husband, Franz, was forcing himself into her with his body, a full two feet taller than hers so their faces were not level during the act of love, which to her felt more like an act of hate, but she knew no better, or other, and so trebled her admiration for all the mothers and wives in history, among them many Marias who suffered love every night in the name of God and family. *Onder dewelke was Maria Magdalena, en Maria, de moeder van Jakobus en Joses, en de moeder der zonen van Zebedeus.* Her face was squashed under the sharpness of his collarbone, a bone broken and healed up harder than before, now pressing down against the cartilage of her nose. Under a rock-fall of emotion, yes, she was prone since childhood to vigorous joys and sadnesses, it was difficult for Maria to determine which was worse: being suffocated under the weight of her husband or the pain of dry fornication. Am I dead, in hell, or am I really here with this man in me? she asked the vision of three desolated Marias that hovered in anguish at the crucifixion. *En bij het kruis van Jezus stonden Zijn moeder en Zijner moeders zuster, Maria, de vrouw van Klopas, en Maria Magdalena.* There was the cross of splinters, and then there was the bed. At home in France Maria's mattress, modest as it was, had been filled with feathers and covered, the breezy duck down coddled in velvet. This man's mattress was packed in cotton sacking, stained, and stuffed with straw and horsehair. Earlier that day she'd seen a porcupine, heard its shaking quills, for the first time, and now it felt like the man she was destined to live out her life with was shoving quills up her body. Swirling around her were all the noises of the seven-devil wind, the bristle-faced man, his jolting, sackcloth bed whose craggy sheets sang out in abrading cotton notes a deafening song of humping. At 16 she was fond of laughing. Where is the joke in all this? Confounded, she asked all the Marias still standing at the crucifixion, and strained to hear their answer over the noise of copulation of which she was the subject, but in which she was playing little part. Some lump in the mattress needled her spine. *En Maria Magdalena, en Maria, de moeder van Joses, aanschouwden, waar Hij gelegd werd.* Maria tried to move her face, desperate for air, but Franz was too heavy with muscles and lust. Her fingers clawed at his jacket as if trying to dig a way out of the avalanche, but the wool was thick and her husband felt nothing. Before passing out, Maria thought, 'Mary of the bees and thorns, Mary of the porcupines and nubbly roots, Mary, Mary, Mary and your son, bless me with quick death rather than life with this brute.' In the din of asphyxiation and unceremonious climax, the angels over Jooste farm didn't hear Maria's prayer: Franz came, he sighed, unrooted himself from her and rolled over. Oxygen filled Maria's lungs and she survived to turn her head and pity and hate the exhausted man with unbuttoned trousers passed out at her side. We are trapped, she imagined telling him, you and I, and this horsehair bed is our four-sided island of matrimonial bleakness. She looked at their respective feet and laughed, for hers were tiny and wistful and his were solid and brutish. I will remember this moment of looking at our feet for the rest of my life. 'Husband,' she said and found the word unsavoury and uncomfortable in her mouth. 'Husband!' It sounded as unnatural as having him inside her had felt. When he did not reply and she was sure he wasn't awake enough to hear, she said: 'Husband, Mary and God forgive me, but I wish you dead.' *En aldaar was Maria Magdalena, en de andere Maria, zittende tegenover het graf.* There they were, the holy Marias staring at Franz's grave, then they turned in a blaze of guilt, and Maria, feeling a wretched sinner, stared through them at the reeds in the ceiling and took a tally of the situation of being married and no longer a virgin. He didn't even kiss me, she thought, glancing at him again, and unable to oust the word die from her wishes. To hell I'm going, and that made her laugh – to a hell of aching hipbones I've already come. The fine skin over those hipbones was turning a shade of bruise. She offered a prayer, begging the Marias' pardon for entertaining murderous thoughts. When she had beseeched the three ladies sufficiently and convinced herself she would make amends for wishing so out of turn, she realized she was glad Franz had not kissed her. While willing to offer Christian sympathies for his human plight, she would have been dishonest if she hadn't admitted that his breath, his feet, his clothes, his bed, all aspects of him, but especially his blebby lips, were rancid to her. He was a knurled farmer, who spent his blessed savings on negotiating for a bride. Pity me, Marias, if you care, that I am the one. A tear ran down Maria's temple and into her hair. It was bitter in that room with no furniture other than a bed and a table for a humourless Bible in Dutch, Dutch, Dutch! In it, Mary's dead son issued the new commandment on love: *Een nieuw gebod geef Ik u, dat gij elkander liefhebt; gelijk Ik u liefgehad heb, dat ook gij elkander liefhebt...* But it was not in the language of Maria's heart, it was in the language of her keeper, the dialect of bondage. Franz, who had stripped her of clothes to fondle, squeeze, prod, suck, suffocate, vandalise and admire her, and now slept fully dressed with his pants still unbuttoned and his mouth hanging open, he would not speak to her in any language other than Dutch – upon her arrival at his farm, he disallowed her mother tongue, French. She pulled up a blanket. Maria had imagined for herself a younger, kinder, more handsome and wealthier husband: a man who understood the significance of a kiss. It was pointless being angry with her family for binding her to such a lot, they had needed money, but she was angry with the Marias. Emphatically, she was angry with the three Marias, always tending to their beloved's crucifixion. And what of my wounds? As wicked as she knew it was, she could not excommunicate the then present notion that all three Marias, Jesus and his God had abandoned her. Why? She repeated her question again and again as she fell asleep, but no answer came to the windy room.

Morning came in place of enlightenment, and it was icy. Before he went out to feed the cows, Franz, made of chilly skin and cold rough wool as if he'd been dragged from the frosty outside, slid on top of Maria, driving her spine against that lump in the mattress. She had been dreaming until she realized she was dying again. I cannot die on bad terms with the Marias, she thought. *The tongue is a fire!* I must pray, and hastily, or risk eternity in God's gloomy dungeon, waiting for judgement for the crime of killing my husband in words. *De tong is ook een vuur, een wereld der ongerechtigheid; alzo is de tong onder onze leden gesteld, welke het gehele lichaam besmet, en ontsteekt het rad onzergeboorte, en wordt ontstoken van de hel.* Panicked, she tried to open her mouth to call her prayer to the mothers and prostitutes of heaven, to ask for help, but her lips were held closed by the avalanche weight of her husband. This second splitting, second coming, was more painful than the first for Maria, but indifferent Heaven's weaver birds were singing in a multitude of nests hanging from Franz's trees. He, her husband, was in as good a mood as he had been in for as long as he could remember. Agony, unlike any Maria had known before, caused tears to flow from her eyes, but Franz's woollen jacket absorbed them all. Dear Marias, why? The lovely mothers spoke only through Franz in unpoetic jerks. Finally he was gone into the wind, out to his cows. Maria shivered, remembering the sandpaper touch of Franz's chapped hands, and got up with difficulty, because her legs ached. Guilty, corrupted by her tongue and ashamed, she pulled the blanket over the new stains on the mattress. She stood, naked, at the window. Never in life had she been so cold. In Dutch, she'd been instructed by her husband to make a breakfast of eggs and bread and have it ready for when he returned from the cows. Even when dressed, she felt no warmer, ice had gone into her bones. Still, she had been raised to be dutiful, so she left the dread room and went to the kitchen. There she met Titus. *Aan Titus, mijn oprechte zoon, naar het gemeen geloof: Genade, barmhartigheid, vrede zij u van God den Vader, en den Heere Jezus Christus, onzen Zaligmaker.* Titus full of grace, he was a slave; there was not much to think of him other than that he was named after an Epistle. Maria didn't think of herself as a slave, she felt she was better than a slave; later she knew she was nothing, no better than a slave. At first, all she noticed about Titus full of grace was his eyes – it wasn't that she admired his eyes, or felt attracted to his eyes, only that she saw dark humour in those eyes. Impish Titus with tapering fingers, who was only three years older than Maria, in spite of everything that was his life, possessed the playfulness of youth. He was a jester, not especially gifted at comedy, but irrepressibly inclined to joke. Chasing chickens around the egg-less kitchen that bleak morning, Titus made Maria laugh until she couldn't breathe.

So Maria left the silent Marias baying at their cross. She grew fond of the Biblical book of Titus, regardless of its Dutch, and from it drew comfort. *Want een opziener moet onberispelijk zijn, als een huisverzorger Gods, niet eigenzinnig, niet genegen tot toornigheid, niet genegen tot den wijn, geen smijter, geenvuil-gewinzoeker.* When her husband beat her, which was often, that line swirled in her thoughts, *geen smijter, geen smijter, geen smijter,* each smack, each punch from Franz, she saw those words: *geen smijter*! Titus danced in the shadows behind Franz's back. He mimicked the master, pulled faces, soothed Maria's pain and dressed her cuts with a lotion made of herbs from the renosterveld. Despite its contradictions, St Paul's Epistle to Titus helped Maria survive life as a wife-slave. *Vermaan den dienstknechten, dat zij hun eigen heren onderdanig zijn, dat zij in alles welbehagelijk zijn, niet tegensprekende; Niet onttrekkende, maar alle goede trouw bewijzende; opdat zij de leer van God, onzen Zaligmaker, in alles mogen versieren.* Master of the house, Franz, refused to buy her clothes, but Master of the farce, Titus, surprised her with gifts from nature: a pretty leaf, a flower, a speckled egg, a feather, a plantling. One day when Franz was whipping Titus for some ludicrous misdemeanour, Maria realized she cared deeply about the other slave's pain. It hurt her to see him hurt, and there was another unexpected gift from Titus – after a decade at Jooste farm, Maria believed she had no feelings left. If only you were to me like a brother, Titus, *dat ik U op de straat vond, ik zou U kussen, ook zouden zij mij niet verachten.* After that, she thought always of kissing him and took to reading the Song of Solomon.

She was the one who leaned upwards and held her lips near Titus's lips. His breath was sweet or maybe it wasn't, but even if it wasn't, it was sweet to her. For an age they stood almost kissing. His lips were beautiful, or maybe they weren't, but even if they weren't, they were beautiful to her. Taken alone, without his being, his lips were perhaps too large, but accompanied by those eyes, his lips were a dream to Maria. It occurred to her that in her life she had borne two children to a wretch, but she had never been kissed by a man whom she loved and who loved her back. *Hij kusse mij met de kussen Zijns monds*; *want Uw uitnemende liefde is beter dan wijn.* Poor Titus, that he has to carry the weight of my dreams, so many dreams I have dreamed about him. Dare I burden him so, and at the same time claim I love him? Still their lips had not touched. It would be a crime; it would be adulterous. God and his Marias will never return if I continue on this course. She wanted to open Titus's jacket to touch the skin on his shoulders, but she didn't, she kept her hands behind her back. She looked up at him as a slave looks up to another slave, as beggar to another beggar, with understanding – *I know how it feels.* Maybe his skin was too dark, maybe it didn't matter; no, this wasn't an imperfection to her, it was part of him, and so she wanted to press her cheek against his cheek, her skin against his skin. What is skin, anyway? His skin was perfect, imperfect, looked soft, as did his lips. Tears came to her eyes because of the dearness of the man. 'I'm sorry,' she said. 'Why?' he asked and she could feel the warmth of his question on her lips. 'It is wrong of me to endanger you for a kiss.' Even though she knew she should walk away out of his sleeping quarters, she did not. She stayed there with him, lifted her hand and touched Titus's brow. He closed his eyes. She ran her fingers over his eyelids, then down his cheek. His skin was smoother than she'd imagined. She touched his earlobe. 'Do you know I have waited thirty years to be kissed?' She hoped he would kiss her then, but he did not. Near enough to kiss, but not kissing. She leaned closer to him so that their lips were touching, but still it was not a kiss. She moved her head from left to right, stroking his lips with her lips. In the cold weather her lips were dry, the skin taut, all the more fragile, more sensitive, but his lips were not dry, they were God's lips. Here I am, almost kissing God. Maria tensed her lips into a kiss and kissed him. He did not take his hands from behind his back. She kissed him again and he kissed her. 'We will die for this,' she said, and kissed him again. 'We will surely die for this.' Now, Titus was moved to unknot his hands and stroke her cheek. 'Never mind, we are already dead.' 'Yes, we are ghosts!' she agreed. She kissed him more and loved him more. 'Dear ghost, I knew from your eyes you would be a good kisser.' Oh, what a gentle kisser he was, and so she couldn't help yearning for more of those kisses. Till that minute she had felt her whole life after her sixteenth birthday like Jesus in his final torment calling out to God, Mary and the Angels, *ELOI, ELOI, LAMA SABACHTHANI! Mijn God! Mijn God! Waarom hebt Gij Mijverlaten! My God, my God, why have you forsaken me!* But now all that was irrelevant, God had returned in these lips, in these kisses, God was reaching out to her, embracing her, smoothing her hair, loving her. There was no need for them to ever stop kissing; they would kiss forever on that spot beside the slave's bed, which he, in preparation for love, had stuffed with stolen wool and scented leaves of herbs. The universe was reduced to two ghosts kissing, both ghosts weeping freely, elated, liberated, consoled. No more were they mortal, no more slaves with bodies to torture, there was no human law that could trammel their joy, no marriage contract, no taboo, no judge, no time, all silence, no separation, only union. Their tongues touched and it was thrilling. So much so that she smiled as they kissed, smiled to think how strange it was that touching tongues could be enough to absolve the universe for all the years it had abused her. Delight welled up in her and caused her to giggle like a 16-year-old. It might have been shameful for tongues to touch like that, but she didn't care and nor did she care what heavenly magic made touching tongues so comforting, so happy a thing to do. It was such a simple act, this being close, this kissing, so refreshing in a gloomy life – or death, if she was a ghost. She paused from kissing to look again, then saw in his eyes the spirit she cherished. 'God is in your lips,' she said. The kiss lasted an hour and several minutes – one hour and several minutes of bliss in a lifetime of brutality. The harshness of their mutual existences took the kiss beyond the realms of the regular and into the ethereal. Horses' hooves echoed through the renosterveld. Franz had arrived back. Maria closed her mouth and, before the kissers scattered, Maria and Titus looked at each other, both astonished.

Nothing was the same after that and everything was the same. They kissed many times, with affection, and, when Franz was with his cows, they made love. One January day, though, Franz – 'Schurfde Franz', 'Rough Franz', as he was known by all in the area – assaulted Maria with a poker, whatever for has long since become irrelevant. Titus was too sickened to dance in the shadows any more. He left the room, returned with a gun and fired. Franz groaned, *I'll kill you both*, was bleeding, but the bullet had only grazed him. Maria grabbed the rod from Titus's hand, and together she and Titus killed that husband with his own weapon. It happened quicker than a kiss. They stuffed Franz's body into a porcupine hole.

For months they loved as lovers.

Then, quicker than a kiss, the life was excruciated from Maria Mouton when she became, according to history books, the first white woman to be given the death penalty in the Cape, for killing her husband and bedding his slave. *Doodsangst, doodsstrijd, agonie, geblaker* are the Dutch words to describe Maria's end as prescribed by the Cape Court of Justice, who were mortally affronted by her concubinage with the slave. *Mijn God! Mijn God! Waarom hebt Gij Mijverlaten!* They held burning straw to her face to make her black as Titus, tied her to a pole, throttled her and left her body to disintegrate. Titus is a ghost in history books; little is said of this man, except that he was impaled alive at the Castle of Good Hope and, even with a stake through his innards, he did not lose his humour. After four hours of impalement, the keeper of the castle dairy gave Titus a bottle of rum, from which the slave drank deeply. When advised not to drink too much in case he should become drunk, Titus joked: 'It does not matter, I sit fast enough. There is no fear of me falling.' He lived 44 hours more until noon on 3 September 1714; three minutes past the hour on that spring day he looked beyond the silent Castle walls at the mountain, for the last time, and thought of all the flowers growing there – gifts he would give Maria when they kissed again. His right hand and head were sawed off and fixed on the gates of Jooste farm as a warning to other slaves who might dare to love beyond their quarters. Perhaps it was the herbs he consumed, but what history doesn't know is that Titus's blood was miraculously sweet, and so abundant that bees from near and bees from far were drawn to that pike to drink the blood of his severed head. For weeks there was a perpetual swarm over Jooste farm until every bee had fed off him, and in due course, Titus became honey, only to be gathered by farmers and eaten again.

According to the records of the Cape, Maria and Titus are still criminals – as the interrogator of the court put it, they are eternally 'a contemptible slave guilty of carnal intercourse' and 'a woman who gratified her foul and godless lust' – but, today, they would be allowed to kiss, allowed to love and would surely have been acquitted from the charges of murder, for they were acting in self-defence. They are soulmates. Officials, let their names be cleared! *Wie oren heeft om te horen, die hore. He who has ears, let him hear.*

Alex Smith has lived in China and Taiwan but now lives and writes in Cape Town, where she was born. She has written two novels – *Algeria's Way* (2007) and *Four Drunk Beauties* (2010) – and one non-fiction book, *Drinking from the Dragon's Well* (2008), all published by Umuzi. She received the 2010 Sanlam Youth Literature Silver Award for *Agency Blue*, a teen adventure story set in Cape Town. 'Soulmates' first appeared in *New Writing from Africa 2009*, published by Johnson & King James Books, Cape Town.

Stickfighting Days

Olufemi Terry

THWACK, THWACK, THE TWO of them go at it like madmen, but the boys around them barely stir with excitement. They both use one stick and we find this swordy kind of stickfighting a bit crappy. Much better two on one or two on two – lots more skill involved and more likelihood of blood.

I turn to Lapy. "Let's go off and practise somewhere. This is weak." Lapy likes any stickfight, but almost always does what I say. His eyes linger ruefully on Paps and the other boy – don't know his name but I see him a lot – and then he follows me.

I run almost full tilt into Markham and he gives me a grin, like we're best pals and he's been looking for me. Markham is my rival. We've beaten each other roughly the same number of times. Well, six to five in his favour, but one of my victories was a beauty, a flowing sequence of sticks that even I couldn't follow before I smashed his nose in nicely. Almost broke it. The satisfaction of Markham's watery-eyed submission that day makes me smile easily back at him.

"Wanna mix it up?" Markham's eyes aren't smiling any more; he won the last one and thinks he's on a roll. I know better.

"We could," I come back smoothly, "but it wouldn't mean much." I hold up Mormegil. I've told no one I've named my sticks though I'm not ashamed. I love Mormegil but I don't think the others would understand. "I've only got one stick with me." I cock my head to one side enquiringly at him. To be honest, I've been leaving Orcrist, my other, so I don't have to get into any serious battles. Everyone knows I'm a two-stick man. But I'm not ready to go up against Markham again just yet. Or any of the other top stickfighters. I've been trying some new moves. I feel close to a breakthrough in terms of technique. But it's not quite there and until it is, I only carry Mormegil. Mormegil is as long as our regulations allow, a lovely willow poke, dark willow – that's why I chose the name. It means black sword in Tolkien's language. A sword with a mind of sorts. Turin wielded it, and it would cut anything, anyone, eagerly. In the end it took his own life to avenge those he killed. My Mormegil has little knobs at the joint and one tip is nicely pointed – we're not allowed to sharpen sticks – but this is natural. Mormegil is a killing machine, even though I've never done for anyone yet. But I will. I like Markham, but I'd like to kill him. I dream of doing it in front of a huge pack of boys. Clinically.

Markham's henchman, Tich, is a one-stick man but he now holds up two. "You can use this one." He throws it to me and I catch it easily, angry at being forced to fight. I force a deep gulp of air into my lungs. Fighting angry is bad! Only Simon ever did it effectively and where's he now? I give Lapy a confident look, taking the measure of the unfamiliar stick as I do. It's rubbery, too bendy but unlikely to break. It's also too light. Much too light.

Markham's not much one for warm-ups, he bounces from one toe to another like a boxer, rolls his head, then gestures to me that he's ready. I already see a ring of boys forming around us, keen for a real spar and not that sword stuff.

He comes at me, neither quick nor slow, his arms wide. One of his sticks, an ash thing, is almost as good as Mormegil. He let me hold it once, before we were rivals. Stiff as hell and with a good weight, maybe an inch shorter than my beauty. I fend him off easily. Markham is good but he's cautious. He knows I'll not risk much with an unknown stick. I could keep him off with Mormegil but I feel I've got to try one of my new moves. No one'll attach too much to this particular fight so

I can afford to be bold. But I'm cunning too. That's what got me to where I am. That and good reflexes.

I hold Mormegil in my left hand and the unfamiliar stick in my right, gripped in the middle – an outdated form I know, but very good for riposting against an over-eager opponent. Here he comes, Markham, his sticks a blur more from technique than power. In goes Mormegil to break that rhythm and then I bring my whippy stick in to catch the one in Markham's left. It is too bendy to give me much opening but I am quick, and I know not to go for a body blow; the opportunity is small and he'd be able to retaliate. I bang Mormegil against the outside of his wrist, the bony bit, all the while twirling my right hand to keep him caught up. I try for his knuckles but he is no fool, Markham. He pulls back a step, wiping his forehead with the back of his hand. I watch him change his grip to match mine. There's no sweat on me yet! He's not angry enough to make a serious error but I feel in my gut, now's the time to let him – all the boys – see what I've been working on. I drop my right grip so that I'm holding both sticks sword like. I bang them together once, and advance on him. This is me at my most fearsome: my speed frightens opponents and no one knows exactly what I've got planned so it's now or never. Our sticks clatter against each other left to left, right to right and cross-wise. I use the bendy stick to hold his every thrust and I am glad that the whippiness absorbs much of the power. Markham settles into a pattern and at the last second, I drop one of my parries so that his stick whistles on, at the same time lowering Mormegil so that my face is unprotected. Markham falls for it and doesn't try to halt his stroke, lunging at my face with gangs of force. Trust him to try and maim me – and this contest means nothing. Both his sticks are held high... so I fall to one knee with both of mine ready, my mind blotting out the murmured wave of anticipation from the crowd. I've thought long about this, long enough that there's no need to think now. It's not enough to go for the balls, the most vulnerable spot. No, a quick stickfighter can inflict double damage. I stab with Mormegil at his crotch, relishing its rigidness and the pain it will cause, yet pulling the stroke a little, for I am a boy also, I know what it means to strike full strength there. Better to kill someone with a temple blow than that. At the same time, I bang the bendy stick on the ball of his knee as hard as I can and roll.

I come to my feet expecting to see Markham in the toils of agony. He feigns total indifference at first, then allows us to see he's in some pain, but only from his knee. He hobbles backward a step, kicking it out to ease it. I wait, tasting the moment but puzzled as to why he isn't clutching his balls howling.

A deep voice rolls out, that of the judge: "Halt, boys!" Markham turns to him, a mixture of reluctance and relief on his face. I'm glad, and now every boy there turns toward the judge. He's not a stickfighter. Not even a boy, the judge. His real name is Salad but we use both. I don't know whether he gave us the art of stickfighting, but he knows the rules and enforces them when he's around. Sometimes he's unseen for days, but his word is binding always, and not because we're afraid. The judge has a fearsome appearance, he's all muscle, like carved wood, his arms bulge and this seems the reason for his shabby shirts – it isn't – and the strain of his thighs against his corduroys makes his hands seem normal, fragile even. But the judge, Salad, is sick. At times, he can't stop coughing and, somehow, it is known among us that the muscles have surrendered their strength though they are preserved in form. The judge's voice is what commands our respect, mostly. He is very fair too.

"What's in your pants, Markham?" the judge is quietly stern. He stands with his hands behind his back. Some of the boys are already taller than him. Markham knows he'll be forced to prove that he didn't cheat, so with little ado, he pulls out through the top of his pants a thick sponge, much squashed, and hands it over to Salad. I grin, but joy is short lived. The judge pronounces: "Markham is disqualified. Match annulled." Damn! I was certain he'd award me a victory, but now it's worked against me that the match wasn't a proper one. And everyone who matters has seen my new move too so the element of surprise, my tactical advantage, is lost. I don't waste time trying to appeal to the judge; he's very strict, and this is why we respect him. I walk away too quickly for anybody to speak to me, Lapy at my shoulder.

In the evening I practise my forms with Lapy, who'd be a good stickfighter if he could be bothered. He never says much, but I like him for this. He's no pushover, Lapy. If he tells me something I listen; he knows what he's about. He's got the manner of a champion stickfighter: you can never tell what's on his mind and he never seems afraid. When he feels like being scarce, even I won't see him.

Finally, I light a cigarette butt I found and ask him the question that's burned on my lips for hours. "What d'you think of the judge's decision earlier?"

He stops to glance at me in the middle of a stick manoeuvre. "Pretty bog-standard. He cheated but the judge didn't want to give you a total victory. Psychologically that would have demoralized Markham too much." I watch him ponder whether to say more before he begins to weave his sticks once more. Sometimes, I think of giving up this stickfighting lark altogether. I'm 13 and getting too big to spend hours practising my sticks. The smart boys spend their days poking and scouring the dump. There's a lot of valuable stuff here – it's not just home.

The judge surprises me early the next morning; he's been watching me from behind a car wreck. Usually I'm about early, practising my sticks, snooping on what others are doing. When I notice him, I wonder how he escaped my eye for so long; it's hard to conceal such a bulky body.

He says, his voice hoarse: "Well met, Raul." The judge – Salad, I want to call him as the older boys do – talks like this sometimes. He moves out from behind the wreck heavily, though I know just how agile he is.

"Salad," I say, continuing my single stick forms. I'm not exactly angry, but it won't hurt if he thinks I am. He likes me. I feel him waiting; his silence tells me something of his mood.

"My decision yesterday was based on what I felt was fair." I wait, hoping he'll blurt something. "I know you and Markham are rivals. I know how evenly matched you two are. I know you feel betrayed, you think I've given him the edge because he's seen your new moves." I'm so stunned by Salad's words that my stick hangs momentarily in the air. It's best to neither confirm nor deny, so I continue practising, keeping my face flat. My thoughts race. I now feel sheepish, angry, afraid and resentful of the judge all at once so I push these feelings away. My concentration is so strong that when I stop to breathe a few minutes later, Salad is no longer there. At first I'm glad, and not just because my chest is heaving. But then it hits me that he wanted to tell me something and then didn't. I am hurt rather than curious. Even if it is just more stories – it is Salad after all who tells us about Mormegil, Turin and Beren – he should have said his piece.

I practise with Lapy much of that day, in a remote bit of the dump. He's a good partner, cagey. I use my new moves a couple of times but with no success. By the evening our feet blister from acid waste, and I feel like crap. My sadness has nothing to do with fighting sticks.

I feel no better the next day and decide perhaps what I need is not more practice but to trade blows with someone. I go in search of Markham but before I find him, I come upon a group formed up in a circle around two boys, 15-year-olds. I know one of them, Malick – he's a brute – but I've never seen the other. They're going at it. Malick uses a lone stick, swings it like a club although it's regulation thickness. His fights are popular because he's sly, savage. We've seen the judge pull him off people a time or two. Malick is actually not so brutish, in my opinion. I think he plays it up because he's not liked and wants to disgust us even more. The other boy uses two sticks and is very good. He blends power and finesse very well; he's strong on both hands. I wonder if he's from the dump. Malick will lose and so I stay to watch, even though I'm eager to fight this morning. His opponent seems popular, the crowd murmur his name, Peja, in a way that I detest, despite his skill. When he disarms Malick a little later, it's done without viciousness so that Malick stands empty-handed but unhurt. His eyes roll wildly in his head as he considers his options. I feel sure Malick is on the point of throwing himself at Peja to grapple him to the ground but he doesn't. The fight is over.

Before anyone can move off, Salad pushes another boy forward by the shoulders, into the circle, and points to me. The judge only occasionally proposes fights in this way – it's not the role of a judge, really, is it? But when he does, there's excitement. This boy is a little shorter than me, sandy-haired, compact. His face is bland and I know with a jolt in my belly that he'll be good, probably better than Markham. Salad has put me on the spot but happily I'm spoiling for a fight. I step forward with a readiness that's very like a thrill for blood. I don't know him, I may never see him again but I want badly to hurt him in unusual ways with my sticks. Break his wrist or knock out his front teeth. Around us, as we prepare, lots of younger boys, tens and elevens. A trio of Malick's friends hang about too.

We both take time to limber up. For me it's a chance to study my opponent. With a signal, the judge gets us going. Sandy hair comes right in, quick as mercury, and hits my knuckles, surprisingly hard. He does not dance back and we spar up close so my longer reach is a disadvantage. He manages to catch my other knuckles. He's done something to his sticks, this one; they are somehow very hard. Being hit twice so quickly calms me. I'm sweating already and my mind is blank save for a desire to humble this boy. His quickness is at least equal to mine, I think, without dismay.

I don't know that he'll tire before me either; my stomach is a pit and my vision blurs round the edges. I should've eaten something but that's not a thought for the present. The next time he launches an attack I go back at him equally hard. His right hand is a little weaker, his ripostes less certain on that side, so I force him to retreat with Orcrist, trying to double his wrist back on itself. He sidles away but I follow, banging his elbow. He tries to reply and succeeds in getting his right hand free. The crowd has been quiet and as we take a moment to breathe, it feels like we all take in air together. This time when he closes with me, Mormegil keeps him away, but I cannot do this for long and I only want him to think I'm tired. He is cautious too – his elbow is likely giving him pain and he teases me with his left hand, batting at Mormegil. I launch myself at him once more, feeling like I did against Markham, that it is now or never. I'm not sure what I'll do but I feel confident enough to respond to anything. He's quick as lightning and rash – going for the eyes when he could have thumped my knuckles again. But he's in close once more and we trade blow and parry until my arms feel they might fall from my shoulders and my breathing fills my ears. I force him to aim a blow at my ribs, leaving my left side open, knowing he'll take the opening. It stings – I feel the skin redden almost instantly – and I drop to one knee, reeling a little bit. He pauses – he lacks the killer instinct – one stick above his shoulder; the other is pointed at me to ward off any blow that may come. But my stroke is aimed once again at the knee, too low for his block, and I lunge rather than swing, to jab him full on the ball of his kneecap, twisting Orcrist – not Mormegil – to cause more pain. He stumbles back, almost dropping a stick as he hops to clasp his injured knee. Mormegil comes up as I shoot up off my own knee like it's a launch pad though it hurts like hell to do that. I pull my stroke at the last second, grudgingly.

There's something in his eyes – he's not afraid – but I see recognition beyond fear – and acceptance of what I'm about to do, of what I am. Killer. I pull the blow, or push it rather so I miss his temple – the thought flashes through me, through my entire body like a lash, that I don't know this boy and can't kill him. Mormegil lacerates his ear instead. And having changed the stroke, I drop my stick. My knuckles sear again as if in sympathy with him. And I breathe once more, like a bellows, exhausted and desperate suddenly to sit. Sandy hair still clutches his knee, ignoring his torn ear. He's on the ground now in agony and my sorrow is complete. Salad eyes me gravely but I can't abide his eyes on mine; there's only shame in this win. It takes all my willpower to not leave Orcrist and Mormegil as I walk off. Part of me notices – and is bitter – that no one chooses to follow me, to ask what's wrong.

I feel shunned but the dump is actually a big place and boys here have enough of a struggle to survive not to worry over someone feeling down. I cannot find Lapy and even the lazy search of a day does not turn him up. Hunger attacks my insides suddenly and I hunt for food for hours. I even leave the dump to see what can be scavenged outside. I take Mormegil, tucked under my clothes – for protection. The fearful looks, the clutched purses of the outside are somehow welcome, an escape from loneliness. At least I'm noticed. People on the outside are scared of me but not because I fight sticks. I'm an urchin, a snot-faced, scuffed boy in rags that they want to pity but can't. I stuff my head with stale old chicken and bacon cadged from a greasy restaurant and go back to the dump, hating and enjoying the nervous looks.

When I can't take any more loneliness, I decide to go and find him, the one I nearly killed. That's how I think of him, and I can't shut him out of my thoughts. I'm resolved to go and see how he is. To explain myself. Perhaps to even say sorry, even though I don't know what for. The thing is, I don't know where he stays, perhaps he's not even a dump kid. I ask boys I know and even boys I don't, describing him, hoping they saw the fight. I get a jumble of answers; short sandy-haired boys are a dime a dozen anywhere, I suppose. I give up, then bump into him as I go in search of Lapy once more, just to keep active. He's practising with some mates. They stop as I draw near. He gives me an almost friendly nod, though I notice his eyes are guarded, like when a madman's in the room. Talking is an effort, my tongue feels thick and ashy, and I have to ask him for a word twice before he understands. We go some way away and he makes a show of dropping his sticks, to impress his friends, I suspect. I conceal my smile.

I say it all at once, afraid to stop even for breath: "Look, I don't even know your name, and I'm not sure this will come out the right way, but I just wanted to say sorry. It was a good fight, you're a good fighter. I know what I did wasn't technically illegal, but I feel an apology is needed." I wrestle down the urge to go on. Laconic Lapy. I must be like him. Like the Spartans too. Sandy hair thrusts his hand at me like we've just played tennis or some other cruddy gentlemanly sport. There are no bruises on him; the ear looks whole. For an instant I think I imagined the whole thing.

"Tuor," he introduces himself. I smile again but not with relief, with real amusement. He's no Tuor. Salad's stories! "It was even steven," he continues. "A good fight like you said, and I would've done the same in your place." And abruptly as that there's nothing left to say for either of us. I try to give him a smile that's not so grateful, friendlier, before I swivel and make off. The clacking of sticks starts up again immediately and I feel less guilty.

Days pass before I pick up my sticks again. When I do, I have a strange sense that it's not me that swings Mormegil or stabs with Orcrist, but some unseen beast that slips into me. The feeling leaves me quite numb. I try to explain it to Lapy but he looks at me as if I've lost my marbles. He's not afraid to practise with me though, our friendship is the same. I neither avoid Markham nor seek him out but he's in my thoughts. Concede to Markham, give up this whole racket, my ambitions as a stickfighter, pass Mormegil on to some eight-year-old coming up, and do something less deadly, less emotionally sapping. That's what part of me feels. I too could lose an eye, or be killed.

It rains for what feels like a week and the dump is in wretched mood. There's nothing to do all day but take shelter. I experience strange exhilarations, tire myself with mad quests that keep me out in the rain. Lapy doesn't try to settle me down; he's known me too long. The morning of the third day, I wake shivering, still muddy and wet from the evening before, and with both sticks clenched in my left fist like a lifeline. Lapy gives me water, tries to swaddle me but I'm already too hot. I'm also too weak to push off the stinking kerosene-smelling blanket which suffocates me. I wake from dreams in which the sandy-haired Tuor sets me alight with a burning stick. Other boys I have fought look on, bored rather than excited.

When I wake properly, the sun peers thinly through high clouds. I smell smoke somewhere not far off but the sight and warmth of the sun is rousing enough. Lapy has left me, likely in disgust at my screams and moans. I'm surprised at how steady I feel on my feet. Awake, I remember that Salad was also in my fever dreams and I'm suddenly dying to know what he wanted to tell me when he came to watch me practise. But first I wander aimlessly, hoping for water and perhaps a bite. I know where I can sometimes get food from someone. Not a stickfighter, but he's so good at scavenging he doesn't care if we steal from him. Sometimes.

I'm ravenous and tear at some bread so fresh it must be from yesterday, and not crust either. I've seen virtually no one but a radio is playing nearby, a warbly song I recognize but can't put a name to. I sit next to the scavenger's sleeping den long after I've wolfed his food, somehow more wobbly from having eaten. I stand, and there he is. Tauzin – I think, watching me smugly. He's a lanky, knobbly thing, all bony knees and thrust-out elbows, not at all tough so I don't expect him to try anything.

He speaks before I can thank him. "That bread was

poisoned. I left it as bait for whoever's been stealing my stuff. Rat poison," he adds unnecessarily. "Bet you didn't know I was a master poisoner. Had no idea it was you, but I don't care really. You might not even die." He's talking too much, yabbering on as though we're in a classroom somewhere, or mates, and what he says really matters. I stick my hand down my craw, squeezing my fingers into a point and forcing them as hard as I can past my gullet. He stops, stunned, and I aim the flood of mush that comes spurting out at him even though he's not stupid, he stopped and stood about ten feet away. A second smaller gush of puke rises, and now I'm sure it's all out. I smile.

"Too late," he tells me, but he's no longer so cool, and not just because I took him by surprise emptying my stomach. No, he's shitless now 'cause I'm advancing on him, both sticks suddenly, magically, in my left hand, a trick I've practised loads to get really good at. He backs up a couple of steps, shuffling as though he'll wet himself if he lifts his feet.

"The poison's already working on your system."

"I've plenty of time to kill you though." I don't mean the words; I just want to scare him. I've no idea if he's actually poisoned me, but as I utter the threat, I know with certainty I'll carry it through. No one's around and this snivelling rat of a poisoner doesn't deserve such a quick end as he'll get. If I am poisoned, I'll be too weak later, too doubled-over in pain to kill him.

It's done almost quicker than thought. He turns to run but his long legs are more hindrance than use and I trip him easily, kicking one foot against the other. He falls like a rag doll, making no effort to keep on his feet, and it's contempt at this weakness that sets my arm in motion. Standing bent over him, I swing the two sticks in my left hand easily, a bit like a golfer, I think, and hard enough that wind whistles through the tiny space between Orcrist and Mormegil. The strike is precise enough to kill; I feel the rubbery give of his temple beneath the tip of my sticks. But once more shame comes on me, so suddenly I taste it mingling with the acid of vomit. I walk away without checking that he's dead. I feel weak again, the return of a fever.

A strange wind comes up that doesn't stir the bushes but pulls at my shorts, keens to me like a dead baby. I stand, clutching my head, afraid I'll fall if I try to walk. The dump suddenly doesn't seem empty after all. Boys are skulking all about, may even have seen me kill Tauzin, and they're just waiting for the right moment to ambush me. I would take one or two of them with me, and the certainty steadies me slightly. After some minutes, I begin walking again, with purpose. To find someone who never moves from his spot.

Aias is awake but looks like he's about to die; his eyes are gummy and he holds as ever the tell-tale plastic bottle in his dainty fingers. Aias looks like shit but his smile is that of a boy who loves the world. He used to be one of the very best stickfighters. One of only two legends we have in the dump. There are almost as many stories about him as about Turin. A champion with two sticks or with a single one. You were lucky if Aias fought you with a single stick; very good if he used two. It was before my time, though Aias cannot be older than 17. His smile is jolly, but only if you don't look too closely. He has all his teeth but they are very nearly black, the gums too.

"Aias," I whisper. It seems rude to speak normally around him, to disturb the sleepy peace of glue life. "Aias. Got any glue?" It takes him an aeon to look at me, to turn one muddy and one clear eye towards me. He's got the trembles. I wish I had food to offer him. The hand he extends shakes uncontrollably. He's never selfish with his glue. Involuntarily, I wipe the bottle mouth with my shirt, suck on it hard. There's not much left, barely any in fact. I suck a minute, taking small breaths through my nose and watching Aias turn his head as though it's buried in a slurry of mud. I feel a mixture of pity and stomping contempt before the warmth invades my mouth and throat. It would be easy to kill him, end his half-life, easier even than with Tauzin. I wouldn't even have to use my sticks, he's like a twig. One wrench would snap his neck. Up close his happy smile seems more a grin of pain. Glue's supposed to be a happy drug. It warms you, it's true, it's a help on cold nights. But it makes me think of blood. I get a bit twitchy on glue, my mind's full of gore. The longer you do it, the more it kills the brain, rots it, or those bits of the brain that make you fight. I suck so hard I get a headache with my warm feeling. I hand the bottle back to him, trying not to gag at his stink. His feet are dotted with yellow shit specks. I walk away with a muzzy head, concentrating on putting one foot in front of the other and clutching at the warmth spreading all the way to my fingertips. It feels like a layer on my skin and yet it's gotten beneath the surface at the same time, sending rays into my bones.

I almost bump heads with Markham. He steps back a pace as if to get a good look, says "you have your sticks, good. Salad thinks we should do a rematch." I think my answering nod is calm but he has a bad habit of catching me off guard. He spins and walks ahead. I follow, his two friends moving in to flank me so it feels like I have an honour guard. I clutch my sticks in anticipation. Markham's own sticks hang from the loops of his shorts; he looks ridiculous.

If anything, I start to feel warmer as I walk. When we find Salad my headache is gone. I'm swollen with energy, and even more eager than usual. More boys draw up. Salad has a few words with us, in a stern tone. He's tireder than ever, and coughs hoarsely. His voice is normal and his muscles have the same rubbery hard look they always do. For the first time I notice he and I are almost the same height. His words bleed out of his mouth, I think because of the glue, and I hear nothing of what he says. I need to release the force building inside me. I can't let it escape before I finish Markham, and I know I will. Snarls echo in my head. Markham will never again challenge me.

I don't limber up; Markham eyes me, perhaps taking note

of my confidence. I stand still to avoid wasting the killing essence in me; I don't want it to escape.

So that when Salad gives the signal I go for Markham harder, I think, than I've ever gone for anyone. He's ready though and our sticks swirl faster and more intricately than I've seen in some time. A trick of the glue makes them catch alight. My limbs are weightless and Mormegil, like its namesake, is keen to drink. No wrist blows, no knuckle raps. I go for his throat and he aims for my head. He'll tire before my supercharged arms so I swing and swing, using a good deal of my strength in each stroke. He sweats, I am dry and I watch his eyes dart about trying to follow my sticks.

He doesn't give ground, I admire that. I'm pressed up almost against him and not once does he hunt for space. But I have cunning too, and when the glue in my veins gives me the signal, I switch tactics. I swing with Orcrist a second too slowly, and he rises to the bait. His parry becomes harder, faster, he drives at my neck. I slip the blow, stepping back and aside, tilting my head ever so slightly so that it misses me. He tries to recover – he's almost as quick as I am – but there's time for me to smash the top of his earlobe, to parry his own return stroke and aim Mormegil's tip at his throat. Let the beast slake its thirst. He dives backward to escape, almost as though he's been hit. He thinks I'll give him time to regain his footing, but I don't. Instead I'm on him, and on his back he tries to sweep my leg with his foot just as I stab again, for his groin. Mormegil catches the inside of his thigh – the twisty fucker – and before I can strike again, with perfect accuracy this time, Salad's arm is in front of me, a barrier of muscle the size of my head. "Fight over," he announces, his voice coming from a long way off. "Raul wins." My skin tingles with the remains of the glue's warmth. My arms, my body still hum with unused force. I close my eyes a second for calm but I cannot turn away. What happens must. I start to swing before my eyes open, I feel bold, so ready. The judge blocks with his forearm, as if he expects this. It must sting like hell even wrapped in muscle like that. His eyes are on mine without expression but the watching boys release a gasp of shock. I smile. They do not know it but I'm freeing them from the tyranny of authority. My next blow follows so hard on the heels of the first that Salad cannot possibly counter, and he doesn't. To his credit he only falls to one knee; I expected a hit on the temple would end him. Stunned, he's at the right height now for me to use maximum power and I hit him again cleanly across the nose. He keels forward not even putting out his hands to catch himself. I give him a chance to roll onto his back, but before I can pick my next spot, another blow lands. Markham's. He hits the judge's knee, a downward chop like an axe stroke, and then pokes at his crotch with the other stick. A spasm crosses Salad's face, the first one. He pulls himself into a ball, his knees up as I stab for his eyes. Markham is circling, looking for an opening, and it's like we're the only two alive in that place, the other boys are all frozen, so still as to be almost empty shells. Markham thrusts into his other eye and Salad's face splashes blood. He still makes no sound.

I'd dreamed of a killing blow, the single cut that cleanly ends life, but I've done that already, with Tauzin earlier. It was sweet. But now's not the time for precision. I swing and thrust, mindlessly raining blows, and Markham is with me, shares my aim for we club at the judge's head with no thought for accuracy. Even when he no longer moves, Markham and I swing for some minutes. Then I stop.

Olufemi Terry was born in Sierra Leone of African and Antillean parentage. He grew up in Nigeria, the UK and Côte d'Ivoire before attending university in New York. He now lives in Cape Town, where he is writing his first novel. 'Stickfighting Days' was first published in *Chimurenga*, volume 12/13, Cape Town 2008.

The CDC Caine Prize
African Writers' Workshop Stories 2010

The Plantation

Ovo Adagha

1

THE PLANTATION GREW FROM the moist underbelly of the Jesse swamps. That place where a luxuriant mesh of greenery blocked away the sun and surrounded everything in sight; just as it surrounded Namidi that morning as he moved about to inspect his trees and traps. He walked across the winding tract of grassy soil – beaten out of the forest at the onset of planting seasons by the young men of the village, with hoes and machetes, spurred on by the bullish power of the native beer. It was the *harmattan* season; the parching land breeze charged at him from the rubber trees and made the hairs on his skin bristle.

This place was an emblem of life to him – the high-pitched whistle of the birds; the cold drizzle of early morning dew; the soft, earthy, muskiness of the air; the endless reams of foliage and the rubber trees that glistened with sap. The plantation seemed to glow with a curious mysteriousness which followed him about as he moved abstractedly, slashing at the banners of plant-leaves that heaved across his path, his face a picture of dark brooding.

There followed a small moment of prickling silence, when it seemed as if the murmur of the plantation was suspended in a state of waiting; as though giving audience to some novelty event. Namidi's nostrils picked up an odd, sickly smell that set his stomach on edge as he moved about; and with it floated an alien, trickling sound. He paused in mid-stride and cocked his ears at the trees. He stood still for a long time, listening, watching and sniffing, until, perhaps touched by an uncertain impulse, he looked behind a thicket a few feet away.

If the trees had started talking to him he would not have been more surprised. A stream of fluid burst forth from the ground and splashed all around in a wayward arc. It flowed across the adjoining greenery, which seemed to shrink away from the onslaught. He watched as a puddle of fluid gathered around him and washed across the plantation. With his senses invaded by the strong stench, he realized it was petrol.

Once, many years ago, some men from the city in khaki uniforms had come to the village with long pipes and heavy trucks. Their spectacle had held the attention of the village people for many days. They had dug across the village grounds, through the plantation and the nearby forests; buried the pipes and then left. A pipe must have broken, was the first thought that came to Namidi; he must ask the village head to do something about it.

But such noble thoughts soon evaporated as he turned the matter over in his mind. Yes, it was surely petrol, but of what benefit would this be to him? There was an opportunity here, if only the meddling of the villagers would let him. Then a small grin lit up his face. Yes, he knew what to do.

He filled the rubber gourd with some petrol and then started towards the village. When he emerged from the plantation the early morning sun was rising confidently in the skies. He walked on, scarcely responding to the greetings of the village women going to their farms. He, who usually lingered over greetings, now wished the women would all disappear and leave him alone.

'Greetings, Sir,' a group of women rallied at him.

'Greetings, good women,' he replied and hurried on without a glance in their direction.

'What is wrong with him?' one of them asked as they appraised the retreating figure. Namidi was moving briskly on the narrow path, his head thrust forward, like it was going to fall away from his neck.

'He looks like he has seen a ghost,' another said, clapping her hands excitedly.

'And he has this smell around him,' another one added.

'It smells like something they use with their rubber,' said another one. They stared at the departing figure and shook their heads in puzzlement.

Namidi moved as quickly as he could, his heart full of intent. Some riches are too hard won, he thought to himself, too long waited for to be shared, especially in this village where no man lacked the capacity for greed and treachery. Of what use is it to come upon a herd of bush meat, if it will only serve the main course of a public feast? For long he had wandered and waited in the plantation for a chance to redeem himself from the poverty that had beset his adult life. Now it was within his grasp to settle it. He would not share his discovery with anyone, he decided.

To avoid detection, he left the road and started walking off into the bush track: a steep, snaking slope of dense foliage and caked mud. He laboured up the path until he reached the village clearing; all the while nodding his head and whispering to himself.

The village itself was a cluster of thatched roofs, no more than a clearing in the jungle. Namidi had lived there all his life and knew all about it: the small huts that were eked out of red clay, with their shaggy cabbage of palm-frond roofs that seemed to recede as one approached – stretched on a paltry piece of land with minuscule space between them; the rainfall and gossip that ploughed on endlessly without season; and how the very ground on which the village stood seemed eternally swathed in a blanket of rust. Ah, he knew all about it – the indescribable weariness and dreariness of it all.

'Ochuko! Ochuko! Where in God's name is this boy?' Namidi called out when he got to his house.

'Papa!' a small, breathless voice rang out from behind the hut.

Namidi turned and regarded his six-year-old son as he came bouncing towards him from the backyard with the reckless abandon of a child, his over-sized knickers flapping against his thighs as he ran. Two years ago some missionaries had built a new school on the outskirts of the village. But the fees were expensive and he could not afford to send any of his three children there with the meagre earnings from his rubber farm. Namidi felt diminished each time he saw his boy playing in the sand while the school bells rang in the distance. It seemed as if the bells in his mind started clanging loudly at this thought, willing him to return to the plantation with the utmost haste.

'Go and call your mother for me,' he said.

The boy set off again, humping and jumping towards his mother's kitchen.

'What is it?' his wife, Mama Efe, enquired as she emerged from the hut. She was a thin, shrivelled woman with a hardened look about her. Years and years of toiling in the sun had drawn the skin taut over her cheek-bones so that time and suffering seemed etched on her features.

'What's that smell you brought home today?' she asked, with a wary, suspicious frown on her face.

Namidi was gazing at his hut; at the lines of rotten bamboo that stuck out of its window panes. It seemed like the thatched roof and clay-red walls were cowering before him and the smell of new money. He turned around with a perspiring face and told her about his findings.

'We must go there now before the busybodies get wind of it,' he added, trying to infect her with a sense of urgency.

'What if a fire starts, eh?' she queried, worriedly. In her mind, there appeared a flash of blurred images writhing inside a great flame; of grotesque-looking figures being planted in the ground; and of grey-clothed people standing around the fresh mounds of soil, with a charged, funereal quality.

Looking at her, at the doubt and anxiety that suddenly clouded her face, Namidi experienced a brief pang of foreboding; but he tossed the thought away quickly from his mind, without repining, and said:

'It won't, I am the only one who knows.' His eyebrows arched menacingly, admonishing her to say no more.

She asked no further questions, but she thought within herself: this thing is a ghoulish business and will come to no good.

Namidi, his wife and three children carved an odd, almost patriarchal procession as they left the house with huge, empty cans. Namidi led the line, towering and frowning, as he strode determinedly down the bush path; his children followed, awe-struck and excited by the scent of adventure, picking their way bare-footed over the rough path; his wife completed the moving line of ancient slave-rite figures, tagging along on hardened feet, her face brooding and disturbed. Their advance took them to where they were greeted by an ensemble of close-knit trees that stretched and heaved into the track, forming an intimidating profusion of branches, fronds and creepers. The air was stale and thick with damp sweat. Yet Namidi retained all the doggedness that was upon him since the time he made the discovery. It was the road that would lead them to riches, he thought cheekily to himself. And as his wife and children trudged mechanically behind him, his mind was closed to all else except his destination.

In the stroking brightness of the sun, an owl in full glide flapped its brown-streaked wings, turned its head and then sounded a doleful note as it flew past the trudging party below.

2

The narrow path they followed was surrounded on both sides by a flagging ledge of greenery. Mama Efe cast a pallid shadow on the ground as they worked their way back and forth from the plantation to the house, with large hauls of petrol. She followed him, without a word, saying nothing of the storm that was gathering in her heart.

Trouble lay in wait in for them, she knew. She felt herself sapped of all will, and of any sort of resistance. Her heart throbbed with anxiety; yet not a word of complaint came from her. There was a time when she could have derided or opposed him in some way, but long years of waging lost battles in her marriage had doused her spirits with meekness and tiredness. Why, she knew how stubborn her husband could be; how he would never change his mind once it was made up. She used to think it was his strength. But she knew all about it now – all the ruin his rigidness had cast upon them.

On the third trip to the plantation they were accosted by Jackson – a greasy-looking youth from the village with a Boy Scout scarf tied around his neck. He was always up to no good and spent his days chasing birds and grasshoppers in the plantation. The lad took one sniff at Namidi and his eyebrows stretched wide.

'Why, are you working in Shell now?' he said, and grinned knowingly at Namidi.

Mama Efe was watching her husband as he eyed the youth with a look of baleful hatred.

'What business of yours is it?' he countered in a cold voice, and surveyed the youth disdainfully, like some errant, wayward fly.

'You should know, anything that happens in this village I make it my business,' Jackson said, and rubbed his hands.

Namidi looked annoyed, like he had been insulted. He advanced towards the youth, eyes blazing, but held himself together with some effort when his wife placed a restraining arm on him. He turned away and continued walking, stiff-necked, down the narrow track. The youth followed at some distance, his eyes darting at about, searching for clues. Mama Efe, a few steps behind her husband, was trembling with dread. He said not a word but she knew that darkness was brewing within him – the way he flicked his head with irritation, and slashed his cutlass at the swaying creepers. It made her all the more nervous, the entire business. And she wished she could depart from it.

Already, the smell of the petrol had reached them; so too had the hissing sound from the plantation. Jackson uttered a cry behind them and then ran off in the opposite direction towards the village.

3

Not long after, the local people from the village and nearby fishing villages converged at the spill site to fetch petrol. The day had progressed to a burning noon, with the sun gliding overhead like a circle of fire. The market, the school and the farms were all deserted. Fishermen, artisans, farmers and women abandoned their wares and swarmed to the plantation, which seemed to glitter with a wave of sweat-drenched, dark bodies. Away to the right, to the left, and all around, the plantation sparked with keen contests as the people jostled and fought each other for space around the site. Metal pans and buckets clashed and flashed in the sweltering heat like weapons of survival.

The petrol was gradually swallowed by huge cans, pans and any element of storage the villagers could muster. But it flowed on still, steadily giving in to the ceaseless mania of sucking, the avid thirst of animals long deprived of nurturing milk. The plantation reeled from the endless trampling of feet, but took it all in; except for the petrol, foreign to its depths, which was resisted and only allowed to brim over the soil surface; enough for the villagers to swim or sink in.

Namidi, his clothes dripping with perspiration and petrol, stationed Ochuko at an embankment, some distance away from the bustle. He was to watch over the family possessions while his parents and siblings did their best at the pits.

But the boy wandered about intermittently and played with his friend, Onome. It was in their manner to climb a tree wherever they could find one. They could not resist the lure of the plantation and the rubber trees. Up they climbed, laughing and swinging playfully from branch to branch, while the villagers below bubbled and brawled.

To the children, the fortune-hunters presented hearty entertainment. They giggled with glee at the sound of high-pitched voices drawn tight with tension; as grown men charged and shoved riotously at each other; as here and there a woman lost her footing, and rolled in a heap in the slimy soil. Onome taunted Ochuko with mimicries of his father's belligerent displays in the heat of battle. 'Hey you, get away from there. Is this your plantation?' Namidi barked at anyone that came close to him. 'Hey you, get away from that tree. Is this your plantation?' Onome screamed at Ochuko in parody.

They lost interest in the brawling at the site and kept themselves busy with all manner of play. Soon they were playing soldiers, launching between branches and taking mock shots at each other – their fingers serving as makeshift guns. Onome took aim at Ochuko and fired. And as Ochuko swerved to duck behind a branch, there was a flash of light from inside the spill site and a deafening explosion that shook the tree he was hanging on. His young adversary fell headlong from the tree, screamed and lay still.

Ochuko froze. There followed a brief moment when the world seemed engulfed in a blanket of yellow light. And then it broke loose with a gut-wrenching choir of yelling that rang out all at once. The boy stared at the growing roost of figures that broke out frenziedly from the smoky interior, running and swaying in scattered directions. He watched it all with a childish fascination.

But it was the heat that finally got to him – the hot, stifling sensation that suddenly seized him in a tight, airless embrace and threw him from the tree. In a flash, he was up on his feet and running off towards the village clearing. He ran, followed by the acrid smell of burnt chicken feathers;

by the long grasses and the screaming demons that leaped up and down behind him. The sky had turned grey and cast over him like imminent nightfall; but instead of easing down stealthily, the demons picked up pace, screaming and gathering behind him in a swift veil of smoke and blackness. It made him run faster and faster towards the village and the familiar outlines of his father's hut.

Huge billows of smoke rose from the heart of the plantation as the dust-laden boy – his eyes itching with soot and tears – emerged from it. He ran into the hut and hid himself under his mother's bed.

4

Ochuko and his twin, elder siblings, Emi and Efe, were like young musketeers. On many occasions, they would scamper home from an adventure gone awry. Once, during a village ritual festival, they had lit a masquerade from behind, and then torn away in different directions, as the violated masquerade skirmished with the flames and roared its indignation to the world around and beyond. Usually they would arrive one after the other at their mother's bed, breathing heavily and shaking with mirth. It was there, under the bed, that Ochuko waited for them. He was breathless, but elated by his escape from the smoking demons. A little while later, after the sweat had dried from his body, he began to feel cold. He ventured to go outside, but then it was already dark. He heard the sound of running feet. Terrified, he whirled around and dived under the bed once again.

His were the pair of eyes that blinked and shone all night in the darkness. He tensed for a long time, listening for the fleeting, brush-like sound of his mother's footsteps and the grating, angry thuds that were his father's. Mother will be home soon to bathe him, he thought with some conviction. He waited and listened to the silence, occasionally broken by the distant wail of a woman crying, and the sound of feet running past the hut.

At the corner of the cooking sill, a small hurricane lamp – which his mother always kept alive – waned and flickered gallantly for long periods. But the dim, smoky light petered out as the night wore on. Soon, a gang of rats, unbridled by their invisibility, celebrated by squealing and rustling up and down the earthenware. The boy lay paralysed by terror, every fibre of him trembling at the scrambling noises they made. Still, he lay in a stiff and innocent concealment. From the holes in the earth floor of the hut sprang a line of ants. It was their time of the night and, roused by the fresh smell of dried, oily sweat, they poured forth from an underground hub. He shivered in helpless immobility as their scrawny legs climbed and formed a defiant trail across his back; as their droppings stoked and moistened the thin hairs on his skin. He lay very still as they walked over him.

It was pitch dark for a long time. And even in the treacherous silence that followed, the boy waited and listened; but all he heard was the faraway bird-call of the coming dawn.

Ovo Adagha is a Nigerian writer. His short stories, poems and non-fiction works have been published in several online and print journals. He recently co-edited a multi-national anthology of short stories, *One World* (New Internationalist 2009). He lives in London.

Soul Safari

Alnoor Amlani

HER EYES HAD ALREADY told him everything he needed to know. She needn't have uttered those unforgettable words.

They were on safari back from the Coast. Adam was driving; Zara was sitting in the passenger seat next to him. He couldn't stop the scene replaying in his head. Yesterday while a strong sea breeze whipped the palm trees and the ocean swept the sands he had told her how he felt. She had drawn her eyebrows up, stuck her chin forward and thrown her head back.

He remembered her turning away, her long neck stretching out as she looked far into the ocean. In her eyes he had seen something that had stopped him dead.

It was as if a fire had suddenly gone out. The ocean waves crashed across his thoughts, scattering them and clawing them back into their depths. A crab scuttled sideways away from the approaching water into a safe crevice in the coral shore. Only a short while ago he had been sweating in the equatorial sun on a boat in a completely calm sea searching for dolphins. Now he was shivering in the violent wind coming across the ocean. He had seen a chilling coldness in her eyes that he could feel spreading slowly throughout his body.

The coldness deepened and surged and his shoulders shook. With a start he realized that tears had crept into his eyes. He tried to fight them back but couldn't. Blinking rapidly, he stood up, turned away from her, and walked towards the ocean. He didn't really know why he was crying. Of course he was feeling rejected, but he'd been through that before. This was something new and he couldn't control it.

Adam remembered walking for a long time along the beach where the tourist hotels stood. She didn't follow him. Finally he realized that the tide had trapped him on a lonely stretch. He couldn't go forward; there was no way back. There was a beach bar on higher ground, not far from him, built out of a restored Swahili Dhow. The name across the driftwood-framed entrance said 'Shipwreck'. Appropriate, he thought. He sat at the bar and asked for a scotch. He offered the solitary barman a drink and had another. Two young American divers came in and took up a table.

The wind howled and suddenly big warm salty raindrops filled the air, accompanied by intense drumming on the thatched roof. They listened to the storm together. It was too loud to think, let alone talk. He found some peace.

Adam remembered having a few more drinks after they left but then it started to get fuzzy. He remembered the barman waking him up and the haggard look in his eyes when he washed his face in the gents' room. The storm had passed but the tide hadn't gone out yet. He waited a bit more and her words came back again.

"I don't think of you that way at all. You're a very good friend, maybe the best friend I ever had, so yes I love you, but I'm not *in* love with you."

Zara's eyes told him a thousand stories in an instant. Sudden unexplained moments appeared in his mind too. Images he couldn't understand; images so vivid that he could not forget them so he was compelled to re-examine them. Somehow, he knew that they weren't coming from his imagination. How could his imagination create such vivid transcendental moments? Once when they were having dinner and laughing at something together, in his mind's eye he saw two children playing and swimming in a river next to their thatched village home. He was seeing through the eyes of one of them and the other was definitely her. She had a completely different face, plain and raw, with a flat nose and small Oriental eyes but the look in her eyes and smile on her face was exactly the same. He didn't know where he was exactly but he could feel the cool water on his skin and the sand on the river bank between his toes. He had never been to the Far East, at least not in this lifetime...

Adam didn't remember much about the early evening walk back along the beach except it seemed to take forever and the sun stung his eyes because he had lost his sunglasses somewhere on the beach. Finally he made it back to his room and fell onto his bed gratefully. He did not open his eyes until the next morning.

When he got up he found her in the hotel lounge talking animatedly with the receptionist. Her packed bags were on the floor right next to her.

"Oh, there you are. I was worried about you. Are you OK? Where did you go last night? I came and knocked on your door but you didn't answer... I thought you had abandoned me!"

He just smiled and said simply. "I'll get my bags and we can leave." She nodded.

* * *

Now they were back on the road again. He had arranged for the next night in a secluded luxury campsite deep inside the famous Tsavo national park. He had planned this safari for over a year, choosing the route carefully and booking places he knew were well managed. He had wanted to make sure everything was perfect. Until yesterday things had been going fine. He hoped it would get better today.

Zara was leaving soon for London to complete the final year of her Film Studies degree. She had grown up in Kenya but her family had emigrated to England five years ago. Her parents lived in Kent and she visited them as often as she could, which was rare since she worked for a small media company part-time as she attended her classes. Zara wanted to be a documentary film maker.

Tsavo approached: 20,000 square kilometres of bush country; bigger than Wales and completely wild.

Adam tightened his grip on the steering wheel and eased his foot off the accelerator pedal as he spotted the police check ahead. The skinny junior officer by the side of the road lifted his hand to stop them. They always stopped him because of his Range Rover. A big car meant a big man and maybe a big bribe...

"Let me see your licence."

He had it ready at hand but the policeman was leaning over the bonnet trying to examine the insurance sticker. Adam had stuck it right in the middle of the huge windscreen to make it difficult. He couldn't be sure but he thought he saw this policeman sneaking a long, lustful stare at Zara's legs while he was pretending to look at the insurance sticker. It infuriated him but didn't seem to bother her. Finally the guy walked around the car and came to his window, smiling broadly.

"Mr Adam, this is a nice British car you have! But do you know that your left rear tyre is worn out?"

He didn't believe him but he knew the routine. He got out of the car. The tyre was only slightly worn. The policeman smiled. "It's still roadworthy but you better change it soon. I'm doing you a favour here..." He held on to Adam's driving licence. "You don't look very grateful. Maybe I should make an example of you?"

The policeman stared at Zara applying lipstick using the passenger side mirror and licked his own lips, apparently waiting for Adam's response. Adam felt like boxing his ears but he knew a better way.

"Look, officer, is this enough?"

The crisp thousand-shilling note in his hand elicited a wide smile from the cop. He handed over the licence as he took the money gleefully, slipping it into his pocket before the other policemen saw how much it was.

He waved Adam back into the car. "Safe journey, Bwana!"

Adam turned the key and slammed the accelerator down, leaving a cloud of dust behind for the fellow's benefit. These were life's little pleasures, he thought.

A rustic wooden sign appeared in the distance. They were at the Park Main Gate.

Adam pulled up and returned the park ranger's salute. The ranger's face was lit up by a perfect set of large white teeth which curled into a wide smile for Bwana Adam, whom he knew well enough. "Jambo Rafiki." Adam bolted out of the car with their identification documents to pay the park fees and came back soon enough.

Just as he reached for the keys in the ignition a Common Bulbul landed on the bonnet softly. It hopped about on the hot surface, chirping shrilly. Zara picked up her video camera. They spoke in whispers, admiring its electric metallic-blue feathers. It was only a few inches from them. Zara kept her camera trained on it until it flew onto the roof. Peering through the sunroof they spotted it for a moment hopping along rapidly. Apparently it intended to examine the whole car.

A moment later it reappeared, perching on the edge of Adam's large side mirror, examining itself. Then curiously it started preening itself, turning and posturing like a person. It was strange behaviour. Zara caught it all on her camera. They were both smiling. But then the ranger approached them and the bulbul flew away instantly.

"Don't you want to enter the park?"

Adam explained that they were watching the bulbul. Zara replayed the footage for the ranger. He agreed it was strange behaviour.

When they were driving inside the park Zara exclaimed thoughtfully, "I wonder whether it knew it was looking at itself."

Adam scratched his head. "Maybe it thought it had found a girlfriend?" He said it aloud before he could stop himself. She giggled and then burst out in laughter.

"Don't laugh; it's a cruel thing to do."

She stopped laughing. They were silent for a while. Zara picked up a packet of sugar-coated baobab fruit she had earlier bought from a roadside vendor in Mombasa and began sucking on them. Every few minutes she loudly spat a bunch of seeds out of the window.

He was sure she was doing this to annoy him.

"Zara, you're distracting me with all that noise! Can't you be quieter?"

She spat out another bunch of seeds. "I'm planting baobab trees."

They drove through the virgin landscape dotted with young acacia trees, shrubs and the occasional baobab. Zara thought there should be more baobabs. They were her favourite kind of tree. They were truly ancient trees, growing wide and craggy. Adam reckoned if her seeds did sprout they would live through generations of humans, as long as they were left alone. Yet the seeding was an intrusion, he thought. They themselves were an intrusion. This land belonged to Nature.

Whenever Adam went into the wild open plains, he relaxed. It seemed to him that the natural world was fairer than the world of people. Animals were simple. If they were hungry they hunted or foraged. If they were upset they did not hide their feelings. Human beings, he thought, were often vindictive, spiteful and greedy.

The sun dipped on the horizon, turning the landscape into a light blue, pink, grey and orange pastel painting. Their camp approached.

They took up two adjacent single tents facing the watering hole and agreed to meet for dinner.

When Adam arrived at the main tent he found Zara talking to a guy at the camp bar. Adam got himself a stiff scotch and introduced himself. He was an old friend of Zara's. They had even dated when they were together in high school. He felt a stab of jealousy when, after the introductions were over, the guy ignored him and focused on her. He could see how he looked at her. After a moment or two he decided he couldn't stay there and excused himself. He walked to the blazing campfire alone. The night air was still now but the watering hole was busy.

Adam watched a troop of elephants that had taken up the entire watering hole. There were two matriarchs – one must be the troop's grandmother, he thought. The old bull was clearly marked out by his massive bulk. Two smaller bulls and three females protectively surrounded a very young elephant. They drank noisily, spraying themselves liberally with water and mud. He could hear Zara laughing gaily at the bar behind him. He wondered why he had gone through all the trouble of planning this safari for them together when she was not going to share these moments with him.

The camp manager came over to say hello. Adam asked him to set up a table for the two of them apart from the rest of the guests and he went off to the restaurant. He returned and told him the table, and dinner, was waiting for them. Adam went to the bar and told Zara, who picked up her camera and followed him.

"Why don't we sit near the rest of the people?" Zara asked, pointing to a large table occupied by her high-school friend and his family.

"Well, actually I wanted to talk to you alone."

Zara sat down and buttered her toast.

"I'm sorry I snapped at you when you laughed earlier at the bulbul. And when you were spitting out the seeds... I guess I didn't find it funny because of how I feel about you." His voice trailed off.

"Well, I'm sure the bulbul is happy by now but here you are still sulking and keeping an eye on me! I don't like this Adam. Why can't you just be normal? I just want you to be my friend."

Adam finished his soup. "Have you seen the elephants?"

"What's that got to do with anything?"

"Well, just look at them. They are a happy family – and that's all I am after. Isn't that what you want too?"

This was too much for Zara. Thankfully the main course arrived and interrupted the conversation. The waiter cleared the soup, refilled their wine and water glasses and set out the food, giving her time to cool off. "You're just not getting it, Adam. I'm not ready for another relationship right now with any man. My last boyfriend was a total disaster. I had to call the police to get him out of my apartment."

Adam saw the coldness he had seen in her eyes yesterday.

"Look, you've sorted out your education and finances. I've still got to finish my degree and move out on my own this year. If you want to get married and have kids, just do it. Find a nice woman who can cook for you and give you bouncing babies."

Adam wasn't listening any more. "What happened with your last boyfriend?"

Zara played with her necklace. "I don't want to talk about it."

Adam was silent for a while. Then he suddenly spoke. "It's just that I get these visions that I can't understand."

"What visions?"

He told her about the village in the Far East. She listened with eyes growing wider. He saw her fear but he couldn't stop. After all, it was the truth.

"I know it sounds crazy but I believe we have been together in many lifetimes," he finished. She had stared at him with a frown frozen on her face all through. She had a distant look in her eyes.

Adam could not take the silence any longer. "Well, say something."

Zara spoke finally. "What can I say? It is crazy. You're reminding me of my old boyfriend, Adam. And it's scaring me."

They were interrupted by Zara's friend approaching their table. Zara stood up to greet him. Adam stayed in his chair. The guy invited them both over to the bar to join him and his family. Adam declined; he didn't feel like making small talk.

Zara decided to go to the bar with him and have one drink. Adam stayed at the table and ordered another scotch. The elephants trooped out of the watering hole just as she reappeared at the table. "I'm going to bed. Goodnight Adam. See you at breakfast?" Adam just nodded.

He watched her walk away. She stopped at the bar and said goodnight to her friend. Then she walked towards her tent escorted by one of the park guards. After a while he was the only guest left at the main tent.

Adam lingered over the fire watching the watering hole. It was deserted. The wind had died down completely and the whistling of crickets filled the night air. The stupendous array of bright stars that had dominated the sky earlier had disappeared. There was nothing to distract him from his troubles. He wondered if he would be able to sleep.

He took a large scotch with him to his tent. He drank it slowly and settled down to try to sleep. It wasn't easy. He knew now that it was truly over with Zara. She thought he was obsessed and even delusional. Who knows? Maybe he was.

Adam finally drifted to sleep after midnight and had a vivid dream that lasted until dawn. It was a strange dream which confused him because he couldn't be sure if it was real or not. He dreamt that he heard a lion roar right next to his tent and he thought he heard Zara scream. The next moment he was outside her tent looking at the open flap. Then he panicked and went looking for her using his torch along the pathways between the tents but he could not find her. There seemed to be more than one lion. He could hear at least two roaring as he walked around. Suddenly he heard a rustling noise in the bushes next to him and jumped. He ran to the main tent but there was no one there. The fire was still going so he sat next to it and waited for a park ranger.

No ranger came. The lions kept up their racket and seemed very close so he kept shining his torch around but he saw nothing. Finally he dreamt that he fell asleep next to the fire.

He was surprised to find himself in bed when he woke up.

He quickly scrambled out and peeked at Zara's tent entrance. The flaps were open, just like in his dream. He panicked and shouted out her name. There was no answer. He looked inside but she wasn't there. Now he was really worried.

Maybe Zara was right; maybe he was going crazy. He couldn't help himself. He ran to the main tent without brushing his teeth or packing his bags.

He was relieved to find her safely sitting at the table finishing her breakfast.

"Thank God!" He exclaimed.

She looked up startled. "What happened?"

Adam told her about his dream. She listened silently, with an expression on her face exactly like last night, until he finished. "I remember hearing lions just outside our tents. I woke up and sat on my bed scared for a long time."

"Do you still think I'm crazy?"

Zara burst out laughing. "No – I just think you're in love."

Adam laughed for the first time since last night.

The sun rose rapidly in the sky. A herd of zebra arrived and took over the watering hole. Then, quite suddenly, a bulbul landed on the table and pecked at a piece of bread that had fallen off his plate. Zara fished out her camera.

"I wonder if it's the one from yesterday."

Alnoor Amlani is a third-generation Kenyan of Indian origin who lives in Nairobi. He has worked in East Africa as a management consultant and written articles and opinion pieces for over a decade. He began writing fiction in 2009. He is currently writing his first novel.

A Life in Full

Jude Dibia

LADIES FLITTERED ON THE streets, restless as dust, and the voices of children playing sometimes found their way into the homes in Macaulay Avenue. Mabel Osondu wiped the sweat that gathered on her brow with the corner of her waist cloth and sighed deeply. It was not so much that the sun bothered her, but rather it was the effort of planting seeds that refused to bloom or bear fruits.

She tilled the small garden at the back of her son's house. She cleared the weeds and watered the soil until it was damp and swallowed the tomato seeds with little difficulty. This would be her third attempt, since she came, planting vegetables on the small patch of land in her son's backyard; first she had tried pumpkins and okra, then garden eggs, but each time just when she thought there were signs of hope, the plant stalks would stoop like aged folks, turn pale yellow and by the next day would be as dry as the scent leaves – *utazi* – she used while cooking pepper soup.

Mabel grabbed the railings by the fence, using them for support as she stood up. She stretched, throwing both her hands behind her back, resting them on her waist and turning slightly. Across the fence, the flourishing tomatoes and peppers with their uncompromising fullness and redness smiled at her. The ground there seemed so rich to Mabel, not once had she observed the garden without the hues of fertility. It gave her hope, though, that all her efforts were not in vain, that surely her tomato seeds would flourish and bear fruits.

Mrs Bassey, the young wife of Dr Kenule Bassey, who lived in the house across the fence, was hanging some bed sheets and laundry on the clothesline not far from the fulsome tomatoes and peppers. Mabel admired her, like she always did, thinking how fortunate that Dr Bassey had married such a beautiful and hardworking woman. And they had two lovely children already. Sometimes Mabel would hear the squeals and laughter of the Bassey children right in her son's living-room, drowning out the ones of the street vendors, and in those moments, she would imagine that they were her grandchildren.

"Good afternoon, Mama Osondu," Mrs Bassey said the instant she noticed Mabel. "How are you today?"

"Thank you, my daughter," Mabel's voice sounded as sweet as birdsong. "I am well. How are your children and husband?"

Mrs Bassey assured her that everyone was fine. Mabel nodded and continued to smile, her eyes moving from Mrs Bassey's face to a bunch of ripe, drooping tomatoes begging to be plucked.

"Mama Osondu, I can bring some fresh tomatoes and peppers to you if you like." Mrs Bassey said, noticing how engrossed Mabel was in the tomatoes.

"You are too kind, my daughter. But no, thank you. I have just planted some of my own and maybe this time they shall bear fruits."

"Yes, Ma," Mrs Bassey responded, like a good daughter, before she turned away and entered her house.

Mabel watched her leave and all she could think of was how much younger Dr Bassey was than her own son, Victor. Victor was 38 this past January and yet he remained unmarried and without children. She had worried endlessly about Victor and wondered why he, after so many years, was still without a wife.

In the early years, just after he had graduated from university, his excuse was that he was still trying to find his footing in the world, he needed to secure a job and at least a level of financial security before he considered marriage.

After Victor had worked for a year, she had broached the subject of a wife with him again. He had told her then that it was too early, that he still had no savings and it would be foolish to start a family without the basic necessities. She had smiled then, thinking what a responsible man she had raised. She had decided to wait; after all, Victor was not yet 30. And she had consoled herself with the knowledge that, even if he did marry in his early thirties, he would still be very eligible, still be considered fresh, unlike women, who would have passed their prime and would be considered old maids.

But Victor was no longer in his early thirties. He was fast approaching that age when an unmarried, childless man was considered less than whole.

Mabel looked away from the bountiful garden across the fence and stared briefly at the bareness that was her patch. She grabbed the hose beside her and watered the ground one more time before she retreated into the kitchen.

* * *

Later that evening, Mabel cooked Victor's favourite dish, mixed vegetable rice and fresh fried fish. She made sure she could taste the salt in the food; it was how Victor liked it, though she always cautioned him of the harmful effect of too much salt. She also ensured that the fish was cut in big chunks, which were then marinated in the special sauce that Victor favoured before she fried them to a crisp. The entire house smelt of spices and fried fish by the time she was finished.

Satisfied with her work, she sat in the living room and waited for Victor to return. It was already past seven in the evening and she knew from his usual habit that he would soon be home. Tonight, after Victor had settled down and had had his dinner she hoped to speak to him again. She could no longer hold it in and pretend to be happy about this solitary existence he had carved out for himself.

And she was ready for him. She knew he would try as usual to avoid discussing this issue with her. He would say he was tired after working so hard. He would even try to laugh it off and assure her that they would discuss it tomorrow. Or he might lose his temper, just as he had the last time she had brought the topic up.

"What business is it of yours, Mama?" Victor had snapped. "Must I marry?"

"Don't raise your voice at me, Victor," Mabel retorted. "I am your mother and yes, it is my business if my first son can't see that people are laughing at us because of his actions."

"Let them laugh, who cares? It's always what people say that matters most to you, Mama. Are these people even real?"

Mabel recalled how she had wanted to walk up to Victor and slap his insolent mouth. He had sounded very much like his father when he had spoken. His father always made fun of her, putting her down when she spoke about certain things.

Mabel sighed. She thought about Victor's father, George, remembering how their conversations and interactions now resembled a sport: a back and forth of blame, noise meeting noise, moving in lofty spirals and strident leaps. But George's were more energetic than hers, more hurtful and tainted with arrogance. She was puzzled by this, wondered at what point in their life it had crept in. It certainly wasn't there when they were in their twenties and he had been pursuing her. One thing she had loved about Victor's father was his politeness and manners. When he took her to bars and restaurants, he would make sure to pull a chair for her to sit on. And he always wanted to show her off to his friends as if she was his most prized possession. She had loved that, being the most important thing in his life.

A car stopped. A door opened and slammed shut. Mabel walked to the huge window and parted the curtains. It was not Victor. The neighbour, Dr Bassey, had returned. Mabel knew that it would not be long before she heard the sound of his children. She could imagine the excitement that always greeted his return; his wife, genuinely happy to see him and maybe giving him a peck on the cheek in front of the children. Mabel could imagine them squealing in laughter, happy in the warm circle of their family.

Happy. That was all she wanted for Victor, for all her children. Happiness and a full life. It did give her some comfort that Thelma and Patrick were both married and had produced grandchildren for her. She saw them often, but not since she had come, two months before, to nurse Victor back to health.

Mabel recalled that it was Victor who had needed her. He had sounded really bad when he spoke to her over the telephone and his half-hearted attempt to assure her that he would be fine did not stop her from entering a taxi the next day and journeying to Lagos. It had been a welcome escape for her from Asaba, from the monotony of life there. It took nine gruelling hours on bad roads, but that did not trouble her. The smile on Victor's face when he saw her had more than made up for whatever discomfort she had experienced during the journey.

If Victor had had a wife and maybe children, Mabel would not have come, or even if she had, she would not have stayed for as long as she did. She had tried and failed to show Victor the importance of these things, the importance of having one's own family at such times. She had mentioned this to Patrick once, when she had visited him.

"Mama, why don't you let him be?" Patrick had said. "Victor is a grown man. He will get married if and when he chooses to."

"It's exactly because he is a grown man that I worry," Mabel said. "When will he settle down? When does he want to start having children? It's every parent's wish to see their grandchildren before they die."

"But Mama, you already have grandkids!"

"Yes, and they are all beautiful," Mabel said. "Yours and Thelma's, but I want to see Victor's children."

"What if that is not what Victor wants?"

"What else would he want?" Mabel asked.

"What if he doesn't want children? What if he doesn't want to marry?"

"Why?" Mabel's fear was obvious in her voice. "What kind of a man would not want to get married and have his own children?"

Mabel drew the curtains and returned to the sofa. She wondered what mood Victor would be in when he got home. In the last couple of days she had noticed a change in his countenance – the way he would grudgingly greet her in the mornings, his muffled words, or when he simply ignored her and pretended not to have heard her while she was speaking to him. His father acted the same way, treated her as though she were invisible. She had often wondered at what moment Victor had changed from the caring, dutiful son she had nurtured into *this* man.

Yet, in those tense moments when Victor's issue came up between Mabel and his father, she was always blamed for whatever shortcoming Victor may possess.

"He is *your* son," Victor's father would say. "It's your fault he is the way he is. You turned Victor into a mama's boy, now he can't find a woman for himself."

Mabel looked at the wall clock. It was now almost eight. Victor was never this late. He had left that morning before she was awake. He had been grouchy the night before, complaining about personal space and chiding her for rearranging the furniture.

Personal space. That was the problem with Victor; he already had too much personal space, Mabel mused. He lived alone in a big house. It had four large bedrooms and a servants' quarter at the back. Victor had no live-in servants, his cleaner and cook came in only on Saturdays. The living room alone was bigger than the first house that Mabel and Victor's father had lived in. Apart from two abstract paintings that hung by the bookshelf, the walls were bare. How much more personal space could anyone need?

She recalled the little house they lived in after Thelma, her second child, was born. It had only one bedroom. The room was just big enough for a bed and Victor's old cradle, which was then Thelma's. The room had only one window and at night it usually got very hot. Most nights, the heat woke Thelma up and she would cry and cry.

"George," Mabel had said to Victor's father on one of those nights. "We need a bigger house. We need more space now that our family is growing."

"We can't afford a bigger house, woman. You talk as if you have no sense sometimes."

"If you let me, I could look for work so that we can have more money."

His laugh had been long and scornful. "Who will employ you? Sometimes I wonder at you, woman."

Mabel had always found Victor's father's snide remarks hurtful. She found it very strange that he could quickly forget that she had had to sacrifice going to university for him, so that they could get married and that it was, after all, her father's money that had helped with his education at the expense of hers. They had been in love then and she was already pregnant with Victor before the wedding. Now, when she looked back, Mabel realized that they had rushed things when they were younger.

This was why she had not thought it strange when Victor had insisted on getting a job first, after he had graduated from the university. In those days, it was Victor who reminded Mabel of her complaints about how poor and miserable she felt in the early years of her marriage to his father. Yes, she recalled how difficult things had been for them and how she and Victor's father had thought it was silly of them to have jumped into marriage without first planning properly. Those were bad years, years that saw her back in her parents' home more than twice with her young children, Victor, Thelma and Patrick. Poverty was not a fabric that a young family should cover themselves with, she had often said. It was easy for Mabel to understand then why her son would not want to make the same mistake by starting his own family so early.

But that was many years ago. Victor had achieved so many things since then – but not the one thing that really mattered, settling down.

Mabel looked at the clock again. It was just past eight. This was not like Victor at all. He would have called her to say he was going to be late. She got up and walked over to the end table by Victor's favourite chair, the one he always sat on when he read his newspapers or watched television, the one he never allowed anyone else to occupy. She noticed the phone on the table, and hesitated briefly before she picked it up. She had a sense that she was further invading his space. But the urge to speak to somebody was greater than her need to respect Victor's wishes.

Mabel sat on Victor's chair. Carefully she dialled a number. She waited until someone answered the phone at the other end.

"Thelma," Mabel said into the phone. "This is Mummy."

"Mummy, I was just thinking of you. How are you?"

"I am fine. How is America?"

"Fine, Mum. Are you back home with Dad? How is he?"

"Your father is fine. I'm still at Victor's place. In fact, it's because of him I'm calling…"

"Hasn't he recovered yet? It was only malaria he had. Mum, how does Dad feel about you staying away for so long?"

Mabel took deep breaths to contain the growing annoyance within her. Why did all her children treat her as though she were a child? When she was away from their father, even for a little time, they would always express their surprise that he allowed her to go anywhere on her own.

Mabel decided not to lose track of why she had called. In a calm voice, she told Thelma about the changes she had noticed in Victor. She also chipped in her growing concerns about Victor's enduring bachelorhood.

"Oh Mum, are we still on this Victor issue again? No wonder he is behaving funny towards you."

"What do you mean by that?" Mabel sounded petulant. "What is wrong with a mother wanting the best for her children?"

"There's nothing wrong with it, Mum. It's just that Victor is no longer a child. If you keep treating him like one, you'll end up alienating him."

"I only want him to be happy." Mabel said.

"What makes you think that he is not happy?"

Mabel wondered why her children had such views. She wondered whether it was the education they had that had planted such opinions in their head. She wondered also whether she too would harbour such radical beliefs if she had had a chance to finish schooling.

"Mum, have you considered that maybe Victor enjoys his life the way it is?"

Mabel sighed.

"Or," Thelma continued, "he may have been hurt before by a woman and is no longer interested in pursuing a relationship. Some men are like that, you know!"

"But he has not had a girlfriend since he left university."

"Or he may even be gay, Mum."

"What kind of foolish talk is that?" Mabel cried. "Be serious, Thelma."

Mabel knew there was no such thing in her family. Homosexuality was one of those outlandish things one heard about and never gave a second thought to. It was typical for Thelma to rouse her like that, saying silly, unnatural things.

"There could be all sorts of reasons why Victor is single," Thelma added. "But he is an adult and I am sure he is quite happy with himself and with life."

"What kind of happiness is that? People will think something is wrong with him, a man of nearly 40 still unmarried and without children."

"It is no one's business, Mum!"

Mabel let out a deep sigh. She had had it with holding back.

"You would say that, wouldn't you? What have you ever known about responsibility? Wasn't it you who went and had an abortion at 18 and we had to live with the shame?"

"Oh Mum, there you go again trying to live by other people's standards! What a *good* example you and Dad showed us when we were growing up! We could see how unhappy you both were, especially you, Mum. If we were to use you as a model for happiness, none of us would ever get married."

Mabel recoiled at her daughter's words. A long silence punctuated by the ticking of the wall clock ensued. All her life she had hoped to shield her children from the disappointment she had always felt about her marriage – the sacrifices she had had to make; enduring the scorn of a man that did not love her or see her as an equal; her frustration with dreams unfulfilled. In a moment of clarity, she realized that in pursuing the happiness of her children's lives and their marriages, she had been trying to find fullness in her own life.

"I've got to go, Mum," Thelma said. "I need to get to the mall to pick up some things."

"OK, goodbye, my dear."

"Will you be all right, Mum?"

"Yes. Greet my grandchildren for me."

As Mabel hung up the phone, she felt a sudden lightness. She got up from Victor's chair and made her way again to the window. She pulled the curtains aside and instead of seeing the lawn and walkways, or the pole across the street that had the green sign with Macaulay Avenue inscribed on it, she saw the different stages of a young woman's life – marrying the man she thought she loved; giving up on becoming a teacher and choosing motherhood. Mabel imagined that no matter what little happiness this woman found in the course of her life, she would never be whole. Because in giving up on something, one could never be complete.

Across the street a young boy peddling mobile phone top-up cards aided a frail old woman as she crossed the road. Mabel watched them. She recalled when Victor was 12 years old. He had come home from school one day, while Thelma and Patrick were napping, to meet her crying in her bedroom. It was the day she got the news of her father's death. Her husband was away and there was no one to comfort her.

"Don't worry, Mum," Victor had said. "I will always be here for you."

Mabel's eyes brimmed with tears. Victor had always looked after her. He sent money to her regularly and made it a duty to call her at least once a week when she was back in Asaba. She always knew she could depend on his calls even when her other children forgot about checking up on her.

Mabel still spoke about him with pride to the other mothers who convened after Sunday Mass. When Victor was younger it had been about his exceptional performance in school. In the later years, it would be of his promotions at work or the new car he had bought. She had been proudest when, after she had asked him, Victor had helped secure a job for one of the other mothers' son who had been seeking employment for more than two years after graduating from the university.

"Mama Victor, I still can't thank you enough," Simi Taylor had gushed. "I'm surprised Victor gave my Richard a job in his office. It must be good to have such an influential son."

Mabel had smiled, soaked up the praises and basked in the glow of the other envious mothers who joined Simi in thanking her. It occurred to her that her exalted position among the women was due to Victor's success.

"May he find a good wife who will bring him so much joy," Simi had continued.

"Amen!"

"May you be blessed with many grandchildren..."

The headlamps of an approaching car cast a spotlight on Mabel. The car came to a halt on the driveway. The lights dimmed before becoming round sockets of darkness.

As she made her way to the kitchen to heat up Victor's dinner, Mabel knew her time for farewell had come. She thought fleetingly about her small garden at the back of the house; how no one would tend to it when she was gone. She knew somehow that the tomato seeds would never come to fruition.

Jude Dibia is the author of two novels, *Walking With Shadows* (Blacksands 2005) and *Unbridled* (Blacksands 2007/Jacana Media 2009). In 2007 he was awarded the Ken Saro-Wiwa Prize for fiction and in 2008 was a finalist in the Nigeria Prize for Literature. Dibia lives and works in Nigeria.

Mr Oliver

Mamle Kabu

I'VE ALWAYS WANTED SUCH eyes. They are part of the face I think I should have, not this one that's beautiful to others but not to me. Just look at them. Even wide open, the lids are so hooded that you feel like applying eye shadow to them like the actresses in the Eighties soap operas. Dark shades along the arc, lightening towards the sweeping lash, the contrast glossing the curve so a blink makes you lean in for the next flash. O, if they were mine, I would dip my eyelids reflectively in conversation, oblivious that the observer caught his breath every time.

"Madam."

"Yes, Mr Oliver, sorry, wetin you dey say?"

What's he doing with such eyes? What did he ever need them for? It's as if they went to him by mistake, robbing some woman who never knew she could have been the next Angelina Jolie if her eyes had not been stolen by a ragged old Ghanaian mason.

"Madam, please, we dey need more cement."

This is what I don't like. Why do they have to come and ask for these things when Alex is not here? I try to don his perennial scepticism but I know it doesn't sit well on me. I'm just too half-hearted about it.

"Cement finish just now? Mr Oliver, are you sure?"

"Yes Madam," he says with his shy smile, humouring my efforts at cynicism.

"You no ask Mr Nii?"

"Mr Nii say money finish."

"And you no fit wait till Master come?"

"Mr Alex say make we finish de work before he come back," he says with eyes half averted.

Indecision makes me irritable. "I dey go for saloon and I make late. You dey worry me ohh, Mr Oliver."

"Sorry Madam," he shuffles with another good-natured smile but he stays put. His cordial tenacity is oddly reminiscent.

Surely Alex would have left enough money for them? I am torn between just giving the guy what he needs to finish the job and being told off by Alex later on. "Why d'you always fall for their tricks, you know he'll only go and drink it as usual."

Is he really an alcoholic, I wonder, not for the first time, coveting yet again that deep arc of his eyelids as he looks at the floor. Nii says he is and he brought him to us so he must know. It's just hard to imagine in such a gentle person. Maybe he's only gentle to me, because I'm Madam. Maybe gentle people are alcoholics too.

I give him the money for one bag of cement and he reaches for it with his right hand, supported underneath by his left in a gesture of respect. I feel a momentary awkwardness. He could be my father.

As I drive back through the gate two hours later with a glossy blow-dry that has made me forget the envy of Mr Oliver's eyes, I gasp. He has finished the facing stone on the front wall of the new screened porch. Instead of entering the house, I walk over to the site of the new extension. He moves quickly out of my way, balancing his mortarboard in one hand ridiculously, like a waiter with a tray of drinks.

"*Ayekoo*, Mr Oliver!"

"*Yayei*, Madam!" he smiles, looking down quickly after his unguarded reciprocation of my artless admiration. The warmth of the moment gives me that fleeting sense of familiarity again, this time accompanied by a sense of loss.

I feel like thanking him but it would seem absurd. How

can I tell him the ecstasy it gives me to look on his handiwork without sounding ridiculous? He's just doing his job. And it's not even all his because the blend of earthen tones, the gold, rust and ochre revealed when the stone was split, have nothing to do with him. But the way they are fitted together, how does he do that? He must rifle through dozens of them to slot them together like a puzzle. It's hard to imagine an illiterate old drunkard of a mason taking such pains, such pride in his work. I can't explain why the soft harmony of colour and texture gives me that feeling, it would sound ridiculous to anyone. How do you explain what colour can do to you, how the purity of a shape, the curve of the neck of a clay pot can put you on a high, to someone who just doesn't feel it? I gave up with Alex after he told me I was irrational about pots. Maybe I am.

I enter the doorless porch, looking around me and imagining the potted plants and wrought iron furniture that will soon be standing here. Palms. It's got to be palms all around, different species at graded heights. I've seen some amazing ones at the new garden centre in Airport Residential, huge and in pots I would display even empty. Varieties I've only ever seen in garden catalogues, probably flown in from South Africa. I can just picture them in here, arching over the heads of my visitors, throwing feathery patterns of shadow around the room. I glance upwards, lost in my vision and in lowering my head, catch his eye or think I do. He seemed for a moment to be looking in, perhaps concerned that I was unhappy with some detail of the masonry on the interior. I wonder what he would think if he knew the price of those plants that will soon be in here, setting off the warm tones and textures of his stonework. Just one of them is probably equivalent to several months of his income.

My phone rings. "Hi darling," Alex crackles down the line.

"Hi…" I feel self-conscious with the sudden intrusion of his presence and hurry out towards the house.

"I'm at the airport, can't wait to see you tomorrow."

"Me too."

"Wait till you see what I'm getting you!"

"Oh."

"You'll wear them for me tomorrow night."

They turn out to be diamond earrings and the latest French perfume from the duty free. The price tags are still on. He wants to spray the perfume on me himself but not till he has removed every stitch of my clothing. I don't like it. It's too flowery. After two years he still refuses to recognize that I wear only one fragrance. Or to know my own scent well enough to pick up a bottle and say no, that's not her, that's never her. Because it's not the smell that excites him, I reflect, as the golden mist raises goose bumps on my naked skin, no, it's not even my body, it's just the thrill of spraying liquid money all over his wife.

I am ticklish when he starts caressing me. It's not the first time and I feel panic rising from somewhere near the back of my neck. I know what it means when I get ticklish and I've never been able to reverse it. I summon all my powers of self-mastery to suppress the shrill horror of giggles welling up inside me, to control the jerks that should be undulations, to fight down the overpowering impulse to smack his hand away. I try to ignore the florid scent cloying my senses, and focus my mind on conjuring back the current that once made me gasp when he placed his hand on my bare flesh.

I tell Nana about it over the phone the next day.

"Ticklish?" she echoes, "Oh shit, you know what this means. Remember when you got ticklish with Yaw?"

"Yes, yes," I say impatiently. She's meant to be making me feel better, not worse. But what a memory, I marvel, she tracks my life better than I do. That's why it's so easy to talk to her.

"So what happened?"

"Well, he went down on me in the end so that finally did the trick."

"I bet it did!" She laughs a dirty laugh and I join in. It makes me feel better, lighter. I was right to call her.

"Yeah, so it was kind of OK in the end, I'm not sure he even noticed anything was wrong," I say, knowing it's myself I'm trying to convince.

"Well thank God for that!" Then she turns serious. "But you do still love him, don't you?"

I feel irritated by the articulation of what I've been evading asking myself. It used to seem so simple but now, it sounds so inane. What is love anyway? As if just saying I do would make everything OK.

"We need to talk, Nana."

"Uh-oh."

"No, it's not like that, I just mean face to face, not on the phone."

The prospect alone is a relief but can I finally admit even to her what has been happening in my head? Can I tell her about the diabolical "It's not working, it's not working" buzz going round and round like a mantra? It's not that I can't trust her, it's just that saying things out loud has a way of making them real.

I head back towards the house and then change my mind. I always call Nana from the garden so the house staff don't hear me but this time, although the call is over, I don't feel like going back. I pluck a bright pink hibiscus from the ten-foot bush near the fishpond and sit on the warm stone step twirling it while trying to order my thoughts. I consciously clear my mind by focusing on the gentle swish and spray of the fountain blowing its drops even beyond the edge of the pond. There was a time when I thought there was no pain I couldn't heal with the sound of water.

If it's time to make it real then Nana is the only person. I can still hear her with that same question two years ago – "You do love him, don't you?" She was the only one who dared ask if I knew what I was doing, marrying such a man. She didn't go as far as to call him nouveau riche, because she didn't need to. I could see the wonder in her eyes, the questions, but I was too in love with what was happening to me. I couldn't imagine life without him, his cocky charm that made everything else unimportant and would make me suddenly want him at the most unexpected of moments. I admired him for making a fortune from nothing and yes, I was seduced by the thought of being the mistress of that fortune. I close my eyes and brush the softness of the petals over my face. My yes to that question was no placebo at the time.

I jump at the vibration of the phone in my pocket. It's Alex reminding me about the reception. "I'm on my way home, just leaving the Chief of Police's office. He says to greet my lovely wife, by the way. I want you to look gorgeous tonight, darling, why don't you wear your new earrings?" I walk back to the house, brushing pollen from my face.

I turn them over in my fingers a little later, unhooking their clasps. Flashes of gold and sparks of rainbow fire answer my dressing table lights as the glamorous trails dance freely on their delicate chains. But I seem to see it only from a distance. I feel like someone watching a gorgeous woman get ready for a cocktail party. Alex stops dead coming out of the bathroom.

"I knew you would look like this."

His eyes scan downwards over my waist and hips, moulded by the two-tone shades of my silk Givenchy dress, turquoise and grey in mesmerizing competition. I turn away so the memory of what used to happen at times like this will not be mutual. "You need to get dressed quickly, darling, we're running late."

In the car he is in excellent spirits. "You're going to love the new ambassador's wife, I'm sure you two will hit it off great." I cringe slightly at his faux American twang. It always gets worse when we're heading towards an event like this. "In fact, you know what, you should invite her to coffee on your new porch!"

I think he is jumping the gun as usual but I make the noises he wants to hear and then add in sudden recollection, "Oh that reminds me, I had to give the mason some money while you were away."

"For what?" he asks, in irate surprise.

"Cement apparently."

"But I gave Nii all the money they would need while I was away."

"Well, I don't know, maybe he needed more than he had thought. His work is very thorough. I knew you wouldn't be happy, darling, but you weren't around and I wasn't sure what to do."

"Don't worry, Babe," he says, taking his hand off the gear shift and pushing it softly between my knees so I know he still feels we have unfinished business. "They know you're a softie but I can handle them."

I'm off the hook, he's too intent on what he wants to pick a fight with me, even if he won't get it till much later. But I'm still restless.

"His work is beautiful, you've seen what he did while you were away, haven't you?"

"Oh yes, he's a master, tops, just like Nii said. Too bad about the drink, he could go a lot further with that quality. It's so rare in this country. I could even recommend him to some of these rich *bronis* but the problem is they don't know how to handle these workers like we do. They're all polite and fair and nice-nice and next thing they know they're being ripped off. No, I don't want it on my head if he goes and misbehaves."

I suffer a moment of disorientation. The word 'misbehave' applied to the doe-eyed Mr Oliver steers my thoughts in unusual directions. It's not that I can't believe he drinks, in fact I've sometimes thought it must be when he has that sleepy look that he's had a bit. But 'misbehaves'? Mr Oliver?

"Where does he get such a name anyway, it sounds so British. Is it some nickname?"

"No-no-no, it's his surname. He's an Oliver, can you believe it? Nii told me."

Now I'm dumbstruck. "You mean he's related to the Olivers?"

"Yes, he must be, they all come from Teshie originally, just like him."

Dusty-kneed Mr Oliver, related to one of the most prestigious families in Ghana. Legend has it their British ancestor was a slave trader and ate with golden cutlery off golden crockery in his Jamestown mansion. Alex savours my disbelief.

"Yes, black as he is, he's an Oliver. Maybe he drank all the money away!" and he chuckles his infectious chuckle, the last thing left that I can't resist.

It's amazing what genes can do in a few hundred years, I think to myself, and not just genes, fate. I think of the light-skinned, stylish Olivers living a few streets away from us and the Member of Parliament who is now the head of their family. Our Mr Oliver's branch of the family tree must have lost the money many generations before he had the chance to drink it away but still... I feel like asking a dozen more questions but Alex won't know the answers – I'd be better off asking Nii. Besides, his jealousy is so irrational, I wouldn't put it past him to take it the wrong way, even with an old husk like Mr Oliver, and I wouldn't want to put the poor guy in that kind of trouble. I venture a different kind of question.

"Did you tell him you liked his work?"

"What? He doesn't need praise from me, just money. Which reminds me, he came for his final payment while we were getting ready this evening, apparently."

"Oh really?"

"Yes, but I told them to tell him I was busy."

"So when will you pay him?"

"Oh, no hurry, he'll get his money."

"But soon please, darling."

His silence implies loss of interest in the topic.

I take a deep breath and continue, "I hope you're not going to do go-come-go-come with him."

He raises his eyebrows with a hurt look and then opts for a chuckle. "So I do go-come-go-come, do I?"

"You know you do, Alex."

"I see," his mirth trails off a little lamely, "Anyway, I can always give it to Nii. He lives round the corner from him. Good thing you told me what you gave him."

I start in my seat and look out of the side window. "Round the corner from Nii? But that's here! Nii's house is just down the road from here."

"True, we're in Nima already, aren't we."

"Yes, slow down darling."

I peer out at the ramshackle buildings lit up by smoking milk-tin kerosene lamps on food vending tables. Behind them I can just about make out the silhouette of the cavernous, filth-choked sewer running parallel to the road. I've often imagined how it would be a scenic canal with boats and ducks in the developed world. I'm struck yet again by the proximity of this vast slum to the gentrified luxury of Airport Residential where we are heading.

"D'you know where Mr Oliver's house is?"

"Yes, as a matter of fact. Nii showed me."

"Oh darling, let's go and pay him now, it will only take a minute."

"Are you crazy?" His tone changes to wheedling when he sees my expression. "Sweetheart, what's got into you? Stop at Mr Oliver's house in Nima now, like this?"

"Why not?"

I watch alarm, exasperation and disbelief chase each other around his face. "Well, on top everything else, it's you who said we're late."

"Yes, but how long does it take to hand a few cedis over?"

"OK, you know what, if it matters that much to you, we'll do it on the way back."

"But won't that be too late?"

"Course not, it's a cocktail not a dinner, and anyway, you think he'll turn money down even at midnight?"

The event is every bit as tedious as I expected. A motley crew from senior Ghanaian politicians to raggedly ethnic Peace Corps Volunteers constitute the guest list. Alex rushes to greet his buddy the Minister of Foreign Affairs and smiles like a waxwork when a TV camera approaches. "This is my wife," he says, drawing me into the circle and beaming proudly as the Minister's eyes rake my length hard enough to flay me, then direct themselves covetously back to Alex. His wife glowers delicately from beneath her stiff head tie, shifting her weight uncomfortably between her undersize diamanté slippers. I sympathize, though not seeking any solidarity, because my heels are at least three inches higher than hers and my calves are already beginning to ache from the endless standing and chit-chat that make me hate these events.

A voluble lady swoops over and kisses me on both cheeks. I greet her brightly because she seems familiar and likeable enough and the only problem is I can't remember who on earth she is. Fortunately she doesn't seem to know my name either. "You're Alex's wife, aren't you?" she drawls. "How absolutely gorgeous you look tonight, and isn't this just exquisite," she breathes, fingering the fringes of my kente stole. I stammer to return the compliments, my eyes tripping over her bony body and colourless attire. "And how are your adorable children?" she rushes on, to my simultaneous relief and consternation.

"Actually we don't have any... yet," I say as diplomatically as I can.

"Oh, no, of course you don't," she says with a flustered laugh, reddening a bit. "Silly me, I must have been thinking of someone else, I do beg your pardon." I reassure her till she feels comfortable enough to resume the chit-chat but I'm not really listening any more, just nodding. She has unwittingly sent my mind back into hostile territory. In the first year

Alex quite enjoyed the idea of waiting, it made him feel like a white man. "There's no rush," he'd say airily, enjoying the nods of his white colleagues and the puzzled glances of his less sophisticated countrymen. "This way we can enjoy each other for a bit first," he would add with a leer at me. The airiness dissipated a bit in the second year but he didn't dare pressure me after Daddy died. The idea of having babies I couldn't give him as grandchildren made me sink even deeper into depression. He had never been able to look me in the eye when we talked about Alex but I knew a grandchild would make it different. I never expected the stroke – he was going to be a fun, hands-on granddaddy.

I look up quickly to banish the threat of tears and find my friend whose name I've already forgotten again looking expectantly at me. I realize she has just asked me a question.

"How exactly d'you mean that?" I improvise. It works but my mind can't stay with her for long. Alex has become more insistent about children lately. I'm sure his family are giving him hell. I can just hear his mother – "So now she's too good for babies too, eh?" I've stalled mainly by dragging my feet about getting my birth control implant removed but I can't keep that up much longer. I haven't yet given myself a concrete reason why the time still isn't right. I love babies but all I know is, it's the last thing I want right now.

As she gabbles on, my mind goes back to Mr Oliver and I look discreetly over her shoulder at the ornate clock on the wall. I wonder what she and the other people standing in this banquet hall would think if they knew my main preoccupation at this moment is getting a paltry sum of money to a scruffy old mason in Nima. Absurd though it may be, the prospect of staying here much longer does not appeal. The lady reaches the end of a sentence and I excuse myself as politely as I can to go in search of Alex. He is in his element, introducing me to excellencies, honourables, ministers of this and CEOs of that and I wonder once again if he ever bothers finding out their actual names.

I play along, initially for Alex's sake, but end up quite involved in the discussion about Ghana's oil discovery and its implications. I enjoy the surprise of the men and the bristling of the women as I hold my own in the argument it becomes. I feel an invigorating confidence that I realize I have missed and it makes me resolve to approach Alex again about going back to work. He is watching me with that odd mixture of pride and embarrassment. He likes to boast about my academic achievements but at the same time I know he feels my proper place is with the wives at the coffee mornings and garden parties. I fizzled out soon enough on that circuit. I could hold my own on the elegance front but their interests and petty politics overcame my wifely sense of duty. As Nana summed it up, I could walk the walk but I couldn't talk the talk. Good old Nana. Alex will never understand why I "waste my time" on friends like her.

He ends up in a cosy clique that lingers after most people have left so it's past ten when we finally head home. He is bubbling with his latest conquests, especially his best buddy the new American ambassador. He drives as fast as he chatters and seems surprised when I interrupt to remind him about Mr Oliver.

"Oh come on, Babe, you can't still..." He takes his eyes off the road as if to see for himself a person who could want to do such a thing after coming from such a place. I look silently out through the windscreen. He clicks the indicator to the left.

"OK, my Princess, you know I can't say no to you." I can't help smiling. Pleased, he takes his eyes off the road again. "Especially when you're looking so gorgeous," he murmurs deeply, stroking the back of my neck with his right hand as we pull into a bumpy dirt road beside an open gutter. He hoots loudly and then clicks down his window, jerking his head backwards as the stench invades the car. I can't stop myself wrinkling my nose either. "Well, you wanted to come here sweetheart," he says, beckoning over a young lad who has appeared in response to the noise. The sight of the Hummer chases the sleep from his eyes.

"Call Mr Oliver, quick-quick. Tell am say Mr Alex come." The boy scuttles off and I follow him with my eyes. In the car headlights I see what looks like a compound house partitioned between different sets of tenants. Browned with dust and rust, the roofing sheets look like fossils of their original metal. The exterior of the building is unplastered and the worn cement bricks look indecently exposed.

Mr Oliver walks towards us in a light *djellabia*. I have only ever seen him in torn working clothes of that indefinable colour all workmen's clothes seem to share, a blend of sweat, dust and their occupational travails. He seems taller in this robe, and has an altogether different presence here in his own territory. This man is the head of a family and the master of his home, it occurs to me for the very first time. He walks over to Alex's window and greets him over the noise of the engine. "Good evening, Madam," he adds, looking over at me with his gentle, starlet eyes. I respond, feeling deferential for the first time this evening. Alex interrupts me, pulling some notes from his wallet.

"They tell me say you finish the work Mr Oliver, and Madam, she like am well-well," he says, handing over the money, "Take dis one and make you count am."

Mr Oliver leafs through the notes and then looks up, disquieted. Alex jumps in smoothly.

"Madam tell me say you come collect money from her the time I travel." Mr Oliver nods and Alex continues before he can open his mouth, "Mr Oliver, you know say me I no like dat kin' libi-libi." He is holding up a forefinger now, "So I commot dat money for inside. Dis one be your balance." And he stashes his wallet away and revs the car. I am frozen to my seat. As he begins to reverse, mortification seeps through, jolting me into action.

"Stop!" I shout, opening my door to force him to brake.

Kicking off my stilettos, I jump out of the car, feeling the still warm sand and the jab of tiny stones beneath my feet. It is only later I will wonder what I might have been stepping into and how lucky I was not to fall into the gutter. "Mr Oliver!" I hobble round the car, fumbling inside my silk evening bag for the wad of notes I keep tucked in the inner recesses of every one of my handbags. I have no idea how much it is but I deposit it all in his hand. "Thank you," I say, feeling a foolish impulse to cup my outstretched arm in my left hand.

I stumble back into the car, exchanging not a word or a look with my husband as we roar out of the tiny alley.

Mamle Kabu was shortlisted for the Caine Prize in 2009 for her short story 'The End of Skill'. She grew up in Ghana and later in the UK where she studied at Cambridge University. She has had five other short stories published. She currently lives and works in Ghana and is a mother of two.

Happy Ending

Stanley Onjezani Kenani

I

TWICE HE HAD WALKED within a few yards of the hut and twice he had returned. It was a heavy thing to do. *Should I or should I not?* he kept asking himself. He was a devout Catholic for whom such thoughts should be anathema, but then he knew many devout Catholics who did worse things, like those priests who slept with little boys – not to mention the Archbishop, who recently was embroiled in a well-publicised affair with a married woman, a mother of seven. *Catholicism has nothing to do with this*, he declared. He turned to face the anthill again. *This time, I'll not return.*

He took one step after another. The make-up of the place was quite scary, as scary as the very idea he was coming here for. Towering trees mixed with shorter ones, shrubs and tall elephant grass, making the anthill look like the unkempt hair of a mad man. Owls hooted and hyenas laughed not so far away. Strange. One expected these things to be laughing and hooting at night, but now the sun's position suggested it was midday. In the middle of all these was a hut of Simbazako, the most famous man in Chipiri and even beyond.

"*Odi!*" He announced his arrival a yard or so from the hut. The hut's door was made of dry grass, like that of any other house in Chipiri. The thatched roof was rotting, judging by the strong smell of decomposing grass it emitted. This was not surprising. Branches of the tall trees formed an umbrella, blocking any ray of sunshine that could have been injecting some warmth for drying the roof after the rains. As a dwelling its days were numbered. It leaned heavily, one would even say sadly, towards the ground. If a strong wind were to grab it by its neck and shake it hard, it would be no more. Again, the trees played curator well, for they trapped and frustrated any malicious winds that might think of delivering the final blow to the hut.

"*Odi!*" He shifted on his feet and coughed. *What if the hyena sprang from this bush and landed on me?* he thought. He knew he did not possess the strength of the biblical Samson, so he stood no chance.

"Who is there?" The voice startled him. It was deep and husky, making him tremble a little in fear.

"My name is Dama Chikwangwala," he answered.

"The son of the late Kampango Chikwangwala of Mtenthe Village at the foot of the Chipiri Hills?"

"Yes."

"Grandson of the great Birimankhwe Chikwangwala who took part in the John Chilembwe Uprising against colonialists?"

"Yes."

"Great-great-grandson of Chimkombero Chikwangwala, he who fought fearlessly with the Zwangendaba Ngonis and chased them further north of the Mabvumbwe River?"

"That is me." *This man is a volume of history in his own right*, Dama thought.

"Come in, my son."

There was sound of some movement inside, like feet being dragged with great difficulty. The door opened. Dama walked in.

Simbazako was very, very old, maybe a hundred years or older. When youth and blood were warmer, before age had written its ruthless signature on his face, he must have been tall and slim and handsome, but now he leaned heavily on his stick, thereby hiding his true height. His grey hair curled in accidental dreadlocks. *Maybe Samson's hair looked like this*, he thought as his eyes wandered about the hut. There was a bamboo mat that served as Simbazako's bed, to which the host dragged himself and painfully sat down. A fireplace less than a yard from the mat had no fire, except a heap of cold ash. An old, threadbare blanket, a pair of heavily patched trousers and a shirt that must once have been white were bundled on a line just above the mat. Unwashed plates and a pot coated with heavy black soot lay in the corner, providing an excellent playground for house-flies. A heavy tobacco smell hung in the air. Simbazako pointed to a spot just next to the mat. Dama walked there and sat down.

"Is there anything I can do for you?" Simbazako spoke, revealing his surviving four teeth that were heavily brownish.

"Yes, *gogo*," Dama replied. Like any old man in Chipiri, Simbazako would certainly feel good to be addressed as grandfather. Or so Dama thought. "I have a big problem," he continued. "I need your help. Urgently."

Simbazako stared at him. "What is the problem?"

"A lot of people have told me that you have herbs that can cure any problem, even my kind of problem," Dama said. He had grown up hearing about Simbazako's immense capabilities in healing all manner of problems. Simbazako could cure headaches, toothaches, stomach-aches, rheumatism, syphilis, appendicitis, epilepsy, diarrhoea, hernia, gonorrhoea, pneumonia, malaria – anything. He could heal snakebites, from puff adders to boomslangs to black mambas to king cobras to vipers – any kind of snake. Many Malawian politicians, even presidents, were said to have used Simbazako in more ways than merely persuading him to vote for them. He had magical herbs that laundered the soiled image of politicians, such that even if they stole public money and enriched themselves, the public should still love them and keep them in power. But some of the legends were heavily embellished. There was one about his capabilities to block rains from falling. Catholic as he was,

Dama knew that only God decided when rain could fall and where. There was another about helping people to get rich using magic. Why, then, was he himself so poor? There was fact, yes, but there was also plenty of fiction.

"What is the problem?"

Dama looked down and said: "My wife is cheating on me."

II

Should I, or should I not?

It was in the evening. Dama sat on a short-legged stool by the fireside in his home. In the pocket of his long-sleeved black shirt, there was a small plastic packet of a powdery substance blacker than his shirt. It was a variety of *chambu*. The full name of this specific variety was *kutha-mokondwa*. Any man who touched Tithelepo would die in the act, at the peak of ecstasy. Dama had had to choose among several varieties. There was one in which the man could die as if stung by a puff adder a few hours after the act. There was another in which the lover could be tortured slowly, feeling like a million needles were pricking his stomach. The torture could go on for a month, every second, every minute, until death put the victim out of his misery. Dama, however, had decided not to be so cruel, so he'd settled for *kutha-mokondwa*. *The man should die in the act*, he thought. There was the advantage of a long-lasting psychological impact on the part of his wife, because, surely, the image of a dead man on top of her seconds after the height of passion would live in her mind forever. She would never want to touch another man, except Dama alone.

He clutched the rosary hanging around his neck and began to utter a prayer: "*Áve María, grátia pléna, Dóminus técum...*" his lips moved without the words coming out. Just like many Pentecostal Christians preferred quoting Scripture from the King James Version to make it sound godlier, he liked the Latin version of Hail Mary which Father Vittorio, the benevolent Italian, had taught him the few years he spent at the all-boys Mtendere Catholic Secondary School.

"Why are you so quiet?" Tithelepo's sudden question made him look up. "What are you thinking about? Are you worried that Abisalomu did not come today as promised in his letter?"

It was only then he remembered that his beloved younger brother was supposed to come home today for the summer holiday. Under normal circumstances, he should really have been worried that the boy had not arrived at such a late hour. But the Simbazako business had made him forget. Looking up at his wife, he coughed, shifted in his seat and said: "Er, yes, I am really worried why he is not in by now." He realized there was no conviction in his own voice.

Tithelepo continued walking about, now in the kitchen, now out, the sound of plates being washed just outside the kitchen, footsteps into the main house and back to the plates while humming *Ave Ave Maria, ah, kudandaula kwathu Maria Ave*, her favourite hymn. All the while, the pot of her *therere* boiled over the fire.

Dama's right hand tightly held the *chambu* packet. He sat staring in the pot for a moment, the steam hitting his face. He decided against it. The packet went back into his pocket, just in time, because at that precise moment, Maria walked into the kitchen.

"When you next go into the house," he said, "bring me the Holy Bible."

Simbazako's words came to him. "It will be pretty harmless to you," he had said. "You can eat it with her. But the moment she eats it, no other man can sleep with her and live."

"How long shall this last?" he had asked.

"Until the day of her death. But let me warn you. If it turns out that she does not cheat at all, say for one year, you will be the one to die. You can only proceed if you are absolutely certain that she is going out with someone."

Tithelepo was back in the kitchen. She walked out just after passing on the holy book to him. It was as he received the book from her that he realized his hands were shaking. He opened it accidentally. Initially, when calling for it, he had wanted to find comfort in something nice, like the poetry in Solomon's songs. But, owing to his clumsiness, the book had landed in his lap open. He decided to read the page anyway, as there was plenty of time to still get back to Solomon. He held the book with both hands, noting in the process that he was on the 20th verse of the 13th chapter of Ezekiel.

"Therefore this is what the Sovereign Lord says," he shifted a bit to lean towards the fire for better reading light, "I am against your magic charms with which you ensnare people like birds and I will tear them from your arms; I will set free the people that you ensnare like birds." At this juncture, the trembling became so intense that the Bible slipped from his hands, heading straight into the *therere* pot. With the agility of a skilled goalkeeper, he went for it, but it was a little late. One tip had already dipped into the slimy *therere*. He fished it out, at which exact moment the packet in his shirt pocket decided to obey the Newton's Law of Gravity he had last heard of in a Science class at Mtendere. It landed in the *therere*, its black contents spilling all over the place as it did.

"*Nchiyani?*" Tithelepo had heard the commotion.

"It's nothing," he said. "I was a bit clumsy, that's all."

He fished out the now empty plastic packet, all covered in the hot, slippery stuff, hid it in his trouser pocket, stood up and, Bible in hand, left the kitchen.

III

"This *therere* is yummy!" Tithelepo said at supper a short while later. She dipped her well-kneaded morsel of *nsima* into the *therere* soup, bit off a chunk, chewed and went for more.

"I agree with you," Dama remarked. "But then I know of nothing you cook that is not yummy."

I hope, he thought, *the charm does not work*. It was a heavy thing to kill another man, even one who was so inconsiderate as to snatch his one and only Tithelepo from his hands. Yet the letter he had stumbled upon one day, written in Tithelepo's own hand, now neatly folded and hidden in the back pocket of his trousers, rekindled the strong feelings of hatred for the other man. *I hope*, he thought, *the charm works.*

The letter had been well hidden. If it were not for the missing 500-kwacha note he turned the house upside down to look for, he would never have known the truth. Luckily, the truth came to his eyes in the form of a small blue envelope, well hidden under the bag of maize flour in the kitchen.

He'd read it so many times, leaning against the wall and repeating the words sentence by sentence, like he was reciting a poem, the way they used to do in primary school. "I love you," his lips quivered. "I will love you forever. Don't worry too much about my husband. He will never know." Each word was a knife stuck into his heart and each sentence was like twisting that knife for a more lasting effect. Shame there was no name. If there had been the name of the addressee, he would have shot off that very moment, sought him out, grabbed him by the throat and squeezed it real hard until there was no more philandering left in him.

That evening, there was a small civil war in the Chikwangwala home.

"Tell me the name of the man!"

"There's no man!"

"I said tell me the name of the man."

"Haven't I said there's no man?"

"You want me to die like my father?"

"I don't care how you choose to die."

"If there is no man, why did you write that letter?"

"I was just practising letter-writing."

"If it was mere practice, why did you have to put it in an envelope and hide it where you did?"

"I didn't hide it."

"You did!"

"I didn't!"

Slap!

But in the end, no name was given.

And now, after agonizing over the issue for several days, it had culminated in all this.

"You have really wiped that plate clean," Dama said to her. "Yummy indeed."

"I like *therere*, but I've never tasted anything as sweet as this."

Lord, he thought, *let there be light.*

IV

Light came as he lay on his bed lost in thought. The sun had risen. Its rays filled the room. He felt too lazy to drag himself from the blanket.

1985 was in his mind. For a few years, they had heard on the radio of a disease that had just been discovered in America which no medicine could cure. At that time, the only information the public had was that the disease was passed on through sex. America sounded so far away. Nothing discovered there could concern them, everybody thought.

Dama's father was one of those Catholics that are Catholic in name only. He never prayed before eating. He never wore the rosary around his neck. He drank irresponsibly. In the evenings, Dama could hear him quarrel with his mother, angrily denying rumours of a new sexual relationship with one of the women of the village. Often, this would end with the sound of his mother sobbing, which could go on and on until Dama fell asleep.

His father slept his way into the books of history. He became very sick and thin, so thin that one could count his ribs without difficulty. He coughed endlessly and spat blood. He went to the Kamuzu Central Hospital for treatment. It was here that he became famous for becoming the first person in Malawi to be diagnosed of the incurable disease that had just been discovered in America a few years earlier. Nobody understood how a man who had never been outside Malawi had contracted the virus. In the villages of Chipiri, the news was received with derision:

"Let him die. He slept with women like it was the only thing God created him for."

"We'll be lucky if he hasn't spread the disease to the whole village already."

"Isn't it such a monumental shame and a colossal disgrace? Why couldn't he emulate the heroic life of his father, Birimankhwe, hero of the John Chilembwe Uprising? Why not live the life of Chimkombero, the patriarch of their family?"

"He sought heroism elsewhere, in skirts and things."

Kampango's name was always used by the greybeards of the village to advise the young:

"Beware, lest you die in shame like Kampango."

Dama's hatred of his father increased tenfold after his death. Whenever he walked about in the village, where two or three were gathered, voices would die down, only to resume after he'd gone a few steps past, sometimes followed by loud laughter. *I'll never die like my father*, Dama vowed. *I'll marry one woman and stick to her.*

Then the worst thing happened a few months after his father's burial. His mother became so ill that it was not possible for Dama to go to school. He decided to look after her. Abisalomu, his only sibling, was five years old then. Dama cooked for the family and bathed Abisalomu. He washed his mother's and Abisalomu's clothes.

One morning, he found his mother's body stiff and cold and utterly lifeless. His shrill attracted a few elderly women in the neighbourhood. They confirmed she was dead. They bathed her body and dressed her in better clothes. The following day, the village buried her. Any thought of Dama continuing past his Form Two at Mtendere was buried together with her. He chose to stay in the village and look after Abisalomu.

He also made another snap decision.

Though he was only 17, he decided to marry. He needed a woman to help him raise Abisalomu responsibly. Since the Scriptures forbade sin, he also wanted to avoid the temptations of losing control and starting to sleep with the girls of the village. *I do not want to die like my father*, he'd always thought. To him, most of the girls he knew were very good only at drilling a hole through one's pocket before drilling it through one's heart.

He married Tithelepo, the only girl he had ever loved in his life. She lived in the neighbouring village. They used to share a desk in the village's primary school. She was as tall as he was, full-bodied, with big, beautiful lips and big eyes. Her skin was the lightest in all the villages of Chipiri. She had a tiny voice, sweeter than any of the girls Dama knew.

With Tithelepo in his life, things became easier. She was an incredibly understanding woman who was very slow to anger. She looked after Abisalomu with as much affection as if he was their own child. She helped Dama to till their gardens where they planted maize and groundnuts. She helped him to sell some of the produce after harvest, enough to raise money for new clothes for everyone in the family. The remainder of the cash was spent on meeting the expenses of educating Abisalomu, who was really doing well at school.

Despite the happiness of those early years, Dama and Tithelepo discovered there was a problem: she could not conceive. A year passed. And another. And another. At the village well, at weddings and other places where people gathered, they whispered about their barrenness. It was amazing how Tithelepo took it. "Let them talk," she said. "They have their lives to lead and we have ours. When the time comes for God to give us a child, we will be grateful for His mercy."

It was now 12 years. Still no baby was forthcoming. The innuendos had reached a deafening crescendo at some point, but now they were dying down. Twelve years is too long for a subject to headline people's talk even in a village such as theirs, where everyone seemed to have an excellent idea about how other people should lead their lives.

When Abisalomu was young, the vacuum of childlessness was not felt so much. He was like a son to them. Now he was no longer young. He was in a boarding secondary school and visited only on vacation. During one such occasion a couple of years ago, as they sat around the fire one evening, he'd said:

"I cannot forget my last night's dream."

"What was it?" Tithelepo had asked.

"I dreamt I was with a very beautiful girl in the bush behind our house. She kissed me and then . . . and then . . ."

Gosh, he can't be discussing a wet dream in front of Tithelepo, Dama thought. "And then what happened?" he asked.

"She turned into a python!"

"Eish, that's scary," Dama said.

"What happened next?" Tithelepo asked.

"I woke up."

After a lengthy silence, Dama said: "Scary dreams like those should not be discussed in front of women, especially just when we are about to retire for the night. Tithelepo, like our late mother, hates snakes, real or imagined."

Tithelepo let out a brief, bitter laugh and said: "Am I still considered a woman?"

That was the first night Dama and Tithelepo had an argument about their barrenness. "You can't say those things in front of a boy!" he said, when they went to their bedroom.

"Don't they say in the village that any woman without a child is not a woman?" Tithelepo asked.

From that day, the thorn of childlessness began to pain a little more than it had before. Could this be the reason Tithelepo was cheating on him? He sighed. He was glad to have found a way of dealing with the problem.

Still, Simbazako's solution bothered him. He needed to talk to someone about this. He had twice tried to bring it up in the Confessional, but it could not get off his tongue. It was a heavy burden. *Maybe I should talk to the priest as a friend*, he thought. He had known Father Kanjedza of St Joseph Cathedral from the days of their childhood.

The first thing he did that morning was to walk to Father Kanjedza's house. The meeting, however, turned out to be far less inspiring than he had hoped for. "Don't worry too much about your visit to Simbazako," the Father had said. "You may wish to know that I visit him too. The small matter of my appointment as Bishop has been eluding me for many years, so I decided to seek Simbazako's assistance. Already I am hearing some positive news from some well-placed colleagues in the higher offices of the Church." He had added: "I've told you this as a friend, though. Not a word to anyone."

VI

The shrill that pierced the air was so sharp that Dama froze. He had just returned from Father Kanjedza's. Nobody was home. He could clearly tell that the cry, coming from the bush behind their house, was Tithelepo's.

Immediately Dama jumped into the bush and ran. Thorns tore at his clothes. Some scratched him in the face. He ran on, sometimes tripping, rising again, tripping, rising again, on and on, trying to locate the source of the wailing.

Suddenly, he saw her. She sat with hands at the back of her head. Tears came out of her eyes in abundance.

"*Nchiyani?*" he shouted the question, breathless. "Have you been bitten by a snake?"

She cried even louder, unable to tell him what was going on.

He moved towards her. He tripped and fell, landing on top of something. He struggled to get up at once, noticing in the process that the thing he had tripped on was the body of a man, lying face down. Instant recognition made his heart leap.

"What has happened?" he asked, kneeling beside the body

to shake it. "Abisalomu!" he called. "Abisalomu!"

There was no response. He shook the boy by the collars of his shirt. He tried to breathe into his mouth. No response.

It was his turn to scream.

VII

He turned to look at Tithelepo, but she had vanished.

Bucketloads of tears poured onto his shirt front. Still kneeling beside the body, he clutched his rosary and started to utter whatever he could remember of the Prayer of St Jude, Patron Saint of Hopeless Causes: "Most holy Apostle, St Jude, pray for me. I am so hopeless and alone. Come to my assistance in this great need..."

Simbazako. The picture of the old man floated in his mind, obscuring the rest of St Jude. *I must rush to him before it is too late. He can undo this.* He began to run.

He pushed his way through the elephant grass up the anthill.

"*Odi!*" he shouted. "*Odi!*"

He had no patience to wait for a response. He had no appetite for Simbazako's recital of the achievements of the several generations of the Chikwangwala clan. He lunged at the door. It gave without difficulty. He walked in and... froze! Simbazako, recognizable only by the accidental dreadlocks, lay dead and rotten. Maggots feasted on his decomposed entrails. A putrid smell that hit his nose made him throw up immediately. He turned and ran all the way downhill.

VIII

Two weeks after the burial, Tithelepo returned home.

Dama did not talk to her. She went about cooking, washing pots, washing clothes, sleeping, rising up again, day after day after day, with no single word from Dama's lips. He never touched anything she cooked. They slept in separate rooms, he in the main bedroom and she in what used to be Abisalomu's.

Msiyana, Tithelepo's best friend, was paying them a visit. It was a huge effort to greet her every morning he rose. At night, since he still refused to touch Tithelepo's food, he always lay on his bed, trying to sleep, as the women talked the night away in the kitchen.

One evening, tired of lying on the bed for a long time, Dama stood up and paced about. Normally, he paid no attention to the chatter and banter of the women, but now he stood still to listen in.

"I want to die." That was Tithelepo, amidst sobs.

"No, Tithe, get that thought out of your mind," Msiyana responded.

"I want to follow him to the grave. It was my fault. He was so young and innocent."

"Don't cry, Tithe. Don't cry."

"I did it for the love of my husband. We had to have a child. I wanted a child. Abi had the greatest respect for his brother. He never wanted to do it. It took two years to convince him."

"Death comes to all of us, at any time. Don't feel so guilty. You did not kill him. It was his day to die. Nobody can stop the hand of God. Of course, it's a pity he died in those circumstances. But don't feel so guilty."

"I can't sleep, Msiyana. I can't take his image off my mind. He died with a smile on his face. He was an angel."

Dama wanted to listen no more.

With a heavy heart he limped into the main bedroom. Later, he heard Tithelepo and Msiyana retire for the night. After a lengthy period of whisking mosquitoes with his hand, he heard someone walk into the room. She lay beside him. She stayed quiet for a little while.

"Dama," she spoke.

"Yes?"

"Forgive me."

Silent, except for a buzz of mosquitoes.

"Dama."

"Yes?"

"I've missed my period."

"What?" he sat up as if stung by a wasp. "What did you just say?"

She did not respond.

"*Sáncta María, Máter Déi*," he prayed loudly, tearfully, "*óra pro nóbis peccatóribus, nunc et in hóra mórtis nóstrae. Ámen.*"

Stanley Onjezani Kenani is a Malawian accountant who lives and works in Kenya. He was shortlisted for the Caine Prize in 2008. He is currently finalizing his anthology of short stories.

The David Thuo Show

Samuel Munene

THE FIRST BIG QUARREL happened on the eve of my 13th birthday. That was the first time Dad and Mum argued loud enough for us to hear almost every word from their bedroom. Mum accused Dad of cheating and Dad accused Mum of sleeping with her boss.

For a short period after that we didn't talk amongst ourselves. We were silent even when watching television. Then Mum started laughing mockingly whenever watching *The Jeffersons* in the presence of Dad. Initially I didn't understand why Mum had suddenly developed a liking for the comedy until I noticed how Mr Jefferson – short, bald and clumsy – looked very similar to Dad. On Thursdays Dad made sure to come home after 7.30pm, when *The Jeffersons* had been aired but in time for *Love and Hate*, another sitcom.

Dad also started laughing when watching comedies. Previously Dad had looked bored when they aired but now he loved them more than any other programme. Again I didn't comprehend the change of taste until I observed he snickered only in those parts not obviously funny, when the rest of us would be silent, waiting for the punchline. His laughter had nothing to do with jokes; it was just a way of making the rest of us in the family look unintelligent.

We got the flow. Mum raised her game, for that is what it was turning out to be. Mum's favourite programme was *Love Is Made Of This*, a Mexican soap opera. In it, Lorenzo, the lead character, acted the perfect husband; hard-working, rich and showering his wife with lots of gifts. Watching the programme, Mum placed her hands on her chest and moaned softly. The rest of us seemed lost. The fact that we could not connect emotionally to the programme like Mum did meant that we were not able to follow the complicated plot. Mum could. But with her random gasps and moans I doubted if she understood the storyline either.

My sister Sharon preferred to be called Shaz. But I called her Wawira, the African name she hated most. I disliked her because I guessed she disliked me too. And also because she was slow. In her form-one exam she had scored one per cent in mathematics, the lowest score in the school's history.

She loved music or pretended to. She sang along to almost every song played on TV. Other than making me feel bad because I didn't know the words, it was also irritating: she reminded me of the buzz of a mosquito trying to bite. By their frowns Mum and Dad also would have preferred it if she had remained silent, but then again that was her moment of intelligence, and the unwritten rules in our house said she was not to be interrupted.

My moment to shine came during *Who Is Smarter Now?*, a show where participants were asked general knowledge questions and the winners given prizes. I shouted answers to almost all the questions asked. Most of the times I got the answers right. When I flopped, Mum smiled and Dad coughed a little sarcastically. Sharon would sneer then laugh out loud. I was sure by getting almost all the answers correct I made her feel thick. I was not so certain about my parents. By giving accurate answers I truly seemed bright, a fact that may have made them happy though they did not show it openly. That would have been a failure on my part: I wanted to make them feel brainless and annoy them. And so, just to be positive I was getting the desired effect, I branched out into cars: things adults should know about. After a Mercedes E-class advertisement I would say something as arbitrary as: "Multiple supersonic airbags? That's a real car". Dad owned an old Datsun.

The only time we almost talked was during the Trust condoms advertisement. At such times if anybody had dared say anything then the rest would have joined in enthusiastically. But no one did. The advert showed a tall, well-built man inserting a bottle into a condom. Two girls who could not have been more than 18 looked at him giggling while soft music played in the background. If the ad started playing, Dad reached for a cigarette and went out on the veranda to smoke, long enough for the commercial to end.

Mum would reach out for a copy of *True Love* magazine, which she always kept by her side. She flipped through the pages and closed it as soon as she heard *Maisha iko sawa na trust (Life is good with Trust)*, the condom's slogan. Sharon would look at the television but not so obviously. She would pretend to play with her phone but her eyes would be tilted to the screen. I didn't mind the ad, but I was not to be the only one watching it. So I reached for a tattered copy of *James Hadley Chase* I always carried around and fantasized about the pistol-holding girl on the cover.

Shiko, our house help, rarely watched television. She spent most of the time in the kitchen. After cooking she would sit on a chair and knit or read the bible. The only programme she liked watching was *Love Is Made Of This*. She understood very little English and perhaps that's why she smiled sheepishly throughout the programme.

Mum worked as an administrative assistant for Ndovu Tours and Travels. She was light-skinned, with long, healthy hair. Mum left for work at seven in the morning but she woke up at five, to shower and dress. Many times I had caught men ogling at her as she walked, twisting her hips. When walking side by side with Dad they looked ridiculous, the same as *The Jeffersons*. Sharon, 15 years old and with her two boyfriends, looked every inch like Lisa, the Jeffersons' daughter.

The television broke down. It was around 7pm. Dad was not home yet but the rest of us were seated watching the news when the TV went off. For a moment we just looked at each other then Dad walked in. It took him only a few seconds to notice something was wrong.

"What have you done to the TV?" he shouted, walking to the TV stand.

Mum clicked. "You should know better, we left you watching it last night."

Dad fiddled with the TV's cable but it didn't power on. He then lifted and shook it a little bit. But still nothing.

He pointed at Sharon and me.

"Between the two of you, who was the first to get home?"

"But Shiko has been here the whole day. She must have done something to it." Sharon said, pointing at Shiko who had been standing in the room in silence.

"Have you ever seen me touch the TV?" Shiko snapped, her eyes fixed on Sharon. "And wasn't it working some few minutes ago?"

"Why couldn't it wait for *Love is made of this* before malfunctioning?" Mum cried, throwing her hands up.

We all stood up, went closer to the stand and watched as Dad tried to revive it. He looked angry. He hit the television on top, then at the back but it still didn't come to life. I thought he was going to lift it up and throw it on the floor. When it became clear the TV was not going to work, we all retreated to our bedrooms.

There was no television the following night. Dad had called the technician who said he needed at least two weeks to repair it. Dad read the newspaper as if he was to be examined on it the following day. Mum was buried in *Live your Dreams*, a book by Joel Osborn. She placed it so close to her eyes I wondered if she was in fact reading. Sharon was grumpy and locked herself in the bedroom. It was a Monday, the day *the beat* aired. I was crouched on a chair pretending to read a social ethics text book. I would have preferred to talk of my nomination as a class prefect.

Shiko served the food after Sharon had come and sat next to me. Our sitting room fitted two sets of sofa seats. Dad lay on one and Mum on the other. We sat on the smaller individual couches.

"Look at what I bought," Shiko said, and pointed to the part of the wall next to the TV stand. We had been eating in silence.

It was a white sticker written in red *"Christ is the head of this house. The unseen guest at every meal. The silent listener to every conversation."*

"It's good." Dad said without lifting his eyes from the food.

"I like it," Mum said. Her head bent into her food.

"Yeah, I thought it very inspiring," Shiko said. She sounded excited. "The man who sold it to me had so many. What other one can I buy?"

"Get something funky," Sharon said, her voice terse. "This one is just too old school."

"Hear the way your children speak," Dad said, still looking at the food.

Mum clicked. "Aren't they your children too?" she asked.

She then stood up and went to eat in the kitchen. Shiko followed her.

Sharon left with her food to the bedroom. I finished mine and went to sleep, leaving Dad looking at the classifieds section of the newspaper.

The following evening, after Shiko served dinner, I decided to tell everyone I had emerged top in the inter-school quiz competition.

"That is the best news I have heard in this house for so long," Dad said, food in his mouth.

"Sharon, you should work as hard as Maina," Mum said, looking at Dad.

"Are you saying I don't work hard? That's cruel," Sharon snapped.

"Come on, listen to what your mother is telling you," Dad said.

Sharon went out of the sitting room, banging the door behind her.

"That girl is spoilt," Mum said.

After that day Sharon locked herself in her bedroom until food was served. That was the time when we had any conversation. Shiko started most of it and the rest of us joined in.

"I hear Wekesa beat his wife last night," Shiko said one evening. Wekesa was one of our neighbours.

"What kind of men still beat their wives?" Dad said. "It's so shameful."

"That's shameful indeed," Mum said. "A lawyer beating his wife?"

"But worse of all he beat his wife in front of the children," Shiko said.

"In front of the children?" Mum gasped. "What will such children think of their father when they grow up?"

Sharon must have gotten her second boyfriend around that time. Her first one, who called himself G, was a classmate. He wore studs and bounced when walking. He talked like the black Americans I had seen in movies.

The second boyfriend, Tim, lived not very far from home in Buruburu estate, Nairobi. He had been in college but now I supposed he must have finished because he had bought an old Toyota and put on oversized hide wheels. It looked as if it would tip over. The car windows were tinted and the music loud.

I saw Sharon getting out of his car one evening and that's when I first suspected she was having an affair with Tim. I confirmed with Shiko.

"I saw Sharon kiss him in that car," Shiko told me. Her lips were twisted as if talking of something filthy. "Can't he date girls of his own age?"

Shiko was bigger than Mum but I estimated she was ten years younger. She had lived with us for about a year. I always wondered whether she was married or had a boyfriend.

We decided against telling Dad and Mum of Sharon's exploits.

"Let's wait. She will get pregnant and everybody will know. I can't wait to see how your mother will react," she said. I couldn't wait either.

Three weeks were gone without television. The technician had said that the television was an old model and it would take a little longer to get the right spare parts.

Then Mum started coming home late. Shiko would serve us dinner in her absence. Dad praised her food, something he didn't do in the presence of Mum. Shiko giggled at such times. Dad would casually ask us how school was. We answered enthusiastically, though by the grunts he didn't seem too interested. After dinner, Sharon and I would immediately go to bed, leaving Dad talking to Shiko. She slept in the sitting room, on the same seat Dad always sat on.

I had heard Mum say it was the tourists' peak season and there was much work to do in the office.

"I am sure they are paying overtime in dollars," Dad said to Mum one evening when she came as we were having dinner.

She chuckled, and then said, "I wish!"

On Sundays I was the only one left in the house. Mum would leave at around ten. "Imagine, they can't even give us a day off," she said. Sharon would have left earlier, saying she was going for youth service. I was sure she was spending half the day with Tim and the rest with G.

Sundays had always been Shiko's day off. She would leave around 11am, spend the day out and come back in the evening. Previously Dad spent Sundays indoors but now he too left the house, some minutes after Shiko was gone.

I looked forward to Sundays. Dad ran a column in the *Sunday News – This and That, a social commentary by Daudi Thuo*. At the bottom of the article it was written: *The writer is a consultant on social issues*. Dad bought and read the newspaper before going away. I had time to read the column hoping to see my name mentioned.

Sundays were also great for me because I got to read

Emotions, a pornographic magazine, without fear that anybody would bump into me. I bought it secretly from a street vendor.

The Second Big Quarrel happened before the television was brought back. It was on a Friday. After dinner Sharon and I had left for our rooms, leaving Dad and Shiko. I didn't hear Mum come in. But all of a sudden I heard Mum's voice:

"What is happening here? Are you sleeping with my husband?"

The next thing I heard was a scuffle and things falling.

"Don't fight," I heard Dad say in voice that was loud enough to wake anyone.

I rushed to the sitting room. Sharon opened her door and followed close behind. We found Mum and Shiko fighting. Shiko was biting Mum's hand. Dad was trying, unsuccessfully, to separate them. They saw us and somehow stopped.

Mum was crying, "Prostitute! Go get a man of your own!"

"You are the bigger prostitute! Who doesn't know you are sleeping with that boy?" Shiko said.

Mum lunged forward. But Dad held her. "Which boy?" Dad shouted.

"Ask the watchman. She is dropped here by some boy driving Ndovu cars. They always hug!"

I looked at Sharon. She started crying and went back to her room.

"Is that it?" Dad said. He then pushed Mum and slapped her on the face. Mum reached for a framed photo of our family and threw it at Dad. It hit him on the head. He then went for Mum but abruptly stopped and looked at me. "What are you doing here? Go and sleep. Stupid!" he said. I went to bed, not sure who I wanted to win.

There was no breakfast the following day. I woke up earlier than usual. Shiko was not in the kitchen or where she slept. I didn't wait to find out; I just went out of the house.

When I came back from school, the door was open. I

expected to find Shiko at home. But she was not in. I was going to my room when I met Sharon. Her eyes were red, like she had been crying the whole day. She hugged me and started crying. I didn't know what to do.

She told me Mum and Dad had fought again in the morning. And Mum had left carrying her largest bag.

"She said she will never come back again."

"Where do you think she went to?" I asked.

"She said she was going kill herself," Sharon said.

I told her all would be fine. I went and locked myself in my room. I believed Mum was joking. She couldn't just walk out on us like that. I cooked rice. Sharon refused to eat. Dad came when we were already asleep. I left him sleeping on the couch as I went to school in the morning, still in his shoes and suit.

The whole of that week Sharon refused to go to school. Dad came home very late and drunk. I stopped cooking but bought fast food. Dad always left a hundred shillings on the kitchen table.

On the Saturday, a week after Mum had left, Dad came home at seven in the evening. He brought us chips and chicken. Sharon took her share and went to her bedroom. Dad had brought a bottle of Smirnoff. He poured some in a glass, took a sip and looked at me.

"Are you all okay?" he said. It was the first time we had spoken since Mum left.

"Yes," I said "But I could do with some cash."

He gave me a thousand shillings. "Share with your sister." I handed out Sharon four hundred, hoping she would stop sulking. She hadn't spoken to Dad since Mum went.

I went out briefly on Sunday and bought that week's edition of *Emotions*. Dad didn't go anywhere. And Sharon was mainly in her room.

We got used to life without Mum and Shiko. Dad left us money to buy food. I bought chips and chicken every day. Sharon complained that the food was making her fat. She had started going back to school, though when she was home she spent most of her time in the bedroom. Dad came home late every day, always drunk. He gave me a thousand shillings every week, which he asked me to share with Sharon. I always gave her four hundred.

We didn't talk about Mum with Dad. It was as if it had never happened. But Sharon kept asking me whether I thought Mum had committed suicide.

"Don't be silly. I am sure she will come back," I usually told her. I was trying to sound brave but I was missing Mum and wanted her to come back now. I just wanted to see her around.

One Sunday, about a month after the Second Big Quarrel, Dad left home around 8am. I thought he had gone to drink. Sharon and I had become really close, close enough to even play scrabble together. Around one in the afternoon we saw Dad's car park in front of our house. We heard a woman laugh. We rushed to the door. There they were, Mum and Dad giggling, removing a television from the boot.

Samuel Munene is a freelance writer based in Nairobi, Kenya. He contributes to *Kwani?*, a Kenyan literary magazine.

Set Me Free

Clifford Chianga Oluoch

"MUUUUM!"

The scream from Pope, my five-year-old son, jolted me. Fear etched at the end of his squeaky voice and I knew that he was not injured. Nor was he in pain.

"Coming," I shouted as I quickly put on my robe and slipped into my green antique slippers that Dad had bought for me a long time ago. Talking of Dad, or The Honourable David Mavita as he was formally known, the International Criminal Court (ICC) was scheduled to give a press conference on the perpetrators of the 2007 Kenyan election violence.

Pope's scream came again. Louder and sharper, almost a screech. Impatience. A five year old knows only 'now'.

Then my cellphone rang. Nuisance. I decided to ignore it as I walked out of my bedroom to see what my son was up to so early on a bright Sunday morning.

The third scream coincided with the ringing of my second cellphone.

"What is it, darling?" I asked tenderly. My son's stooped back greeted me, Spiderman's web and face taking the shape of a map at the back of his blue pyjamas.

"Look mum," he said softly, pointing at something on the wooden-tiled balcony floor. Pope's head blocked my view so I had to go round him. He, however, did not turn.

It was a bird lying still on its side. It must have fallen from the gigantic *mugumo* tree that proudly occupied the centre of the 16-flat compound, one of Dad's vast investments. The incessant dirge-filled chirping, from the other concerned 'family' of birds hanging on the branches, formed a mournful mood.

A Chestnut Belly Starling. It's the closest I had ever come to one and its deep purple, almost bluish colour felt like God's paintbrush had been too perfect. Its eyes were shut.

From the background I could still hear the persistent ringing of my phones. Who could it be on such an early Sunday morning?

"Is he dead?" my son asked, making me wonder how he had determined the gender of the bird. Pope's eyes bulged and his lips trembled to complement his quavering voice.

I energetically rubbed my hands for warmth, and then gently lifted the delicate bird, the twittering from his comrades in the stooping branches increasing in intensity. The bird was light and its velvety feathers tickled like warm water running down my hands on a cold day. It was no bigger than my forefinger.

"No, he is not dead!" I affirmed. Pope stood up, his head just above my hip, and held on dotingly to my robe. Together we transferred the bird to his room. I drew the purple Harry Potter curtains and sunlight flooded the room.

"Get me a cereal box from the kitchen store," I told Pope. He dashed out.

I took one of Pope's old brown face-towels and gently wrapped the delicate bundle in it.

Both the phones were either beeping or blaring by now.

Pope came back with three boxes of differing sizes. We chose the biggest, a box that I had promised to make a car with.

"Hold him." He cupped his hands to receive the bird like a devout Christian taking holy communion.

I took another, bigger towel, folded it twice and then spread it inside the box. It fitted perfectly – a cosy nest by human standards.

Pope looked at me. I smiled and nodded. He cautiously placed the bird in the box and then turned again to me.

There were many question marks in his teary eyes.

"Let's turn on the heater," I told Pope.

"Mum?" Cracking voice. Insecurity. His bulging eyes blinked continuously.

"No, darling, he won't die! There is a reason God sent him to you." I emphasized the last word as I gently patted the top of his head.

"Can I stay with him today?" he asked. Mary, the housegirl, was the key to that question. She would have to forfeit her day off.

"Yes," I replied absent-mindedly as I moved to my room to attend to the two phones that were still generously soaking in message after message. Like most of my urban Kenyan friends, I owned more than one handset, courtesy of turf wars between the mobile phone companies.

There was a record-breaking number of missed calls and messages. I decided to start with the messages.

"Check the brking news on tv."

"ICC releasd the names of politicians."

"Yr dad on tv."

"What's the latest?"

"Yr dad deserves 2 die."

"May he rot in Hel."

"ICC Prsecuta comng 4 yr dad."

"Ol Poltshans nvr dai – thei rot."

None of the messages, most of them from numbers I did not recognize, were from Tim, my husband, stuck in Australia for his PhD studies. I was sure he would call.

So it had finally come to this. The list of those involved in the election violence had at last been released by the ICC, thus bringing to climax weeks and weeks of debates on every medium in the country.

My dad's name was on the list. My heart sunk at the vitriol that some of those phone messages conveyed. My mind turned to Dad and his vast amount of wealth, some of which I was not only a beneficiary of but also an administrator. The majority of his property was in my name.

Another call came. It was Wangu, Dad's housegirl of more than 25 years. She was sobbing.

"Dad was found collapsed in his room and has been rushed to hospital!" Wangu was almost family and I could feel her distress. Dad, diabetic and hypertensive, had been in and out of hospital regularly since losing in the 2007 general elections – the first time in his 20-year political career.

"I am sorry – I have to rush to hospital to see my dad," I told Mary, who was missing her day off for the third week in a row. She frowned but she knew that I would pay her overtime.

Before leaving the house, I decided to switch on the TV to get the latest news.

"Breaking news: ICC releases 20 names of perpetrators of 2007 election violence" flashed on the screen. Dad's name was the first one: David 'the monster' Mavita – ex-Minister without Portfolio. Thao Matek, Mbaya Mbofu, amongst others. There was no woman on the list.

"More than 1,500 people died and 500,000 were displaced," the scroll bar rolled on. Footage of displaced persons carrying their belongings was relayed.

"The ICC has vowed to use Kenya as an example to the rest of the world on how to combat impunity."

Then they showed some of the political rallies that Dad had held to incite crowds. I flipped channels and found the same stories. I switched off the TV.

"Pope, do not feed the bird," I said as I walked past his room. He turned and waved.

Half an hour later I was at the hospital's reception area, the white walls adorned with uninspiring paintings needed a facelift. Hordes of journalists were there with their cameras and notepads. They saw me and made a rush, questions flying all over. How did they know me? I smiled politely, shook my head and moved past them to the smartly dressed uniformed hospital security guards. One of them blocked me.

"Where do you think you are going?" He thrust his chest forward, raised his chin to ear level and sneered at my small frame.

"I am David Mavita's daughter," I replied in a low tone. The guard straightened up and his look changed to amusement, his lips curling into a wry smile.

The shame of being a politician's daughter had long worn off. The taunting and fights that I got into while in school had hardened me. I flashed my national ID and the guard let me in. I headed to the ICU on the left wing of the hospital. I obeyed the 'Please switch off your phones' sign.

He was there, a small, curled-up figure wrapped in the hospital's green bed sheets. Winding tubes from Dad's body to the noisy machines, in an otherwise serene atmosphere, dominated the room. A clipboard with a chart hung above his bed.

There was a tall, slim man in a white lab coat. Two nurses, dressed in blue pants and white tops, were hovering around Dad and monitoring the readings from the beeping machines.

"Hi," I croaked.

The man turned and his quizzically furrowed forehead and raised eyebrow made me complete my introduction. "I am his daughter!"

The same pitiful look sprung from the three, the two nurses gawking shamelessly. I chose to ignore them. Dr Katana. I read his name tag.

"Are you alone?" Dr Katana asked. His mannerism – a slight bow and the gentleness in the voice – told me that he was a coastal person.

"For now, yes!"

Mum was in the USA with Jerry, our last-born brother, who had stuck by Mum after my parents' divorce seven years back. She had since severed all contact with Dad and the rest of his family in Kenya. I, nevertheless, kept in touch, sending endless emails that had never been answered. Joni, my other brother, was somewhere in Nairobi. I knew I could get him.

The doctor pulled me aside. "I need someone in the family to take legal responsibility of the situation."

"You can talk to me now," I told him. Silence. I could feel the wheels of decision churning noiselessly in his brain as he fixed an intent gaze on me.

"Follow me."

The constriction in my chest became tighter. Was the situation that bad?

Several corridors and turnings later, we were in the doctor's cramped office. He took a seat; so did I, opposite him.

My eyes did the talking.

"Okay," he exhaled heavily. "Your dad is on life support. All his vital organs have failed. He was brought in too late, almost three hours after he was found collapsed in his room. Hypertensive stroke. Very, very weak pulse. No fight." The doctor's baritone faded as he looked out of the curtainless square window into the distance.

"What do we do next?" I croaked, my bulging eyes certainly getting bigger.

"We need permission to switch off the machine," he summarised. He showed me the forms.

"Give me today to round up the family," I pleaded, the strength in me ebbing away.

After exchanging contacts with Dr Katana, I exited via the back door. I needed to contact my brother Joni, my mum and Tim, my hubby. My head spun. A hurricane of emotions overwhelmed me and I had to force my feet to move.

I switched on my phones and again a flurry of messages bombarded my screens. I ignored them. I scrolled down the contact list and landed on Joni. I dialled but the response was a disappointing, 'the number you have dialled is no longer in service!' I tried Mum's number and again there was no response. Tim was also unreachable. I left voice messages for them.

I was home by 3pm and my first stop was my son's bedroom. Pope had fallen asleep next to the box. Still dressed in his blue Spiderman pyjamas, I lifted him and gently put him on his wooden poster bed. He did not stir. I stole a glance at the bird. Possible.

"He did not eat enough," the housegirl told me about my son. "How is *mzee*?" she inquired about my dad.

I shook my head, tears welling in my eyes. "Not good at all."

She understood the mood and did not pursue the story. "You must eat!" she gently ordered me. I sat down and wolfed two platefuls.

"Has anyone come home?" I asked Mary. I was thinking more of the moral support from the neighbours.

"No." I now was fully convinced that the ICC list was acting as a deterrent. Nobody wanted to be associated with those on the list.

I decided to make some calls. Dad's older brother, Uncle Koech, was the first one.

"Hallo Uncle? This is Jackie, His Honourable Mavita's daughter!" I piped.

"Dishonourable Mavita!" my uncle barked. "Ten million shillings of insurance money is what your father sold our parents for! Please do not call me again!" Click.

I knew of Dad's problems with his siblings but I thought that in times such as these they would show more solidarity and less hostility. I decided to call Aunt Maureen, Dad's younger sister. She had always been sensible.

"What can I do for you, Jackie?" Her voice was ice cold and impatient.

"It's about Dad's condition. He is in a coma….." I did not get to complete my sentence.

"Your father, just like he has always been, is on his own. Having both our parents killed just because of money was sheer madness." She hung up. Same frosty tone. I slowly sat down and stared at the blank TV screen. I decided to switch it on to catch up with the latest.

The newscaster sounded excited. "A politician, Thao Matek, whose name was adversely mentioned in the 2007 election violence, was found dead in his home today......

"An ex-minister, David Mavita Mingi, is currently in a coma at the ICU of Kenya Hospital. Reliable sources indicate that the former minister is on life support."

"Another politician has been stopped at the Ugandan border disguised in a *bui bui*."

The images of the dead, displaced people, machete-wielding youth, and hacked limbs dominated the TV screen. It was depressing.

"Muuuuuum!" Pope's scream startled me. Was that a tinge of excitement at the edge of his voice? A breakthrough?

I rushed to his room.

"Look, it's twitching!" Thrill. The feeling of watching the sun rise early in the morning with the promise that the day would be warm.

"Time for you and your bird to eat," I told Pope as I excused myself from the house to go and continue with my search for my brother. It was almost 7pm.

Half an hour later, I was at Hurlingham Shopping Centre, one of Nairobi's Red Light Districts known for all types of peddling. I chose the dimly lit alley behind the shopping mall.

I slowed down my car and immediately a horde of skimpily dressed male and female peddlers rushed to the car, Dad's S-class Mercedes Benz.

"I am looking for Jolly J," I used my brother's nickname. Someone clicked loudly in disappointment.

"Joni is a gigolo and does not screw women!" – an angry voice rose above the murmurs of those mulling at my window.

Finally someone shouted Joni's name and he came lumbering towards the car. He must have recognized the car because he opened the door and took the passenger's seat.

I was excited to see him but he did not reciprocate. He was tense, his eyes darting from side to side. His jeans were a little too tight and his earlobes full of earrings and bling bling.

"Hi!"

"What do you want?" he asked stiffly, his thin voice barely audible. His jaw was taut and I could see the protruding veins on his neck.

"Have you heard about Dad?"

"I have no dad."

I was silent. I knew about Joni, Jerry and major differences with Dad but I did not expect Joni to come out so openly about it.

I ignored his statement. "Dad suffered a massive stroke and is on life support."

"He died many years ago." The same thin voice. The same tautness of muscles accompanied by heavy breathing. It is like he wanted to say something. He turned to look at me. His eyes were fiery, his lips pursed and he kept on nodding his head in slow motion.

"Forget it," he finally blurted out forcefully. He looked away.

I stretched both my hands and held his, squeezing both of them gently. It is then that I realized that he was crying.

"Dad drove me away from home into this life," he said softly, a broken man. "It's like an inner roaring monster fighting to escape."

Joni and Jerry never saw the best of Dad. Their memories were blurred by the political figure that he had become and both boys had had serious discipline problems in school. After my parents' divorce and Mum's departure to the US, Joni had disappeared from home. He was 18 then and had not even written his 'O' level exams.

"How is business?" I asked him.

His shoulders dropped a bit. "There is plenty of money." He left it at that.

He agreed to accompany me to hospital. "What about your clients?" I asked, though I was more concerned about his dress – the black jeans and black top were too tight and too revealing.

"I will take a break tonight," he laughed as he ran out of the car and came back in an overcoat. "But I am only doing this for you."

Fifteen minutes later we were at the hospital. A change of shift and we found another doctor – Dr Maazo – who took us in. Dad's breathing was laboured, the face ashen and the eyebrows taking on a pallid look. He looked peaceful, a deceitful summary to what his life for the last 30 or so years had been. Joni, gazing into the ceiling, stood at the edge of the bed, where Dad's feet were.

"Any improvement?" I asked the doctor.

"None so far." It was a statement loaded with pity.

"Visitors?"

"Nobody." Who was it who said that there were no permanent friends in politics?

"I still have to talk to my mother." I was not mentally ready for the switching off of the life-support machine. I needed Mum's and Tim's advice.

"What do you think?" I asked Joni.

"He is dead, just like the way he had always been in my life." The words were spat out in utter contempt. "Get the fucking machine switched off!" I wonder how he would react if he knew that Dad's will bequeathed me all his wealth.

We left the ward still not decided about the life-support machine. We walked past the reception area – the journalist having long gone – to the car park. I dropped Joni at Hurlingham and then drove home. I was very tired.

I drove into the compound and decided to remain in the car as I made calls to Mum and Tim.

"Hi Mum." The phone connection was very clear. She sounded like she was in the next room.

"I heard about your dad." Detachment. She talked like Dad

was just another person in the streets.

"He is on life support." I mouthed the words slowly.

"Waste of time, money and energy."

"He is my dad."

"Apologies for my poor choice." How mechanical and callous! "Switch off the damned machine and let the man roast in peace." Click. The last one was a shriek. I wanted to talk to Jerry but the coldness in Mum's words put me off.

A call interrupted my brooding in the car.

"Hallo?" a heavily accented female voice punctured the silence.

"Hallo?"

"I have five children with your father and I want to know who will take care of our children." Rapid talking.

I hung up and blocked the number.

Then I decided to read the messages I had previously ignored. There were a total of seven women claiming to have had children with Dad. They wanted to be part of the burial plans and some were blatant enough to ask for maintenance fees. I saved all the messages, took a deep breath and walked out of the car into the house.

"Muuuuum!" Pope's scream greeted me the moment I opened the door. Conquest. Pope dragged me to his bedroom. The bird was fluttering its wings and trying to stand. Pope's face was radiant, his eyes, nose and mouth forming a galaxy on his rotund face. Some food particles were scattered in the box.

My husband, Tim, finally called at around 10pm. Pleasantries, then business.

"I understand that the ICC is coming for your dad some time this week?"

"Yes, and I am very scared." Tim knew about Dad's political involvement and his vast estate, of which I was an administrator. He did not, however, know about Dad's will.

"Have the machine switched off tomorrow," was his advice to me. Practical. That's my Tim.

"What?"

"For what reasons and for how long are you going to keep him on life support?" I saw the sense but I did not want to be the one to sign the forms.

I had a restless night, images of Dad, my son Pope and my two brothers and the bird all merged together. Was that Pope's bird with an axe chasing my father round our compound? And was that Joni and Jerry carrying machetes and joining the bird in the chase?

The first light at dawn found me awake. Monday morning – and I would not be reporting to the office.

"Muuuuum!" Triumph. The roar of spectators when a victorious goal is scored.

The bird was fluttering round the room and testing the strength of its wings. Following the bird round the room, Pope could not stop howling with laughter and contentment.

"The bird is ready to leave us," I told him. Crunch time. Tough love. The mood in Pope suddenly changed. He stopped abruptly like an electric toy that had instantly lost power.

"Why?" Disbelief. He looked me in the eye, his continuous blinking meaning that tears were not far away.

"Because he belongs out there," I said, very slowly but emphatically.

"But we can keep him." Attachment? Selfishness? The bird, oblivious of our differences, continued the adventurous flapping of its wings. A few trial flights proved almost successful. I stole a sideways glance at the bird. Pope did the same.

"What about them?" I pointed out to the tree that still had birds tweeting in excitement at the brightness of the day.

I managed to catch the bird and together with a reluctant Pope we went to the balcony. The overhanging branch was within touching distance. I gave the bird to Pope.

"Mum?" Self-doubt. Desperation.

"Set him free," I told him. He looked at me with his big eyes. Sadness. Loneliness. I nodded and motioned my head towards the tree. Hesitation.

One. Two. Three. He ushered the bird to freedom by giving it a gentle push. It took to the air with an initial dip, struggled briefly to find its rhythm and then naturally circled the branch before landing on a branch not far from our balcony. Other birds joined it in a neat row. The chirping grew louder and we could not tell which bird was ours.

Then the dam broke.

"Muuuuuuuuum!" Pain. Howling cry. Heartbreaking. The sound of a child when a prized toy is irretrievably smashed to pieces.

"Why? Why? Why couldn't he stay with me?"

There were many whys that I had no answers to.

I held him and felt his body convulsing in great sobs. We cried together as we looked at the tree. We cried to celebrate the bird's recovery. We cried for the company that we had lost. We cried for the joy that the bird had brought in less than 24 hours. We cried more. And more.

Pause. Uneven breathing. I felt fresh and washed with relief. My head felt clearer and my heart lighter.

Mourning. "I don't want to go to school," Pope told me. I felt his loss, so I left him at home as I made my way to the hospital. I switched on the car radio to catch up with the latest. The ICC list of shame had claimed more lives: two suicides, and a homicide. One of the cases involved a whole family of five. This was getting quite depressing. I avoided buying a newspaper.

Joni was already outside the ward waiting for me. His black cotton trousers and black shirt made him look elegant. Gone were the multi-layered earrings and the bling bling.

"Thanks for coming." We hugged. Further decongestion in my chest. We moved to the doctor's office. I calmly signed the forms and insisted on being there when the machines were being switched off.

One. Two. Three. Off. Minutes later Dad was dead. The machine went silent and I knotted my fingers into Joni's. His were tight with tension and I could hear his heavy breathing. Two nurses zoned off Dad's bed, ready to wheel the body to the morgue. Joni and I walked slowly to the lobby to discuss the next course of action and to settle the bills.

"Cremation?"

"Yes, Joni. Cremation."

I showed him the texts. The number had reached 11 women with a total of 19 children. We knew that cremation was one of the shrewdest ways of containing such women.

Unanimous. Joni agreed rather too easily and I was not sure whether he saw it as a chance to finally see Dad burn to ashes.

We cleared half the bill. Two hours later we were on our way to the private crematorium on the eastern side of Nairobi.

My phone rang.

"Yes, Dr Katana!"

"Court orders barring you from collecting and disposing of your father's body." The desperate women had already landed at the hospital.

"Who?"

"Five different women. Five different court orders."

"All from the same judge?"

We laughed. We both knew how difficult it was getting any document from government offices, especially on a Monday morning. I was guilty of having a disposal permit for Dad yet I had not gone to any government offices. Money talked.

"They won't find me." I said.

The hearse took another half an hour to meander through the maze of Nairobi traffic. Formalities completed, I noted down the time that Dad went in for cremation. Electric Furnace. 11.17am. Cloudy day. Normal.

Joni and I sat down in the expansive hall. We braved the four hours that it took to get the ashes. We talked about our adult selves and about the future.

Another call from Dr Katana. "Seven more court orders.

And the police are also here."

"The cremation is over." I told the doctor. Tim was right about the emotional toll this would have taken on me.

"The press is speculating a lot. They are going round all the morgues looking for your Dad's body."

"Thanks Doc."

There were many questions that I knew we would have to answer pertaining to Dad's cremation. But life had more questions than answers. Dad's life was a testimony to this.

Finally, the usher brought a silvery urn that would not hold more than a litre of liquid.

"Is this all?"

"Yes. Human beings are very small," he answered as he handed me the urn.

"Thank you." Dad's life – or was it ashes – fitted in my one hand. It felt very strange trying to reconcile the ashes and the person.

I turned to Joni. "Where should we scatter them?"

"Parliament buildings, of course."

He was right, though Parliament buildings would pose security problems. We settled on the building opposite.

It was close to 5pm and the rush-hour madness was about to take over Nairobi. The drive from the crematorium in Kariokor to Continental Building, where most of the parliamentarians had their offices, took more than an hour. I parked the car opposite the building, came out with the urn and walked to the lifts where the bored guards just gazed at us.

We took the lifts to the top and made it to the roof of the 15th floor. The clear view of Nairobi was breathtaking. The spread of the horizon, coupled with the orange-coloured clouds of the setting sun, was a sight that I had not beheld in a long time.

6.40pm. I stood atop the building drinking in the beauty of dotted buildings, cars and people. Sunset. One of the uncelebrated daily wonders of the world.

I opened the urn and turned to face Parliament buildings. I scooped some ashes, sprinkled them in that direction and watched as the wind blew them away.

Within five minutes all the ashes were gone. I felt free as the flocks of birds trapped inside me fluttered noiselessly away and settled on the trees of human wilderness. The whistling wind past me caressed my face and kissed my tears.

I looked down and could not differentiate between Dad's ashes and the speck of dust on the ground.

It was over.

Clifford Chianga Oluoch is a teacher at Oshwal Academy Nairobi Primary in Kenya. He is a published author of five children's books – *The Eastlander Series* – and eight Primary Mathematics books. He writes for the online magazine www.eastafricainfocus. com Clifford lives in Nairobi with his wife, Benedette, and two daughters, Elsie and Lisa.

Invocations to the Dead

Gill Schierhout

THE WORLD WAS EUPHORIC and uncertain. It was the day that Jonas Peterson and Grace Jaffe first met, the day that Mugabe came to power – more than 20 years ago now. If a truck of early celebrants had not ridden right over Jonas Peterson, leaving his pelvis crushed in 17 places, he may never have met Grace Jaffe. And if they had never met, today she would not feel a single grain of affection towards this man who has brought so many troubles upon himself. Jonas Peterson is to be admitted to Strickland Psychiatric Clinic today for a three-day observation. But because their shared history lies across her like a shroud, Grace cannot think of him as just another shirker playing the system in order to obtain a lighter sentence.

Grace stands behind the window in her office – the one that overlooks the hospital car park. She is an old woman peering out from behind a lace curtain. The police van comes to a stop in full view of the window. Jonas jumps from the van's side door – not a spare ounce on him, trusting himself to the air. He leans slightly forward as he jumps, arms splayed outwards to correct his balance. He hits the ground, rather than lands; it is, for Grace, an act of violence to the earth.

There are always two sisters on duty here; Grace, being more senior, does not deal with admission, but with in-depth patient assessment. She takes a breath and goes to the staff bathroom. In front of the mirror, Grace dampens her palms and presses down her quivering dreadlocks. Her hair has recently turned the colour of carrot peelings, thanks to Always Beautiful hair dye. She gives up, turning her attention to her lips, licking and biting them to make them darken. Then, straightening, she frowns and brushes dust specks off the clear whiteness of her uniform. Grace has not freshened herself up so as to please the new patient – far from it – but simply to strengthen herself against the terrors that she is becoming certain lie ahead.

It is no coincidence that, by the time Grace emerges from the bathroom, Jonas has already been sent to the small concrete cell that will be his sleeping quarters. Under hospital policy, patients with 'aberrant behaviour' are not accommodated in shared wards.

Grace envies those who bear no burden of loyalty to actual events, for whom history is not so much made with others, as observed together, happening outside themselves. For these people Jonas would either be deviant or normal, hell-bound or saved, guilty or not – there would be love or no love... And for them, this story would not have to be told. It is not like that for Grace.

As Grace walks home that night, the sky thick with stars, there is a cold slab of anger in place of her heart.

* * *

Many years ago Grace was a young trainee nurse working in a general hospital. She did not yet wear the green rectangular bars that she now has on her shoulder epaulettes, showing her advanced training in psychiatric nursing. Jonas too, a young man, still unformed, was an Apprentice Miner. He had been on his way to night classes when hit by the truck. Lucky to be scooped up off the ground, lucky to be taken by ambulance on a stretcher to Prince Albert Hospital, lucky to be tied to his bed with plastic tubing and weighed down by plaster casts so that he could do himself no further harm.

When Grace came on duty that evening she was instructed not to leave his side unnecessarily; he was a high-need case. All night he jerked in and out of drug-induced slumber. Every now and then he loudly begged for a packet of Aspros with whisky to help him sleep.

"I thought you *were* asleep."

He fell back into unconsciousness without answering, dreaming of whisky fire flying from her hands straight into the bloodstream, cleaning him out from the inside.

Later that night, Grace became convinced that he would not last another hour. She called the priest in for the last rites.

The priest took one look and walked straight out again: 'Not one of my flock,' he said.

So it was Grace who sat beside him, watching the pulsing veins of his neck in the gap between his brace and bandaged head, touching an exposed fingertip with her own.

Jonas made it through that night, and the night after that.

After two months, he learnt to walk again, a nurse either side. He learnt to wee again on his own two legs. He was the ward favourite, the nurses' pet, the charmer. Everybody knew his name. He was discharged after six months, reborn. Grace was sorry to see him go. What was to follow must have been her fault of course, since she gave him her address.

* * *

These days the inmates at Strickland are almost always all up by the time Grace Jaffe arrives for her 7am shift. Many of them do not even take a nap during the day. This is one of the reasons she prefers night duty, it gives her more time to think.

About mid-morning Grace takes the observation book down from the shelf and picks up a blue biro. She opens the book. Hers will be the first entry of the day. She licks the end of the biro, watching Jonas from behind the window. He has taken up a seat on the far end of the hospital veranda, facing away from the building. The tendons and sinews of his neck stand taut, tethering a hungry head. Its familiar sculpted shape annoys her. Grace considers that it is in her power now to say that Jonas shows remorse – that he shows no remorse – remorse – no remorse. It is her own small power and she will most certainly use it. Grace leans forward to rest the book on the windowsill. Before she can enter the day's date, a flamingo feather falls out of her pocket – a small trinket that Jonas had long ago sent her from Kariba.

✳ ✳ ✳

Jonas had walked out of the orthopaedic ward all those years ago, thoroughly medically, if not religiously, anointed, his life saved for a special purpose. He had kept his promise to Grace, writing to her, and sending small mementoes for her interest – this feather, sitting now in her palm, a stone from Great Zimbabwe, gold splinters found in a river in the Lowveld. She wrote back, and unlike other men she knew, he always tried his best to answer each one of her questions fully and with respect.

Grace allowed herself to love him through the veil of his letters. But when she read them later, she thought he could have given more. Sometimes his letters verged on florid – so excited he was with his latest theory, or view of the world. And he had many enthusiasms those days – constructing pyramids out in the veld, lying beneath them to align his energies.

And then one day, as if he knew that Grace's marriage had turned cold as a headstone, he arrived at her door.

Grace was living in a small house in Essick Street. She'd stayed on there after her marriage ended, grateful for small mercies. One morning, on her day off, Grace was sitting on the small concrete strip alongside the house. She liked to sit here in the quiet, leaning against the wall, her flesh turning to rising dough in the morning sun. She had just been preparing to get up, bending forward, rubbing zinc oxide cream onto the varicose veins of her calves, when she felt a shadow fall across her. She looked up. Jonas was there. He stood upright in loose royal blue overall pants, and a white tee-shirt that had gone into the coloured wash. He was quite unchanged in his face.

He was just passing by. He was carrying a small canvas bag. Two years since his discharge. In two years you would think he'd be fully well.

Grace was unused to inviting lone men into her house. Such a man, like the lone elephant, was certain to be unpredictable, distressed. But Jonas was so uncomplicated, so practised perhaps at putting people at their ease, that it would have gone against her nature not to have let him in. And in any case, it was just a cup of tea. And then another cup.

In the late afternoon when rain clouds began to spurt some drops of promise, Jonas leapt up to help Grace bring in the washing. He folded each item as if he had never touched anything quite as fine. This kind of thing counts for more than it should, in a man. At a respectable hour, he pulled out his hip flask and poured all of his brandy into two of her glasses. That first night he slept on a folded blanket on the kitchen floor.

Before long it had become apparent that Jonas wanted, as they say, nothing more than to settle down with Grace in Essick Street. He said he was through with mining, had told the boss where to stick his job, and was willing to try anything new up on the surface. It did not seem to bother him that there were not many jobs around for a cocky miner with no other trade. With time to do it, he took over feeding Grace's chickens, and fixed the run, so that they could not escape to lay their eggs. He replaced the broken washer in the kitchen tap, opened rusty jars and when she came home from work, worn out from being on her feet all day, he had a meal hot and ready, tomato bredie, chicken and potato stew.

He liked to cook with herbs and lots of garlic. In all her adult life, Grace had not felt this nourished.

* * *

Grace opens the slender manila folder that contains the patient's history. There have been no prior admissions. She deciphers the handwritten notes entered the previous day:

Illegally possessing various body organs, for no legitimate reason. Atypical Necrophilia. No evidence found of defilement of a corpse. Patient cannot give an account of his actions. No other compulsive behaviours noted. Some tendency to magical thinking.

It is now up to Grace, and her colleagues, to answer the Magistrate's standard questions. In your opinion, was the act premeditated? Does the patient show remorse? Is this a rigid pattern of behaviours? Is he likely to re-offend? Following which, Jonas may, god willing, be sent to prison; let out on bail, perhaps some anti-anxiety medication will be recommended. Grace is becoming more and more convinced that none of this will do any good. The thing is intractable, even with the light shining on it so that it squirms.

Grace, standing again at the window of her office, looks out at the patients scattered across the veranda. Some are seated in small groups, but Jonas is alone. She notes that Jonas does not read a book. He does not light up – perhaps he indeed has stopped smoking, as he once said he would. He does not seem to be watching the birds in the hospital gardens. Every so often he gets up, walks to the edge of the shade, and spits into the bougainvillea. After a little while, a few of the women patients begin to find one excuse or another to pass by where Jonas is sitting.

Something must be written in this book, or they will think that Grace is not doing her job.

On the other hand, there is no need to over-commit so soon. Grace is about to write 'No abnormalities noted,' but then considers that this could be read in a positive light. She finally settles on 'Nil of note' and, checking that she has signed and dated, she closes the observation book, putting it back on her desk.

Before she leaves the room, Grace takes the flamingo feather from where she left it on the windowsill. As if it may be carrying some contagious disease, she tosses it into the wastepaper basket. Then she crumples some paper from the printer tray and throws that in too, to put the feather out of sight. Grace cannot say exactly why she has kept this feather close beside her all these years. It had nothing to do with the fact that Jonas had given the feather to her; of that she is quite certain. She has always felt some affinity with these shy delicate wetland birds – a kinship now that she suddenly feels she has outgrown.

* * *

It was Grace who had found Jonas the job in the morgue. She spoke to some people in the teaching hospital – it was through someone she knew. And then again, there were not many applicants lining up to wash and prepare the bodies for the pathologist, the ceremonial coffin, the dissecting table.

"It's just a job," Grace had persuaded him, "Someone has to do it."

And anyway, he'd seen plenty dead down the mines, carried the boots out to return them to the families.

The morgue had given Jonas green outer-clothes to put over his own.

"You never know if there might be an outbreak," Grace had said. "Microspores flying all around."

Bodies were wheeled toward him day after day. He made deliveries at the medical school and admired the pictures up in colour in the front of the classroom with every bone and tendon labelled layer by layer – better than a car repair manual. But the real stiffs are so different from the pictures; people just don't take care of themselves, do they, he complained to Grace. There was a lot of debris, things in buckets, a lot of waste. Because these people had died indigent, for the most part they had no names.

In a month or two, Jonas found himself beginning to look forward to greeting the stiffs, the softness of their powdery skin, the way their bellies hung round to either side, plastic bracelets fixed around their wrists. Across the corridor, the pathologist wrote his diagnosis on a clipboard, and Jonas had to copy it over onto the white plastic bangle. "Cause of death: Cirrhosis." Or sometimes "Assault. Intracranial haematoma secondary to cranial fracture." Grace became used to the smell of formaldehyde in the house.

One evening, Grace was late in getting home. Jonas was cleaning up the mess he had just made in the kitchen by mistakenly letting a pan of oil catch alight. In the half-dark of the bathroom, Grace bent down to pick up Jonas' pants that he had left lying in a sour crumpled pile on the floor. As she lifted them to put them into the bucket for washing, something seemed to jump out of the depths of the fabric's folds, and land with a soft thud on the floor. A kind of bald and injured rat, Grace thought at first, its stumpy red tail snaking out behind it. She screamed; she had not known she had so much screaming in her. Then when she noticed that the rat-creature had not moved since falling, her shrieking stopped. It must be dead, she thought. She stepped gingerly backwards and flicked the light switch. Closer, she looked more carefully. Closer, around the other side. It must be, it was, unmistakably the grey and spongy partial lobe of a lung with some surrounding pinkish tissue, a large vein still attached.

By the time Grace emerged from the bathroom, Jonas had slunk off taking whatever he had been able to stuff into the small bag that he had first arrived with. Grace checked beneath her mattress where she kept her money. She checked her silver teaspoons. Nothing was missing.

Grace did not rest until she had combed the house. She

worked her way from room to room. She left no drawer, no box, no cupboard unopened. She found nothing further. Then she went around the house a second time, picking up anything that belonged to Jonas and throwing it into a black plastic garbage bag – his spare socks, a book 'How to make friends and influence people,' his overall pants. Even things of hers that he had touched too often, went in too. Then Grace returned to the bathroom and using Jonas' shirt to pick up the offending lung, deftly placed both into the bag, muttering her apologies to the souls of the dead.

Grace had been about to leave the bathroom when she noticed a dark crevice where the damp had rotted the corner of a floorboard beneath the basin. The floorboard was loose and easily lifted. She brought a torch and shone it into the two feet or so of space between the flooring and the dry earth beneath. A small enamel bowl (*that* had gone missing some time ago), contained something small and red and glistening. And beside it, an old diary. Grace flipped through it. Jonas seemed to have been using this book as some kind of catalogue, much the way some *playa* men, she has heard, record their female conquests. Some pages were filled with diagrams. Grace put everything in the bag, then tied it as tightly as she could. She placed it inside another black bag, just to be sure nothing could leak out. She would put the bag out with the rest of the garbage in the morning. After washing her hands and face with soap and the hottest water she could stand, she went to bed.

* * *

Two months later, Grace Jaffe received a letter from Jonas Peterson asking her if she could send him his military boots. What a nerve! He was living in a small town less than 100km away. Because she was a nurse, because she was a careful person, because they shared a history – Grace decided that she would, after all, write back. In her letter she told him straight out, in case he was not aware, that a head injury from the impact on the tarmac of the road was simply no excuse. Since he was lucky enough to be living in this natural world, she said, he should not do unnatural things. It was simply not the right way to live. Grace held onto the letter for some weeks before she posted it because, while all she said was true, she was one of these ineffectual people who can always see the other side. Perhaps, she considered, Jonas wanted nothing more himself than to be a natural man – and as we all know, the desire for a thing is not the same as having it granted.

After that exchange of letters, Grace heard nothing further for several years. She seldom thought of him.

Then one day, just a few months ago now, not long before he turned up here at Strickland Hospital, Grace received a further letter from Jonas. He had married a girl from a farm near Rusape he said, and he had a son, and here was a picture. And by the way, he had thought a lot about Grace's words, and if she was still disturbed about what had happened in her house he would pay for cleaners, disinfectant, *sangomas* – anything to help her to get over it. Stupid man. He had a decent job now he said, had got his heavy-duty licence and was driving a bus picking up the kids out on the Chegutu Road and driving them into town for school. Grace looked at the picture of the boy for a long while. He had his father's finely sculpted head and delicate features. His skin was very light in colour, glowing. There was something so happy about his face, his soft brown eyes sharp and expectant. This little boy, Grace thought, he has done nothing wrong. Grace has no children of her own.

* * *

Grace steps out into the corridor that leads to the veranda door, pulling her uniform down from where it has caught on the roundness of her hips. She walks, one reluctant foot after the other, until she is standing directly in front of Jonas

Peterson.

He looks at her so fervently that she cannot endure holding the gaze for long.

She looks away, down at his clean khaki shorts, his small well-formed legs. How pathetic that he has shined his leather sandals.

"You've shined your shoes," she says.

"Yes." His smile is crooked. How is it that she had not noticed this before?

The thing sits like a block of rock between them.

"You've done it again," she says.

But she knows as she says it, that it is not so much that he has done it again, but that he has been caught – that is his complaint. The thing is so much in his nature now.

She glances around again to ensure that they are still alone.

"Nobody knows," she says quietly, "what happened before. I never told them."

"I gathered that."

"You gathered that? What exactly do you mean?"

"I did not think it would be in your interest to say anything. You have a nice job here," he says, nodding toward the garden where the purple jacaranda is fully in bloom. Always in October.

"Grace. I'm sorry. I didn't set out to hurt anyone. Do you know what I mean?"

Grace catches sight of Mrs Gush, collecting herself at the end of the veranda, preparing to join them, and she is glad to walk away.

* * *

The next evening, just before Grace goes off duty, all hell breaks loose because it is discovered that Jonas has stolen the Doctor's car. Somebody thought she saw him outside the corridor near the Doctor's office that morning. Somebody else saw him get into the car. Somebody saw the car turn left at the gate and somebody else saw the car turn right at the gate. The police are phoned and they take a long time to arrive. Whilst all of this is going on, Grace leaves. She thanks the good lord that last night she took a detour to get petrol. She has at least half a tank. She sets out on the road she knows he'll take. It is dark by the time she arrives at the Truckers' Inn about 30km out of town.

She drives into the turning circle. In the beam of her headlights, she can see the blue Toyota Hilux. Grace pulls up beside it and walks towards the low building with its small sign above indicating 'vacancies'.

As Grace comes level with the building, she sees Jonas. He is sitting on the ground in the semi-darkness outside one of the rooms. His legs are outstretched and he is hacking open a can of baked beans with a knife. A bottle of Tassies and a bruised avocado sit beside him in the dust.

As he triumphantly pulls the rough serrated lid from the tin, he looks up and sees Grace standing there. As always, as if he can anticipate all manner of human behaviours, Jonas does not miss a beat.

"Madam, you are in time for supper. Just a moment."

He disappears into the darkened room and returns with a blanket which he carefully folds and positions a little further against the wall alongside him.

"Take a seat."

Grace feels shy suddenly, as if she were a girl out on her first date.

"They opened up the kiosk just for me," he continues. "Lucky I remembered to bring a knife."

An oil truck pulls in hooting, his high-beam blinding lights falling directly on them.

Grace doesn't care that she is sitting out here on the ground in her nurse's uniform. She doesn't care that she is sitting beside a man about to be convicted of some form of necrophilia. She is sitting beside Jonas Peterson. And that is all that can be said.

When they have finished their awkward meal, Jonas brings out his bag and they walk together across the zebra-stripes of light and shadows to Grace's car. They drive slowly down the long straight road into town.

The Doctor will fetch his car in the morning.

* * *

The next morning, Jonas is sitting in his accustomed place at the end of the veranda. But today he has prepared a small table beside him, with a few magazines on it. He has positioned another chair alongside his own. He is ready.

Later Grace watches as he shows his little boy how to make colourful birds and boats from torn-out pages of old magazines, folding this way and that like magic. She watches them make patterns with elastic bands between their fingers, laughing.

After his visitor has gone, Jonas Peterson walks in from the veranda, carrying his chair like a cross, the wooden arm of it hooked around his arm.

Gill Schierhout is a South African writer who was shortlisted for the Caine Prize in 2008. Her first novel, *The Shape of Him*, was published by Jonathan Cape in 2009, and was shortlisted for the Commonwealth Writers' Prize 2010.

Almost Cured of Sadness

Vuyo Seripe

ANOTHER ONE OF THOSE days at work leaves Lisa feeling like shit. Her kitten, Foot-Foot, appears from the kitchen and makes its way to her, purring. Lisa wonders whether it's affection or anger from leaving it in the house the whole day. Lisa often wonders whether Foot-Foot has emotions, intelligence and common sense. *Instinct leads it, doesn't it? Intelligence leads us, doesn't it? Emotions are what we blame for not using our intelligence.*

Lisa's little house has a wooden floor. She can't stand carpets. There are cloths draping from the window instead of a curtain in the living room, which is tiny enough for her, Foot-Foot and Hennie. The one room is a work studio, where Hennie paints and she does her sewing. The second bedroom is where they sleep with Foot-Foot when it's not in heat. She's a seamstress and a junior administrator to pay rent.

Hennie isn't home. She decides to give him a call to find where he is. He's at the shops buying wine and chicken wings. She feels like eggs and crackers tonight.

Hennie's been on a diet on and off for two years. He never listens to her, his dietician or anyone else. He went on a diet because he always felt conscious of his weight during sex. The first few months of dating Lisa were complicated – she spent a good few months proving her love for Hennie. He reckoned the only people who liked him were his parents – girls were a different story altogether. Hennie is indeed a sweet man but he doesn't come across as one to most people. Most of Lisa's friends think he's mean, pessimistic and he talks too much. They also hate the fact that he keeps long nails on one hand to strum his guitar.

She hears Hennie opening the door, she gets up to greet him.

"What are we up to on Saturday?" he asks in the kitchen, handing her the wine and the food.

"I'm going for Reiki." She cracks open the Tassies' screw-on cap.

"What did I tell you about that Reiki shit? It doesn't work! How could hovering crystals over a person cure an ailment? That bitch is just wasting your time and money with homeopathy, baby!" he pours the wine into her glass then his.

"Don't call her a bitch... and in any case, I do see Western doctors for serious ailments, c'mon now... why are you asking about Saturday?" She picks up her glass and heads to the living room.

"Josh and Sarah are having a *braai*."

"The same old Josh that called me a different species from you people?"

"Yeah, same one..."

"Not going."

"He doesn't think like that any more."

"Huh? It is what it is... Josh is an arsehole. I'm not going. End of story."

"C'mon baby, we haven't been out in such a long time."

"Can you please let it go, honey?"

"No... we're hermits!"

"What?"

"The only people we see are clients and family."

"Isn't that what we wanted?"

Hennie keeps silent, Lisa is staring at him, expecting an

answer but she knows she won't get one.

"Do you know what's wrong with you?" He is not asking. "You're a hypocrite and you don't even know who you are."

"Excuse me?"

"Yeah, you heard me. You think that everyone's out to get you and that everyone's stereotyping you."

"You're crazy, fucking crazy. Know what? I'll go to the stupid party!"

"Oh, you don't have to... you're just looking for a way to get out of this conversation."

"You call this a conversation?"

"I'm going for a walk." Hennie slams the door behind him.

* * *

Lisa lost her virginity at 14 with a man she didn't even like. She never knew him well or where he was from, just that he was well hung enough to leave her limping for a couple of days. In those days Lisa was known for her flirtatious ways and her ability to juggle multiple partners.

She always went for looks, nothing more, nothing less, though there were a few exceptions, depending on the size of the man's wallet. Soon after Lisa turned 18 years old she fell pregnant. Her mother gave her the option of an abortion and carrying on with her life or keeping the baby, which would mean forgetting about school for a while to raise a child. She chose the former.

One of her escapades at a tavern became a blur. Different people bought her drinks. At some point Lisa needed to use the loo terribly and a man followed her. She sat down to urinate. Her relief, along with being very drunk and high, made her pass out. *Just a few seconds of shut eye*, she told herself.

When she woke, she thought she'd gone blind, her eyes wouldn't open, there was something holding her up against the wall. A bright light shone into her eyes suddenly and she realised it was a man, entering her from behind. She tried to scream but no sound came out. She cried to herself, knowing very well that she wouldn't be able to fight the man off her. Her sobs became louder – he showed her a knife and told her to SHUT THE FUCK UP.

When he was satisfied, he ran off. A panic-stricken Lisa headed straight home and collapsed at her mother's feet. When she woke in her bed, her mother stood over her with a cloth to cool her fever.

"Ma, I was raped..." Lisa cried.

"I know my child... we need to get to the clinic and then to the police station."

Forensic results from the clinic proved that she was indeed raped. There was only one problem – Lisa didn't know who the man was.

"Lisa, I think it's better if you move up to Jo'burg with Auntie Thamie. I can't keep up with you any more."

"As if Auntie Thamie will do anything to erase the pain you've put me through... I don't even know my father!" Lisa raised her voice. "You've been a pathetic mother!"

"Lisa?"

"How do you think I turned out so bad?"

"I'm sorry I have failed you. I don't know what to do any more..."

"I'm more than happy to move in with Thamie."

"I love you, Lisa." That's all her mother could say.

"Well, I hate you! I hate you!"

Lisa had to spend a few days in bed. She was too weak from drugs given to her to prevent HIV from entering her system along with anti-depressants and painkillers.

She had hallucinations and dreams about crying babies, men raping her – all sorts of men. On two nights she tried to run away. Her mother had to lock her in and seal the windows. Lisa's distraught mother blamed herself for what Lisa had gone through. She had no idea how to comfort Lisa, everything she did was in vain.

After her slow recovery, Lisa left her mother in the house she grew up in without so much as a goodbye. Her mother's tears meant nothing to her.

Lisa looked forward to a new start in *Jozi Maboneng* – The City of Lights.

* * *

Lisa's first year in fashion design school gave her something to occupy her mind. She got deep into her drawings and designs. Lecturers were amazed at how quickly she grasped the art of sewing but her designs left them concerned about her mental health.

For a lingerie assignment, Lisa designed padlocked panties and bras which would be made of a type of material which flattened the chest and hips to hide all feminine features. The end-of-year assignment was a fashion show. She had all the models wear masks from horror movies with all the outfits sewn up with a technique that made them look torn and the material was dyed to look bloody. As a result she failed all her design courses but passed her sewing courses. The school advised her against becoming a designer.

She dropped out and started to sew and mend clothes from her aunt's home. She found a part-time job at The Redtree Gallery in Melville, where she met a 22-year-old Hennie. The gallery wasn't an exciting place to work in. Visitors to the gallery were mostly middle- to upper-class art buyers. Hennie wasn't really impressed with the work. Lisa explained each work according to what she was briefed but Hennie wanted to know what *her* opinion of the art was.

"It's all uptight and *square*," she giggled.

"Yeah?" he wanted to hear more.

"I don't like how he has explanations for things I can't even see. Most of this art is ugly and it's priced too high for a regular old Joe like me."

"But it's not for you…"

"Art is for everyone and it *has* to be beautiful."

"Says who?"

"Says me... then what's the point?"

"The artist is making a statement, isn't that what they do these days?"

"Well, the artist is too concerned with his statement and not the actual beauty of the art."

This conversation went on for hours, Hennie waited for Lisa to close up the gallery and they walked to the bus stop together. Hennie invited her to a vegetarian barbeque, hosted by his friend, Josh. She agreed.

Lisa was instantly attracted to Hennie's soft features. He looked like paintings of Jesus she'd seen in an illustrated bible she owned as a child. Blond hair and blue eyes, his pale skin contrasted with her dark brown skin; he was tall, with broad shoulders and a bit of weight he could do without.

They exchanged numbers and met up three days later to head off to the party. She was the only brown person there. She refused to call herself black – she was brown, perhaps a darkie, maybe an African but not a black. She called white people pink, pale, olive or creamy. The world was a palette of colour to her – why would she want to confine it to black and white? Skin is skin. Nevertheless, she felt uncomfortable – she'd never seen so many pink, pale people confined to a tiny little garden.

Everyone there assumed that she was dating Hennie. His friends seemed like nice people, they spoke politely and offered her all sorts of alcohol and food. Josh came over to chat with her.

"So, what are you celebrating?" Lisa asked.

"My twenty-first..." he replied.

"Happy birthday..."

"Thanks... so, how did you and Hennie meet?"

"I work at Redtree Gallery. He came to look at some art..."

"Oh, nice... What's it like dating someone like him?"

"Well, we're not really together but I think he's a cool dude."

"No, I mean the racial thing..." Perhaps Josh had had one too many. "Ya'll are like a different species."

"Excuse me?"

"I mean blacks are like... totally different from us, I'm sure you can tell."

Lisa looked around for Hennie. She couldn't see him anywhere, then her phone rang.

"That's my aunt. I need to take it."

She found Hennie outside when she finished on the phone; they spoke for a while. Her favourite song played on the hi-fi – 'The World at Large' by Modest Mouse.

"I love this song," she said, as he held her close.

They were both barefoot and danced in the garden.

Hennie lifted her off the ground, literally, and swung her around for a bit – perhaps she was hallucinating. Lisa saw something in his eyes that she'd never seen before: sincerity, love and kindness. They kissed. Josh cleared his throat behind them and told them it was time for the party to split.

She and Hennie went out together more often. He showed Lisa some of his paintings and drawings and sometimes drew studies of her.

"I'm very glad you think that I'm so beautiful..." Lisa commented on a portrait of her once.

Lisa felt ready to take the next step in her life, moving out of her aunt's place. She made enough money to move out to a place of her own. She found a little house in Auckland Park and got Foot-Foot after two months. She got bored with her job at the gallery and found a job at an NGO specializing in childhood development as a junior administrator.

Her friend Mangi came to visit for a couple of days to see Lisa's new place. She was keen to meet this Hennie Lisa couldn't stop yapping about on the phone. Hennie and Lisa went to meet Mangi at Park Station then went out for drinks. After Hennie went home, the girls sat on the porch and watched the sun set.

"What do you see in him?" Mangi started.

"Clearly what you don't."

"He's fat, sweaty and stinky and those nails... Yuk!"

"He's not fat, he has a problem with his sweat glands, that's why..."

"I just think he should take a bath, friend!"

"You don't understand. I really like him. He's not a jerk..."

"I think you're with him just because he's white."

"That word isn't in my vocab. I don't have to explain myself to you, anyway."

"I still think he's..." Mangi put her finger in her mouth, pretending to puke.

"Mangi, I don't want to make a decision based on looks and material things. I am content with him as he is. If you don't like it – I don't care. He's my man and I adore him."

"If you say so... I'm glad you're happy and brave," Mangi said, hugging her friend. "That guy's not well."

"He's moving in."

"What?"

"In two months, that is. Depending on where we are..."

"Are you sure?"

"Yeah, well, he hates his job and he wants to focus on his painting. If he moves in with me, he can quit his job."

"Who's gonna pay the rent?"

"Me..."

"You?"

"Yeah me... I have two incomes with the sewing and my nine to five. I'm sure we'll manage. Plus, he'll hustle. Sitting on his balls isn't an option." Lisa's eyes glowed.

"You love him, don't you?"

"Yes, I do."

"Hmmm... you'll be saying 'I do' in a chapel in no time at the rate you're going!"

Two years later, they hadn't entered a chapel. Instead they argued about the pettiest things, like a barbeque hosted by Josh and what to have for supper. The time was never appropriate to socialize, make love, watch a movie or go for a walk but when these things happened they made the best of it.

* * *

After all of these thoughts, sipping wine, staring at a blank TV screen, Lisa misses Hennie. She breaks out into tears. Foot-Foot surely understands what Lisa is going through. Instead of insisting on cat games, it perches itself on the couch right above her shoulder and licks her tears with its sandpaper-textured tongue and purrs.

Lisa often wonders whether Hennie knows how much she loves him. This love is expressed in clinginess, rage and the deepest sadness at times. Lisa never spoke about the rape to Hennie and she mentioned the abortion in passing after too many glasses of wine.

Hennie never forgets to tell Lisa that he loves her. Her clicking tongue amuses him when she mumbles and swears in Xhosa at her angriest moments. When he feels like crap, after a bad day – Lisa finds ways to cheer her man up. Sometimes she tickles his belly and makes silly jokes like:

"What's big and green and if it fell out of a tree – it'd kill you?"

"A pool table of course..." Lisa told Hennie the joke when they first met.

He hadn't planned to fall in love, he was always alone and lonely and felt that he deserved it. Lisa has faith in him and takes his dreams seriously, gives him space and time for his art. When they moved in together, he discovered that happiness is simply a by-product of love, that their love came with challenges.

Lisa's multiple personalities fill his life with colour, vibrancy and drama. The drama comes in many forms, both necessary and unnecessary but she is *working* on the latter. She meditates and constantly speaks about *metta* – renouncing bitterness, resentment and animosity towards all beings. He speaks of the opposite, he hates people and he's told Lisa that she is on thin ice a couple of times.

Lisa has Love, Hennie has Hatred. Yin Yang. Opposites Attract. A negative and a positive. They belong together, for now.

* * *

Hennie returns to the house after a couple hours. Lisa has gone to bed and he finds his wings in the oven, covered and warm. The time is only nine o'clock and Lisa's already gone to bed. He sits down in front of the TV and watches his favourite programme, *Snuff Box*. His peals of laughter wake Lisa up – she has slept in tears, with Foot-Foot right above her pillow purring her to sleep. She gets up to make peace with Hennie.

"Where have you been? I was worried," she croaks, standing by the entrance of the living room.

"I ended up at The Bohemian with Koos."

She likes Koos. He is one of Hennie's friends from high school.

"How's he?"

"He's good."

There is an awkward silence, she shuffles towards the couch and sits next to him, grabs the remote and switches off the TV. He doesn't complain and tell her that she's being a bitch like he usually does.

"I hate it when we fight about crap, we have better things to fight about – don't we?" she smiles at him.

He smiles back.

"I can't imagine my life without you, Lisa. I'm sorry."

She perches herself on top of him and starts to kiss him; his mouth tastes like beer and chicken spices. He holds her, touching her in all her favourite places. She kisses his neck, takes off his t-shirt and works her way down his chest and belly.

Vuyo Seripe is a freelance writer and artist based in Johannesburg and Port Elizabeth, South Africa. Apart from working on co-operative writing projects, she contributes articles to a variety of publications and is a keen observer of South Africa's emerging urban cultures.

The Journey

Valerie Tagwira

IT WAS THE END of the month and she had to make a decision. The more she thought about it, the harder it became. The ring was her most valuable possession, a reminder of happier times. It was the last present her husband had given her. A month later Tendai had been killed; struck down by a drunk driver as he crossed the road on his way home. Two years had not blunted the sharpness of loss.

Shingai stayed by the window, holding the ring against the gentle, morning sunlight. Gold shimmered, revealing a hint of silver around the edges. The red stone set at the centre perfected its beauty. What she loved most was the stone's heart shape, a symbol of Tendai's love. She stayed by the window for a long time, just staring at the ring. Sighing deeply, she slipped it onto her finger and set off.

✻ ✻ ✻

Shingai did not immediately enter the shop. She waited outside, gazing at the display window. A sign read: WE BUY AND SELL ANYTHING. Brand new and second-hand goods were displayed side by side. She slipped off her ring and placed it deep inside her handbag. She walked into the shop.

She joined the people who were looking around. Goods were neatly arranged on shelves. There were television sets, radios, clocks, hair-driers, kitchen utensils and an assortment of other household goods. In one display cabinet were items of jewellery: necklaces, bracelets, earrings, and a couple of rings.

Shingai tried to find someone to assist her. One uniformed shop attendant was smiling as she talked to a customer. A second one was busy arranging goods on a shelf. The third attendant was sitting at a desk in the corner, counting money. Secretly, Shingai hoped some of the crisp notes would end up nestled in her own purse. She approached him. He looked up at her, squinting through a pair of glasses.

'Can I help you?' he asked, smiling politely. His badge said his name was Mr Shamba.

'I would like to sell a ring,' Shingai replied. She dug into her handbag and handed him the ring. Her hand shook. Mr Shamba accepted the ring and scrutinized it.

'Mmm! I need to have it valued.' He called out, 'Peter!' A young man emerged from the back room. He handed him the ring.

'Check the value please.' The young man disappeared back into the room. Mr Shamba offered Shingai a chair. Shingai sat and waited. After what felt like infinity, Peter materialized from the room. He handed Mr Shamba the ring, together with a piece of paper. Mr Shamba read the paper, frowned and scratched his head. Shingai watched with curious apprehension. He asked her to come forward.

'I can offer you $20,' he told her.

'What? For such a beautiful ring?' Shingai exclaimed, shocked. While Tendai had never told her the value of the ring, she had expected more, at least enough to pay the rent.

Mr Shamba nodded. 'I agree. It is a beautiful ring. But it's not made of real gold.' He pointed to the edges. 'That's why you are getting this silver appearance.'

Disbelieving, Shingai grasped at straws. 'The stone? Isn't the stone worth anything? Can you please check again?'

'No point.' He tapped on the stone saying, 'It's a fake ruby.' He shrugged. 'So do you want to take the $20?'

Feeling as if she might just fall into a heap at his feet, she gripped the edge of the desk. Mr Shamba's interest in her appeared to have gone. He looked past her shoulder at an approaching customer. Too stunned to speak, Shingai held out her hand for the ring. She slipped it back onto her finger where it belonged and walked out of the shop.

* * *

Fretful thoughts held Shingai in the thrall of insomnia. As if in tune with her anxiety, her two children who slept on either side of her were fidgety in their slumber. Shingai stared into the darkness. Tomorrow would be the 31st. She had defaulted on her rent payment and faced eviction. Mai Tafa's rules were clear. There were never any second chances.

The tears that Shingai had denied herself in front of her children flowed freely and seeped into her pillow. Earlier on in the day, her friend Nellie had offered to take her in for a while. Although Shingai had had some reservations, she had not turned down the offer. They had grown up together and, over the years, Nellie had become her most loyal friend despite occasional differences of opinion.

She considered her in-laws. It was within their means to help her at that point, but she did not know if they would. Shingai had always had a complex relationship with her mother-in-law. Things had deteriorated after Tendai's death because of his pension pay-out. Her mother-in-law had wanted Shingai to surrender half the money to her. After Shingai had cashed in the pension, she had stubbornly held onto every single dollar for her children. Not that it had done them much good. Within two years everything was gone.

Shingai sighed, deep in thought. Since losing her stall at the market, she had resorted to street-hawking. Although it had sustained her for a while, it had become more competitive. More and more vendors had taken to selling goods on the street. With no sound educational qualifications, she had no job prospects.

She fretted, tossing and turning in the night. Her hand swiped at mosquitoes that seemed to know exactly where her ears were positioned. Eleven-year-old Chenge had settled. She was snoring gently. Nine-year-old Tendai was still restless. Shingai turned and hugged him close. Sleep crept over her just as the township cocks started to crow.

* * *

Shingai was evicted in the morning just after her children had left for school. Mai Tafa ordered her to remove all her belongings from the room. Shingai begged her for an extra day. Mai Tafa was firm. No amount of pleading could change her mind.

Beaten, Shingai packed and cleared the room. She piled four suitcases, a sleeping mat and two buckets containing utensils on Mai Tafa's veranda. She was given till the afternoon to remove them.

Shingai walked down the street to seek out Nellie. She went round the main house at the corner. At the back stood Nellie's two-roomed wooden shack. She knocked. The door opened. Nellie was in a short red night-dress. Her eyes were red, her face puffy with sleep. She was a woman who worked by night and rested by day.

She rubbed her eyes, looking annoyed. 'Eh! What brings you here so early? It's nine o'clock.' She asked, stepping aside to let her friend in. Shingai did not answer immediately. She felt close to tears.

Nellie asked, 'So, is everything all right?'

She listened quietly as Shingai explained what had happened.

'That woman has no heart. Does she not care that you have children?' Nellie clicked her tongue.

Shingai asked if she could move in with her children.

Nellie scratched her head, deep in thought. Shingai waited hopefully.

'I could have you for a week or two. Otherwise it will become very difficult for me to work, Nellie responded, yawning. Shingai remembered Nellie telling her that she now worked from home most of the time. She nodded gratefully. Maybe in a week or two, she would have managed to raise enough money to move on. The only question was, *How?*

Nellie borrowed a wheelbarrow from her landlord so that Shingai could move her belongings. Then she went back to sleep. Five trips later, Shingai had finished moving. Nellie was still fast asleep.

As she sat alone, Shingai slipped back into a contemplative mood. Bringing her children to live here was beginning to feel more and more like something she should have done as a last resort. Once again, she considered approaching her Tendai's family. Baba, her father-in-law, was a benign, friendly man. But painful words had been exchanged between Shingai and her mother-in-law. Although she seemed to love her grandchildren, their interactions were few and far between. Having considered all this, Shingai decided that consulting her in-laws was still the best decision she could make for her children.

✳ ✳ ✳

By the time she arrived at her in-laws' house, Shingai was shattered and out of breath. For a moment, she hovered near the gate, earlier doubts resurfacing. Then her need pushed her past the gate and propelled her forward. She found herself knocking on the slightly open front door.

'Come in!'

The loud, authoritative voice belonged to her mother-in-law. She gave the door a small push and entered the living room. Amai was having an early lunch on her own. *Where is Baba?* Shingai wondered, disappointed.

Amai was dressed smartly in a green dress and a matching headscarf. A mixture of surprise and annoyance seemed to flit across her face. It was followed by her characteristic, tight little smile. The smile did nothing for the lines of bitterness tugging at the corners of her mouth. Although she was slight in build, her manner turned her into an intimidating woman.

She threw a critical look at Shingai's dust-covered feet and frowned. Her slippers had stamped unsightly prints on the polished cement floor. Shingai shifted uneasily and slipped off the offending Pata-Patas. They had originally been a striking orange, with a crimson Bata emblem. Now they were crusted with red township dust. Over-use had carved deep tears into the soles.

Shingai extended her hand, saying respectfully, 'How are you, Amai?'

Amai shook the proffered hand briefly and pointed to an armchair. 'Do sit down.' The veneer of politeness was fragile. She continued with her meal.

'Thank you, Amai.' Shingai murmured, feeling a stab of hunger. She had not eaten since morning. She bit her lower lip, anxiety growing. Then she decided to break the heavy silence. 'Is Baba in?'

'No, he's not.' The answer was abrupt.

Shingai fidgeted in her chair, uncertain how to proceed. The memory of a previous conversation with Amai about her children stirred. It stopped the words she wanted to say.

'So, how can I help you?' There was no sincerity there. Shingai heard the hint of a challenge.

'Amai, I need help. We were evicted this morning and I need money to find lodgings elsewhere.'

Amai had just lifted her glass to take a sip of water. Her hand stopped in mid-air. She carefully placed her glass on the tray, before speaking in a quiet, controlled voice.

'Money? Have I not done enough for you? All these years of doing things for you? Heh?' She clicked her tongue crossly and pushed her half-eaten meal away.

Although she had expected something along these lines, Shingai was still taken aback by the exaggeration. In two years, Amai had given Chenge three second-hand dresses. Tendai had been given two shirts and a pair of trousers. Amai had bought them groceries on one occasion. This was when Shingai had been so unwell that she had not been able to go to the market.

For a while after that, Baba had secretly given them money for food. He had paid rent for their lodging at the slum end of the township. Amai had not taken long to discover this. When she did, she had put an immediate stop to it. Fortunately, by then, Shingai's health had improved and she had gone back to the market.

'I am sorry, Amai, but...'

'Sorry? Do you think I'm made of money? You refused to give us a share of Tendai's pension pay-out, and now you want my help?'

Shingai shook her head. In an instant, and quite irrationally too, the conversation had switched to the real cause of Amai's deep animosity towards her.

Amai stood up, wagging an accusing finger. It trembled with the intensity of her feelings. 'I bet you danced on his grave! That was all you wanted. His money!'

Shingai started to protest. 'Amai, I didn't...' She slumped back, defeated. Amai's words had prodded a nearly-healed wound. She had loved her husband.

Amai continued raging. 'Well, you are not getting any money from me or from my husband. If my grandchildren need money, send them to me. I will give it to them, not you.' She raised her voice.

Shingai was at a loss. It was ridiculous. Chenge was eleven years old, Tendai only nine. If Amai gave them money, would she instruct them what to use it for? What about rent? If they bought food, would she, as their mother, be allowed to cook for them and eat with them? This was as good as being told, *No!*

She shook her head. This antagonism was something she could not deal with. Worn out, she made a last feeble effort. 'Amai, please help us. Can I bring the children here while I look for work? '

Amai sat back in her armchair, pursing her lips. She seemed to be considering this. After what seemed like a very long time, she called out, ' Mavis! Mavis!'

Her housemaid hurried in and greeted Shingai. She knelt by the door. Shingai looked on with a mixture of relief and humiliation while Amai discussed her children with Mavis. It was as if she wasn't there. Mavis was given instructions to prepare the spare bedroom for Tendai and Chenge.

Finally, Amai turned to Shingai. 'Bring them after school with their clothes and uniforms.' She did not ask her where she would be staying.

Relief eclipsed humiliation. Shingai clapped her hands, 'Thank you, Amai. Thank you so much.' There was nothing more to say. She stood up.

'Good-bye Amai.' There was no answer. Amai nodded and resumed eating.

The door slammed behind Shingai, almost catching her heel. She imagined that it wasn't the wind. She imagined that Amai had pushed the door. But she knew that her children would be safe.

*   *   *

Shingai lingered in the shadows of a jacaranda tree at the corner of Fife Avenue and Fourth Street. She was relieved that the street light was not working. She could hide in the shadows while gathering courage. Nellie had brought her here because it was meant to be an easier street corner for learning. There were fewer girls to compete with, and the traffic along the main road was less.

Standing there, she felt abandoned. As soon as they had arrived, Nellie had picked up a taxi driver. He had stopped on the opposite side of the road, flashing his lights. Nellie had pointed at the taxi, 'That's the signal I told you about. Let me go and see what's on offer.' She had run across to talk to the man. After a few minutes she had returned.

'I have a client. I will be back soon. Stay around here,' she had said. Shingai had watched them driving up Fife Avenue. The car had turned into Sixth Street and disappeared.

Thirty minutes went by. She waited. A few cars passed. One of them slowed down. A man looked out of the window and waved at Shingai. He did not stop. A short while later, two scantily dressed girls laughed as they walked past Shingai. Her competition. They were self-assured as they strutted in high heels and swayed mini-skirt-clad hips. Shingai felt mediocre and ridiculous in Nellie's tight dress.

Fear started playing nasty games with her imagination. She saw shadows and shapes that suddenly disappeared. She saw the headlights of a police car which turned out not to be a police car when it passed her. She imagined a gang of girls confronting her and assaulting her for trespassing on their territory. She saw them clawing out her eyes with red fingernails as they laughed through lips that were painted scarlet.

She was a bit worried about actually being picked up. The lines that she had been given by Nellie were a tangled mess in her head. What she thought she remembered sounded pretentious and silly. Nellie had also said something about what miracles could be worked on a man's groin by fluttering eyelids and a gentle sway of the hips. The rest, she could not remember.

She wondered how she would manage to actually do it with a total stranger. Unease swept over her. When Nellie had first made the suggestion two days previously, their discussion had deteriorated into an argument. Shingai had told her that she could not do it. She had told her that she did not like the idea of being touched by a man who was not Tendai. She had tried to reason with Nellie. 'I am a married woman and...'

'*Was*'. Nellie had interrupted emphatically, before dismissing the given reasons. She had said they were trivial, particularly in her situation.

She had added sarcastically, 'And don't be so judgemental, my friend. Where would you be right now if I wasn't selling my body, as you put it?'

Shingai had felt then how close to fragility the bonds of their friendship were growing. They had been there before. But they had agreed long before not to let what Nellie did ever come between them.

Shingai had considered her circumstances again. She had no real choice at that time. Nellie had been right. Life had to be faced in a practical way. She had relented.

Two days later she had allowed Nellie to apply make-up on her face and to paint her nails. She had been given a slinky, tight dress and a pair of strappy sandals.

Before leaving the house, Nellie had shared some practical tips. She had offered her a packet of Protector Plus condoms, saying, 'You must play safe.' Handing her a retractable knife, she had said, 'This is for your protection.'

The sight of the knife had thrown Shingai into a panic. 'I could never use a knife on anyone!' she had exclaimed.

Nellie had calmed her down. 'Listen, I am not saying you have to use the knife. In all these years, I have never had to use one. I just show it when they threaten me, or refuse to pay. And that, my dear, is very rare.' She had added, 'And if you ever meet policemen, just do what they say. They are harmless really.'

Shingai had nodded, too uneasy to raise further concerns. A spray of fragrance later, they had left the house.

✳ ✳ ✳

Now as she stood alone at the street corner, she felt a twinge of regret. The knife in her handbag felt as heavy as a brick. Feeling restless, she moved away from the corner. She moulded herself into the shadows of the next jacaranda tree and continued slowly down the road.

As she walked, she saw headlights flashing a signal at her. It was a potential client. She stopped, trying again to remember her pick-up lines. She pictured herself fluttering her eyelids and planting a hand on her hip. In her mind's eye, it didn't look right.

When the car stopped, she realized that it was a police Santana. On impulse, she started running to escape from the brightness. She headed towards the shadows.

'Stop! Police! Stop!' She froze and turned round. She waited, her heart thudding in her chest. A uniformed officer strode towards her. His bald head glistened menacingly in the glare of headlights.

'How many?' A loud male voice called from the Santana.

'Oh, just one! Lights off please!' The officer shouted, grinning as he approached her. The headlights and engine were turned off.

The officer grabbed Shingai's hand. He pulled her from the road, further into the shadows. He pushed her against a jacaranda tree-trunk. She flinched in his grip.

'ID please?' he asked, business-like. She reached into her handbag and gave him the document with a shaky hand. He flashed his torch, scrutinized it and handed it back.

'And your business here?'

'Nothing. I am on my way home.' Her voice was a whisper.

'Oh! So where is home?'

'The township.' She muttered. Her heartbeat was a roar in her ears. He held out his hand for her handbag and started rummaging. He pulled out a packet of condoms and grinned cheerfully.

'Good brand! Never lets you down.' He winked at her.

'And why are you carrying this around?' He held up the knife, mock surprise on his face.

'Oh! I didn't know it was in there.' Even as she said the

words, she knew he would not believe her.

The officer made a face. He laughed. 'I wasn't born yesterday. Some of you people are robbers, prostitutes, drug dealers... dangerous people. I have to perform a body search.'

Shingai nodded mutely, hoping he would let her go soon. She just wanted to be as far away from this place as possible. A car was approaching them on its way up the street. The officer pulled her deeper into the shadows. They entered an alleyway.

'Raise your arms, spread your legs and keep still.' He ordered. Shingai complied. He looked into her eyes and started working his way down her body. His hands lingered on her breasts, and again on her buttocks. He prised her legs. Putting his hands into her underpants, he fingered her roughly. She felt the edge of a nail, and then a finger went inside her. She trembled with fear and struggled to stop herself from screaming. Suddenly he stopped and stood up, staring intently at her.

'You are really something, do you know that?' His voice was low and suggestive. Shingai looked sideways. She wondered where this was leading.

He held her chin between his thumb and forefinger, forcing her to look at him. 'You have condoms, don't you. If you give me a quick one, I haven't seen you, and I haven't seen the knife. Hey, I can even take you home.'

Shingai hesitated.

The officer drawled. 'Or, I book you in for soliciting, carrying dangerous weapons and threatening an officer. What shall it be?' He waited for an answer. Shingai turned the possibilities over in her mind. What he was telling her was that she had no choice.

She nodded and allowed him to push her against the wall. He undid her buttons and fondled her breast. His hands shifted. He stroked her with one hand as the other one lifted her dress.

'Condom.' His voice was thick. Shingai rummaged in her handbag and handed him one. He undid his zip and quickly slipped on the condom.

Lifting her dress higher, he pushed her legs apart and hoisted her. His hand tugged at her underpants. She felt him shoving himself inside her. He grunted as he covered her mouth and face with slobbery kisses. She smelt cigarettes on his clothes and alcohol on his breath. Then it was over.

'That wasn't so bad, was it?' he asked as he zipped up his trousers. Shingai remained silent. In a daze, she pulled down her dress and fastened the buttons.

She could not look at him. There was a salty sensation in her mouth. She realized it was her own tears.

'My dear, you are free to go.' He said cheerfully as he swaggered away from her. Then he turned and smiled, 'We should do this another time.'

Shingai did not answer. Defeated, she wiped her face dry then walked from the alleyway back into Fife Street. She was drawn towards a street light in the distance. Her purse was still empty, but not for much longer.

Valerie Tagwira is a Zimbabwean writer currently working in London as a medical doctor. Her first novel, *The Uncertainty of Hope*, was published in Zimbabwe (Weaver Press, 2007) and in South Africa (Jacana Media, 2008). The novel won the National Arts Merit Award for Best Fiction title in Zimbabwe (2008). She has had two short stories published.

The King and I

Novuyo Rosa Tshuma

WE WERE FRIENDS AS far as friends go. Stretch the word. Mull over it. Paint it with a soggy-spinach green or a lemon-pickled lime. It doesn't matter what shape or size the word decides to take, whether it is fashioned after envy or joy, as friendships go. The best that one saw in the other, not necessarily the *best*, mind you, by any standard term, was a kind of best that one saw lacking in oneself. Two half-full cups, each complementing the emptiness of the other.

The photograph rests on my dressing table. Not large. Your normal four by six. Two university boys in South Africa, one tall and fashionably dressed (ahem... that would be me), the other unfashionably short and unfashionably thin (that would be Nana). The unfashionably short and unfashionably thin fellow slumps towards the ground in an untidy heap. An arm is hooked around the shoulder of the tall and fashionably dressed chap. Sleepy eyes and an intoxicated grin. The tall and fashionably dressed chap looks on with a deliberated expression, into which you could read anything pleasant you might want to, depending on who you were. An endearing son to a mother. A lover to another type of female. Take your pick.

The humble and the arrogant. A humble arrogance? An arrogant humility? Oxymorons at every turn, at home in the contours of human contradictions.

If the State is going to fall, it is from the belly. Akan proverb, from Kwame Appiah's 'In My Father's House'. Ironically true, don't you think? The wealth of Africa is in the rotund bellies of its leaders.

Those were Nana's first words to me, in our African Studies class, followed by a bubbly, larger-than-life laugh that died abruptly because I wasn't laughing back. I stared at him as he swayed to and fro, like a stalk of grass at the mercy of the wind, stared at the lopsided smile sitting on his lips, and said, "You're drunk."

He burped and giggled.

Very serious about his alcohol, Nana. A regular at the student bars. Teetering with a glass of vodka-and-lime. Blubbering in that heavy diction of his. Slurring philosophical musings whose quality favoured his drunken stupor over his sober state.

Drowning in oversize shirts of a similar make, indigenous prints that bore the agenda of a socialist Panafricanism, Nana called himself The Great King, another Kwame Nkrumah destined to usher the masses towards a United Africa. When drunk, he would shuffle about clumsily and sing:

"*Nana o ba o!*
Nana bre bre bre!"
(*The King is coming o!*
The King bre bre bre!)

Swaying towards the ground into an imaginary seat as he sang, *bre bre bre.*

Most of his agenda shirts hung in the flat of his 'woman', a large Sudanese illegal immigrant named Hannah, with soft dimples that made her look pretty even when she was angry and slabs of flesh that swayed to the rhythm of her body, shivering and shuddering as she walked. She looked after him like his mother, so long as he would look after her like her lover, deliver renditions of eloquently plagiarized, African-flavoured Shakespearean poetry.

It was this great whale of his who sidetracked him, I would tease. She who fuelled his nonsensical polemics posted on Facebook and every other site he could find, and misguided him into staging protests outside any institution that was prepared to entertain him.

This angered him. "You do not take me seriously," he would say to me. "You make fun of my poverty."

"There you go again, off on a tangent. Who said anything about your poverty? True, you must entertain a fat woman old enough to be your own mother in order to subsidize your meagre scholarship. But that is not where the fun is. The fun is in your face, it is so black, I have never seen such a black face in all my life, at night it is only the extraordinary white of your eyes and your colgate flossed teeth that I see."

"It is not funny, shut up, you know you are so ugly, talking *nye nye nye* your A-grade English. You think you are so smart, in your fancy clothes and your fake English Accent. Well, by the time I am through with this place every NGO is going to be backing my cause, you shall see."

"What cause, Nana? You have no cause to speak of. You preach a feeble socialism and you drink too much. In the end all you ever do is run all over the place shouting self-contradictory statements, shooting yourself in the foot, squawking like a chicken that has lost its head, *squawk squawk squawk!*"

"Sipho, I will hit you, do not make me angry now, I swear I will kill you, it is easy for you to stand here and make fun of a poor African man, I hear that your father is one of the Big Men in your country, is he not one of the Big Men raping Africa? And yet you are here splashing money around like it grows in your garden. Whose money are you spending, Sipho? It is certainly not your father's."

"I will hurt you and I'm very serious."

"Only because I speak the truth. I intend to be a great revolutionary one day, and you will be on the wrong side of my table. I represent the true starving masses of Africa. Their cause is my cause."

"Idi Amin said something to the same effect once. So did Joseph Kabila."

"So did your Mugabe."

"You will be the same one day. You only cry now because *you* are sitting on the wrong side of the table. Absolute power corrupts absolutely. Who said that?"

"Lord Acton."

"Must've had some African blood in him then, to know what he was talking about."

They were never ending, our playful little arguments. Wedged in that comfortable place, fashionably named university, where one could mould whimsical notions of finding oneself. *Finding oneself.* Such a leisurely term. A lazy walk down the avenues of life – a Jason Tongogara Avenue awash with jacarandas shedding purple confetti – searching for the name of a street one did not yet know.

So whenever anybody asked, "What are you doing with your life?" I would reply, "I'm *finding myself.*"

A luxurious notion that, Nana would say.

Four years of squabbling over space like a tired couple in one of those dreadful economy university flats. Economy status to the last letter. The low, wide windows afforded a view of a world caught in what Nana called "a play of capitalist chaos". Rats in a race. Caught in an infuriated river of traffic thundering past at all hours of existence. Practising a dodgy entrepreneurialism across the road – a string of Nigerian-owned shops that sold electrical gadgets, among other things. Samsung and Panasonic and LG at the front of the store (no guarantees – but more reliable than the Sumsung and Punusonik and Lg from the Chinese shops). Cocaine, hashish and abortion pills at the back (a favourite among the free-spirited students).

The haves and the have-nots. Mostly have-nots. In the good old minority-bourgeoisie-majority-proletariat Marxist order of things. The *unconscientized* masses, caught in a play of capitalist chaos.

I soaked up the wise teachings of Marx from Nana's bandaged volumes, who in turn soaked them up from his beloved whale. After his first lesson from Hannah in becoming a competent Marxist –

(amidst some raucous love making, while I stood huddled in our tiny kitchen:

"*Down with the bourgeoisie!*"

"*Power to the nomenklatura!*"

"*Em... power to the proletariat mon petit noir.*"

"*Sorry... power to the po-le-tia-rat!*"...)

– we staged a two-man rally outside the Humanities Faculty Office. It was in protest against an award given to a Political Science student for what the Faculty termed "a brave and brilliant piece" entitled *African Despots – The Dynamics of a Failed Socialism*. Two ridiculous fellows in morning gowns on a rainy Sunday afternoon waving a cardboard banner. "*Power to the po-le-tia-rat!*" squiggled across a khaki background in angry red magic-marker. Stomping the ground in drenched, squishy bedroom slippers. Coughing marijuana-induced phlegm into pieces of soggy, disintegrating tissue.

A momentary madness disguised in youthful idealism.

It was a crazy era of reckless experiments – a certain recapturing of a 1960s America. Careless strokes of life smeared beneath a crisp, sky-blue canvas (sometimes polluted by the sooty grey of sullen clouds). An active night life shimmering with disco lights. Daytime illusions in cold, wide lecture rooms viewed through a swirling vapour of marijuana haze.

And a girl or two brought in the dead of night. Hit and run, we used to call it. The kind of pretty, quick little thing you definitely wouldn't want for a wife.

The worst was Nana's insatiable thirst for alcohol. I would receive telephone calls at 4am, a finished Nana dragging out a request to be picked up, he had lost his car, he didn't know where his car keys were.

"But Nana, you don't have a car."

All right, he'd been kidnapped.

"Kidnapped by who, Nana?"

"aaaaah warawarawara….."

"Nana, this nonsense has to stop. I'm not your nanny, do you hear?"

"warawarawara....."

"All right, where are you, Nana? Tell me where you are. This is the last time I'm doing this, you hear?"

Always a last time. Then the next time would be another last time.

On graduation day, I drove a drunk Nana who had refused to remove his graduation gown to the airport to catch his flight back to Ghana.

"You look like a coat hanger holding up that gown."

"Thank you, your compliments are flattering."

"You look like a true African scholar. Well schooled in the theory of life, destined for pauper-hood. All that's missing is your certificate – where is it? Carry it in your hand, so everyone can see that you are a true learned man."

"F. you."

"Now that is not the language of a learned man. They will mistake you for an unschooled loafer, if you continue that."

"A big F. you. Instead of worrying about me, you should be wondering what you will do with your life. You do not strike me as the scholarly type. Will you be returning to your country to continue your father's legacy?"

"I resent that. And no, I will not be going back home any time soon. The comforts of South Africa are rather addictive. I'm going to get myself a little place and work on a little novel."

"You mean you are going to get your father to get you a big place with taxpayers' money and waste time writing a terrible memoir nobody is going to read."

"Your faith in my capabilities is inspiring. Now off with you, or you'll miss your flight."

"You will miss me, come on, admit it. I will not leave until you admit it."

"OK, if it will make you feel better, I will miss you. Now off you go, they don't do refunds here."

Four years bottled in a hurried, untidy goodbye in a half-filled lounge at the OR Tambo airport. A Praying Mantis clutching a leather-bound volume of Kwame Gyekye's *Tradition and Modernity: Philosophical Reflections on the African Experience* in one hand. Flapping the other with intoxicated vigour at a tall-and-fashionably-dressed chap wearing a brave, sad face.

It is never *adieu* between friends, is it? It rather feels like a wet, sky-blue *au revoir* that stings with salty, unshed tears.

We kept in touch, as all good friends do. Nana got a post in the Ghana Trust for Civil Societies as their Project Officer (though what they saw in the poor fellow's radical nature, I do not know). Ghanaian politics were a let-down for him – he would have enjoyed the turbulence of a Kibaki-Odinga Kenya or a Mugabe-Tsvangirai Zimbabwe. He was made for serious politics, the type of jagged landscape ready to be cultivated by his revolutionary ideologies, popularity talk and hate speech and all that sort of thing. Something I was determined to shy away from. My perambulations down the blissful, flowery avenues of self-discovery ended abruptly when my father lost his ministerial post during elections. I received a telephone call from a teary Mama (something she rarely did) lodging frightened complaints about how they were setting up father for the fall, branding him as one of the top government officials who were responsible for the mess in the country. I wondered why she was talking to me about it – what it was she expected I could do.

"We could be thrown out of our home," she sniffled, careful not to call this home government property. That's the problem with these posh government jobs. You never really get to own anything – unless you pilfer a million or two.

I mumbled something akin to sympathy. Mama had always fashioned herself after royalty. To live among the masses, as she disdainfully referred to them, was not something she had ever thought to prepare herself for. She had been deliberately oblivious to the bigger things, which were "really none of her concern"; we all had, actually. I am reminded of the many times we sped through town in one of father's government vehicles, gaping at the churlish crowds hurling themselves against the bank doors, scrunched up into angry fists outside the empty supermarkets, squabbling over bags of mealie-meal and sugar and bottles of cooking oil. Mama always liked to remark how watching these poor caricatures was like watching some tragic comedy on Africa Magic TV. Everyone would laugh, including Oswald the driver, right on cue, as though Mama had made some brilliant and witty observation.

Father did lose the elections, and we had to move out of our ministerial home. They found him some limp post in the government that didn't pay as well but was enough to fare by. I got a post as an attaché in the Zimbabwean Embassy in South Africa, enabling me to stay on. A reasonable salary by average standards, with quite a few perks, such as a little house in Blairgowrie with a front lawn and a backyard swimming pool. Not top market, but upmarket enough.

I got married two years after graduation. I wanted Nana to be my best man. I was sure I could convince him to manage 24 hours of sobriety. By then our conversations had become scattered morsels fed in between extremely busy schedules. Nana was steadily climbing the ranks, and there was talk of him venturing out to start something of his own. He promised to keep me in the loop. Our conversations seemed to become more and more scarce, and when I did send Nana an email vis-à-vis my wedding, he did not respond. When I telephoned his employer, I learned that he had been "dismissed". Rumour had it that he had been caught up in an embezzlement scheme. I sent him a couple more emails, to no avail. I wondered if his rebellious nature had got him into some sort of trouble.

I did hear something about him, some four years after my wedding. An old university friend claimed to have spotted him in Jo'burg, in the drug-peddling precincts of Hillbrow. I was sceptical; that didn't sound like Nana at all. And in any case, if he was in the city, I was sure that he would have made an effort to make contact. I did see him, several weeks later.

He appeared on my doorstep last night.

It was my daughter Bongi who first saw him, kneeling on the window sill behind the dining-room curtain.

"Daddy, there's a scarecrow by the gate."

I thought it was one of the beggars who made door-to-door enquiries. They always appeared at odd hours of the day, such as this, an early evening when one was preparing to wind down and least prepared to entertain their grovelling. They could put up a good show, those chaps, bending over with a few miserable coins clinking at the bottom of outstretched tin cans. Quite a bother. I decided to give the chap a coin or two and send him off.

I would never have recognized Nana without the "Power to the *po-le-ta-riat!*" followed by the trademark bubbly, larger-than-life laugh. Nana precocious as ever, still wielding his ludicrous antics.

I let him in, of course. For old times' sake, I tried to explain to my horrified wife Asanda.

He was as bubbly as ever, in soiled clothes of a varying brown (not the original colours, it seemed). Full of raucous laughter. The grating sounds of a clanking tap coughing out rust-coloured trickles of larger-than-life bubbles.

He literally led me into *my* house. Stepping in as though he had always lived there, his battered, squishy shoes leaving dirt prints on Asanda's carpet.

"That's *Persian*," she said pointedly.

"Lovely," came the audacious reply.

He settled his wet figure in the living room. Stretched out his arms across the back of the sofa. A musty smell overpowered the room.

I stood there, teetering between childish amusement and growing umbrage.

"So," said I.

"So!" said a cheerful Nana.

"Where have you *been*?"

Translated to mean *what happened to you?*

"Oh, around. I was in the neighbourhood and so thought to pass by and say hello."

"Hmm."

He attempted to woo Bongi, who immediately ran to hide behind me. Asanda settled herself at the opposite end of the room and eyed Nana with open disgust.

Even I found it difficult to explain my connection to this hideous-looking – and I'm afraid this is the only word that can capture Nana's appearance with accuracy – *tramp.*

A miserable, soppy figure in dripping, mawkish clothes.

Dilated pupils dancing in kernel-yellow sockets.

A chipped smile displaying brown teeth.

"Where did you get my address from?" I asked, a bit flustered.

"What a question! I do not know whether to be amused or insulted. As my people say, *Obi do wo na oba wo fie.*"

"And what does that mean?"

"The literal translation is, 'If someone loves you, they come to your house'. OK, I got your address from Matthew, remember Matthew? Heavy fellow from our Anthropology class? Apparently he works in the Zambian Consulate, opposite your workplace. Is this your family? Wonderful, you've done very well for yourself, much better than anyone would've thought. You always were a directionless fellow. Without me, you would have probably failed your courses and stayed on in university."

There was a menacing silence, which nobody bothered to interrupt. Nana's eyes moved about the room like compasses out of control. It must have been the drugs and alcohol. Fair and fine to indulge in a little experimentation whilst in university, but some people, it seems, never recover from that road. It is always a shame when brilliance drowns itself in inanity.

"Nana, you look terrible," I said with earnest concern.

"You're not bad yourself," came the jocular response.

"What happened to you? Where have you been? I've been looking all over for you."

He tilted his head, wore an amused expression. Then he got up and began shuffling his feet. He sang,

"Nana o ba o!
Nana bre bre bre!
The King is coming o!
The King bre bre bre!"

Swaying towards the ground into an imaginary seat as he sang *bre bre bre*.

Abruptly, he started laughing. A ridiculous giggle that shook his whole body and ended in a rapturous cough. Blobs of bloody mucus sputtered from his mouth.

Asanda shrieked: "That's it, out of my house!"

"Did Awakhiwe ever tell you the shenanigans he used to get up to at uni? There was a time when..."

"Out!"

Nana raised an apologetic hand. "If you could give me a room for the night, dearest *madanfo*. I'm afraid I'm a long way from home."

I put him up in the garage. There was no other place, really. Asanda was not about to have a madman in the same house as our daughter, and quite right, in fact.

I determined to have a firm conversation with Nana the following morning.

He was gone when we woke up. I found the garage door that leads into the house ajar, knocking against the wall.

I don't know how he left – must've jumped the gate – but he left his musty alcoholic smell in the backseat of my car. And a smoky whiff of marijuana.

Several things were missing. Asanda's encrusted cutlery. My Jack Daniel's. One of my Marx and Engels leather-bound volumes. And some ridiculous, useless things, such as Bongi's Barbie Doll kit.

I drove into the city centre and spent a good hour or so roaming the streets of Hillbrow. Windows wound up, doors locked. Avoiding any eye contact with the rogue-looking types loitering outside the dirty, rickety buildings. One or two brought their fingers to their mouths, pretending to smoke, signalling that they had drugs, if drugs were what I was looking for. I was tempted to get out and ask about Nana, but thought better of it. There is no better way of asking to be robbed than parking a Mazda 3 in Hillbrow and venturing into the streets in a Hugo Boss suit.

I finally gave up my search and drove to work. It was my hope that Nana would be back again.

Later that evening, I sieved through my shoe box, where I keep my old photographs. I found the photo at the very bottom. It was dog-eared and crumpled. Two university boys, one tall and fashionably dressed, the other unfashionably short and unfashionably thin. A soggy spinach-green lemon-pickled lime. I sat for a long time by my bedside, chin in hand, staring at that snapshot. A picture is worth a thousand words. A million to friends.

Novuyo Rosa Tshuma is a Zimbabwean writer currently living in South Africa who has had short stories published in several anthologies. She was the winner of the Intwasa Short Story Competition 2009. Her musings may be found at www.novuyorosa. blogspot.com

Indigo

Molara Wood

AT A PARTY ONE night, in a room full of women fussing over the Kolapos' newborn, Idera spoke against the accepted wisdom, and wished she had never opened her mouth.

Lagos, to which she had relocated with her husband Jaiye three years before, was a hive of celebrations. She found the naming ceremonies particularly tasking, especially the industrious, cramped atmosphere of the nesting room, where a decorous huddle of women would always be cooped up with mother and child. The Kolapo naming ceremony was no different, and about ten female friends and relatives were holding court in the baby's room when Idera entered.

"Congratulations," she said to Bola Kolapo.

"Shhh!" Bola's aunt, in whose arms the baby nestled, placed a finger to lips that seemed to occupy half her face. Her baggy *boubou* attire did nothing to hide the tyre-like circumference of her midriff. A mole perched on top of her left earlobe like an audacious fly.

Idera thought she saw a hint of pity on Bola's face at the aunt's reprimand, and wondered when the equation changed between them. When she came from London with Jaiye to attend the Kolapo wedding, Idera had been the sophisticated merchant banker who lived overseas and travelled everywhere. Bola could hardly keep her admiration from showing then, but now only a self-satisfied air remained, and this look of pity.

Idera had seen a similar look on her father's sister, Yeye Koleoso, many times, except that Yeye always seemed to pity herself also.

"We are in this together, this continuing matter of your childlessness," she had said, when last Idera visited her fabric store in Balogun Market. Yeye rose distractedly to wave away a haggling customer, then dragged her chair to sit directly in front of Idera.

"I'm just going to come out with it, Idera; something must be done, for your parents in heaven will never forgive me if I continue to watch you like this and do nothing." Yeye ignored another potential shopper who, taking offence, moved quickly on. She looked intently at the bustling market scene outside before continuing.

"My dear child, I blame myself. I blame myself for sending you to all those fancy schools, in my desire to give you everything I could never give the child I was not blessed with. But now I see I have shielded you from reality, and you're suffering for it."

Tears started to roll down Yeye's face, veins stood out on her neck and her voice quivered. She wiped the tears with the corner of her wrapper but they continued to fall. Idera leaned closer and touched Yeye's knee but the older woman would not be consoled.

"Don't you see? A woman cannot be married in our society and have no child to show for it. And that high-class diplomatic family you married into with their snooty ways, their determination not to behave like regular folk, they've only aided your refusal to face the truth. A five-year marriage without issue! Child, have you ever wondered why I did not last in my husband's house?"

"But there's no problem, Yeye," Idera said gently.

"Yes, my daughter, but enough! It is only a snake that crawls around without offspring behind it. Let's *walk* concerning this thing. Let's go the traditional way. Jaiye needs never know."

Yeye fixed herself up, closed up shop and hailed a taxi. An hour later, Idera shivered as they sat in front of an Ifa priest with sharp cheekbones and small, piercing eyes. The *babalawo* was dressed in white, with a dog-eared cap of the same colour. A chunky white shawl was draped on one shoulder. His voice when he started to speak reminded Idera of soft rain on a warm night, and a calm settled on her.

"Once in Ife they divined Ifa for a chief who wanted to know why his favourite wife was not with child. He was told: why sacrifice, when talk is the solution? If he would talk to the wife, the way would open. No need for sacrifice when talk will do."

Yeye shifted on the raffia mat and frowned at the babalawo's parable.

"Ah, Baba, this will require more than talk-o. Five years, Baba. Five years and no sound of children." Yeye started to rub her palms together in supplication. "Please, see what can be done for my daughter."

The babalawo's forehead creased as he looked from Yeye to Idera, then cleared his throat. He started to recast and rearrange his *opele* on the *opon ifa*, speaking as if to his moving hand on the divining chain.

"That being the case, *Ifa Olokun Asorodayo* – Ifa of the sea who turns all things into joy – your daughter seeks a solution beyond talk."

He said Idera would have to go to a small village shrine near Abeokuta. She would have to make the pilgrimage herself.

"Nobody can go there for you."

Idera put Yeye's ambush out of her mind on her return home. She told herself she'd merely gone to the babalawo to please the superstitious Yeye. She could not imagine going to some shrine in order to conceive; it was ridiculous, the stuff of home video films produced in Surulere.

✳ ✳ ✳

"He wants breast," Bola's aunt said, when the baby stirred. She got up ceremoniously to settle the infant onto its mother's lap.

Wrapped in a fluffy white shawl, only the baby's face showed, pale pink with downy hairs. Johnson's baby oil applied to the fontanelle had slicked forwards, glistening the tiny forehead.

Bola, the mask of pregnancy not yet lifted from her face, hitched up her lace *buba* and, unzipping the front panel of her maternity bra, held an engorged breast to the baby's mouth. She winced as he latched onto her. The shawl loosened a little, exposing one brown ear and a tiny, balled fist.

"The ear indicates the eventual skin shade," said the aunt. "He is going to be the exact colour of his father!"

Idera looked at the baby again as the others made agreeing noises. Bola once said her husband got teased as *oyinbo* back in his school days because of his fair skin. How could brown ears now be his?

"Ah, look at him!" The aunt continued to coo. "He's the carbon copy of his father, this one!"

"Actually, the features are not quite set yet," Idera said with a smile. "It may be too early to tell who the baby resembles."

The last few words dropped haltingly from her mouth, as she became aware of the frozen stares in her direction. Several women raised their eyebrows.

"Excuse me, but what do you know?" The aunt planted one hand on her hip and jutted out her chin at Idera.

"I'm sorry?"

"I asked you a question: what do you know about babies? How many have you pushed out? How dare you contradict me?"

Bola shifted, adjusting the baby's head in the crook of her elbow as she did so. "Aunty, please..."

"No!" The aunt thrust a hand at Bola, whose mouth clammed shut. "Let me deal with this, this so-called woman." She poked the thumb of the other hand at Idera and enquired of her niece, "*Abi*, is this not the one that came from London and thinks she's European? The empty husk you told me about, parched as a fallen leaf in Harmattan?"

Bola lowered her gaze, unable to meet Idera's eyes.

"I, I'm not sure I know what you're getting at. I don't have to be a mother to comment about babies." Idera's hands were in front of her, palms facing up. "Not that it's any concern of yours, but my husband and I choose not to have children yet."

"Don't give me that! What kind of woman chooses not to have a child?" The aunt looked at the others; they stretched their lips thin, shook their heads and averted their eyes. Idera could almost imagine them posing the same question: what kind of woman chooses not to have a child?

"Next time when mothers are talking about children, a barren woman keeps quiet," said the aunt.

"I'm not barren!"

"Are you sure? I'd get myself checked, if I were you."

Idera felt the sting behind her eyes as she fled the room. The aunt's voice came after her in a finale delivered to Bola. "What are you doing with her type anyway? Pathetic. Pointless as a friend in a Nollywood movie!"

* * *

When Jaiye's parents visited London early in his marriage to Idera, it was his dad, shedding his crested blazer and fingering the cufflinks of his Savile Row shirt, who first broached the subject of a grandchild. Idera left it to Jaiye to explain that they wanted to enjoy each other's company first. Jaiye's father lost his usual reserve that day. His thin moustache twitching, he cast aside his gentility and spoke like a village man.

"Ah, you two are selfish," the old man said in a tremulous voice. "When your mother and I first married, we were as much in love as anyone, but we were not selfish about it, or you would not be here today."

What did that man from another age know, Idera told herself as she snuggled up to Jaiye in bed that night. This was much too good. Just the two of them. Perfect.

"We don't need kids to be complete, do we? At least not yet?" Jaiye's voice intruded into her thoughts. "We're happy, aren't we?"

"I'm happy," she replied cautiously, "aren't you?"

"I am, whyever not? As long as we're together, that's the

deal, right?" He spoke with a directness that puzzled her, like an actor delivering a practised line.

His father's death was the catalyst for their relocation back to Nigeria. Jaiye's mother told them after the funeral, "About time you did what all your mates are doing and come back home." She wore mourning colours and sat with a resigned air in her vast bedroom at the family home in Bodija, Ibadan. But her voice grew more animated as she looked from Jaiye to Idera and back again. "I am an old woman, my ears are full. I am hoping you've enjoyed each other's company enough to be able to think beyond yourselves now. Come back home. In England you can deflect issues with all manner of new-fangled ideas. Things will be so much clearer here. Come back home."

Jaiye started to make preparations for their relocation within 12 months.

"It's the only thing my mother's ever asked of me," he told Idera.

* * *

Only the full headlights on cars illuminated the Third Mainland Bridge as Idera drove back from the Kolapos' Victoria Island home to hers in Ikeja GRA. Nothing could be seen beyond the railings, where the darkness of the Lagos Lagoon merged with the pitch-black sky.

Were things that much clearer now? Idera wondered as the car eased off the Third Mainland onto the Oworonsoki Expressway. What did her mother-in-law mean by the need to think beyond themselves? What filled her ears – people's talk? The same talk that enabled Bola's aunt to call Idera barren? She had certainly never thought of herself as such, although her supply of the pill had run out within six months of their relocation and she had never gone to the doctor for more. She relied instead on her clumsy policing of the natural rhythm method.

Idera stopped at the traffic lights in Maryland and street

beggars filed past the rolled-up windows of her car. It hit her then: no solid birth control for two-and-half years and not one missed period. Idera's hands started to shake on the steering wheel.

As she pulled into the driveway of their GRA residence, Idera saw without varnish the sterile life she and Jaiye lived there. Four bedrooms, three bathrooms and a visitors' toilet, two receptions and hedges tended by the gardener, yet something was missing. Had she lied to herself all this while?

Jaiye was away on business to Accra and the house was cloaked in silence. Idera gripped the stairway balustrade tightly and her eyes swept around as she walked up, feeling hollow inside. How she loved this place, all airy rooms and minimalist flair. She never could stand the homes of couples like the Kolapos, overrun by kids screaming, breaking things and sticking forks in the DVD player. But now hers was the unsatisfactory place, too ordered, devoid of spirit. She slumped into a heap on the steps, her cries echoing through the hallway into the rooms.

* * *

Idera was awake most of the night, rolling the babalawo's divination around in her head. How foolish to have scoffed at his words, she thought bitterly. She didn't feel confident driving a long distance in unknown terrain, so she went in search of transporters in Oshodi. She arrived at the small village at midday, face and hair powdered with dust blown into the hire taxi on winding dirt roads. Following directions from the locals, she found the shrine, its perimeter delineated with palm fronds. A male acolyte in a Yankees T-shirt, jeans and rubber slippers, met her at the entrance.

"I have come to make a request of the *orisa*," Idera said, wondering if she had used the appropriate words.

The acolyte shook his head and came forward, so that she had to step back.

"The orisa cannot be consulted by a woman with a visitation in the body," he said.

"Visitation?"

"Yes, a visitor." He moved one hand over his groin area. "A woman must be clean in the presence of the orisa."

Shame washed over Idera as his meaning dawned on her: she was in her period. She didn't quite know what to say to the all-seeing diagnosis. Her menstrual cycle had never been discussed with anyone but her husband, and not often, since they had never talked about conception. It took some effort to meet the acolyte's eyes after he spoke; it surprised her that there was no embarrassment on him, just the simple execution of his folk duty. He probably turned 'unclean' women like her away daily, all part of the job.

Idera rued the wasted journey as she started back down a narrow path between a grove of trees. She had come to a clearing before realizing she had missed her way to the main road. Nearby was a thicket where a lone tree stood, and from there came the gentle rush of water. Idera started towards the sound, comforted by the thought that she might freshen up. She stepped gingerly around the tree onto small rocks that led to a narrow stream. Then a young, clear voice startled her.

"Take off your shoes."

Idera turned round and raised a hand to shield her face from the sun. A girl of no more than 12 stood under the shade of the tree. Her hair was short, like a boy's. She wore a flowing tie-and-dye dress with long, roomy sleeves. Ritual chalk had been used to make a line of white dots from her forehead to the tip of the nose. *Adire* patterns on her dress replicated the long fingers of the tree's leaves.

"This is the peregun tree. It lives forever." The child touched the trunk; she had noticed Idera looking from the foliage to the motifs on her dress. "You are standing on sacred ground. You must take off your shoes."

Idera hurriedly stepped out of her slip-ons. "I only want to wash my face and my hands."

The girl gestured to say: carry on. Idera hitched up her wrapper and hunkered down to scoop water with cupped hands. Her fingers parted and the water seeped through: it was a deep, dark blue.

"This is Odo Aro, the indigo stream," said the girl in answer to Idera's unspoken question. "This is the place of the life-giving dye. Indigo, like the peregun, never dies. Do you know about indigo?" Idera only half shook her head as she rose slowly. The girl, now picking her way across on the rocks, continued, "Indigo is medicinal, you can drink it. Everything flowers with it. When you're in love with your husband, you wear indigo."

The girl, now alongside, regarded Idera with narrowed eyes. "People come here to seek all sorts of things. Fortune, children... What is yours?"

"Actually, I got lost. I just want to freshen up with clean water." Idera looked at the dark stream again with apprehension.

The girl waded suddenly into the water, only turning round midstream. She looked like a floating statue. "Why wash face and hands alone when you can bathe in the living dye, as many have done before you?" She pointed at a small screening bush downstream. "You can bathe there. I'll just stay here and talk."

Knee-deep in water shortly after with her clothes spread on the bush and the girl's incessant talk, Idera wondered what had come over her. But she felt reassured by the rush of dark water on her skin, and gave in to its spell.

* * *

Back at the house, Idera told Jaiye about her ordeal at the Kolapo party, some days after his return from Accra. As she spoke, she looked out of the window where the gardener clipped the hedges, keeping the facade of their lives intact.

"What Bola's aunt said to you was evil, totally uncalled

for," Jaiye said. "I'm sorry you had to go through that. Maybe now you understand why I don't attend these things any more."

Idera turned round. It was Jaiye's first admission of his growing social avoidance, that perhaps he'd noticed the looks too, the talk, the innuendo. Like his mother, his ears had become full.

"You mean, it bothers you too?"

"Damn right it bothers me." He let out a joyless laugh. "I mean, people might think I'm not man enough or something. How to tell them the Mrs is a 'modern woman' – no time for kids?"

"How could you say that? You didn't want any kids!"

"I'm sorry to have to break it to you, darling Idera. It was you. I've endured all these years, denied myself – for you. For better, for worse, no?" There was that laugh again.

Idera told him about the birth-control situation. She'd not done much in a long time to prevent pregnancy; it just never happened. He shook his head repeatedly, covered his ears and backed out of the room. She followed him to the dark upstairs reception where he'd sunk into an armchair, his face in shadows.

She would not allow him to blame it all on her. She wanted children, really, and she would convince him of this if it was the last thing she did. What was that parable about the need to talk? And so, in a measured voice, she told him about the babalawo and the shrine where a visitor impeded her progress. She lingered over her recount of the peregun tree by the indigo stream, the child with the white dots on her face, and how she bathed in the water and came out with bluish skin.

"I thought I knew you, Idera," he said after a long silence. The light from the window illuminated his face as he leaned forward. "I thought you went to school, travelled, lived an enlightened life. If there was a problem conceiving surely we could have tried IVF? How could you go seeking *juju* men for an ailment you would not even admit? How could you compromise us like that?"

"You compromised us first, Jaiye, remember that. We were fine in England, only for you to turn me into a 'barren' woman here – you and your misguided relocation!"

Jaiye stalked off to the bedroom and started throwing his clothes into a suitcase.

"I'm out of here." At the door he turned briefly to say, "Funny thing is, I would never have left you because of some kid we couldn't have."

* * *

The house lost what little vitality it had after Jaiye left. Idera stayed mostly in the bedroom and left the once-a-week cleaning woman directionless while she worked. The washer-man looked puzzled when he noticed that Jaiye's clothes were not among the dirty laundry, but said nothing. Food went stale in the fridge as Idera watched *Africa Magic* on DSTV. Hackneyed scenes of black magic were a staple of the Nigerian films shown back to back on the channel, and set her thinking about the rift with Jaiye. Would he ever forgive her? she wondered.

Idera was at the clinic six weeks after Jaiye walked out on her, when his mother called to say she wanted to see her in Ibadan that weekend. She had not been feeling too well, she told the doctor, after she came off the phone. "We'll run some tests," the doctor said.

The gravel crunched under the tyres as she parked in the Bodija compound days later. Her mother-in-law was out, but in the cavernous living room where four arched doorways led to different wings of the house, Jaiye was seated. Idera caught her breath.

"Mother said you'd be here today, so I came." He gave an uneasy smile as he rose.

"Oh," was the only sound she could make.

"Idera, I've missed you..."

The ringing of her mobile interrupted him. It was the doctor calling, and Idera fled for the privacy of a bedroom. Jaiye poked his head through the door a while later.

"Are you okay?"

"Yeah, yeah, I'm fine." She quickly mopped one cheek with the back of her hand, hoping he'd go away.

"Sure?" He came inside.

"Oh yes, just a little under the weather, is all."

"'Under the weather' – reminds me of England, the way you say that."

"Oh well, we did live there." Her smile did not reach her eyes.

"Yes, we did live there, and look at us, eh?" He sat on the bed and touched her arm. "Did the phone call upset you?"

Idera could not hold back. She told him everything: her visit to the doctor, the tests. He'd just called to inform her she was pregnant, first trimester. The doctor was certain. Her body was racked with sobs as he held her tight, her tears wetting his *adire* top.

"We'll call her Indigo," said Jaiye, his voice breaking.

Idera drew back and searched his welling eyes. It was the first time she had seen him cry since his father's death.

"Don't you see, darling? This is going to be the best thing," he said. "I hope it's a girl, beautiful as you. We'll call her Indigo."

Idera and Jaiye did not know when his mother came home. They had fallen asleep in each other's arms, birds chirruping in the garden outside.

Molara Wood won the inaugural John La Rose Memorial Short Story Competition. Her work has been published internationally in journals and anthologies, including *One World* (New Internationalist 2009). She lives in Lagos, where she works as the Arts and Culture editor of a national newspaper.

Rules

The prize is awarded annually to a short story by an African writer published in English, whether in Africa or elsewhere. (The indicative length is between 3,000 and 10,000 words.)

'An African writer' is normally taken to mean someone who was born in Africa, or who is a national of an African country, or whose parents are African, and whose work has reflected African sensibilities.

There is a cash prize of £10,000 for the winning author and a travel award for each of the short-listed candidates (up to five in all).

For practical reasons unpublished work and work in other languages is not eligible. Works translated into English from other languages are not excluded, provided they have been published in translation, and should such a work win, a proportion of the prize would be awarded to the translator.

The award is made in July each year, the deadline for submissions being 31 January. The shortlist is selected from work published in the five years preceding the submissions deadline and not previously considered for a Caine Prize. Submissions, including those from online journals, should be made by publishers and will need to be accompanied by six original published copies of the work for consideration, sent to the address below. There is no application form.

Every effort is made to publicize the work of the short-listed authors through the broadcast as well as the printed media.

Winning and short-listed authors will be invited to participate in writers' workshops in Africa and elsewhere as resources permit.

The above rules were designed essentially to launch the Caine Prize and may be modified in the light of experience. Their objective is to establish the Caine Prize as a benchmark for excellence in African writing.

The Caine Prize
The Menier Gallery
Menier Chocolate Factory
51 Southwark Street
London, SE1 1RU
UK
Telephone: +44 (0)20 7378 6234
Fax: +44 (0)20 7378 6235
Website: www.caineprize.com